T ◆ H ◆ E

SCHOLASTIC

RHYMING

DICTIONARY

SUE YOUNG

SCHOLASTIC
REFERENCE

New York Toronto London Auckland Sydney

Design: Brock Waldron, Bill Smith Studio
Illustration: David Sheldon

ISBN 0-590-96393-7 (pb) / ISBN 0-590-49461-9 (SSE) / ISBN 0-590-49460-0 (POB)

40 39 38 37 36   6 7/0
                        Printed in the U.S.A.   23

Table of Contents

cheer
fear

How to Use this Dictionary

Welcome to the world of rhymes. We encounter rhyming sounds everywhere — in song lyrics, advertising jingles, rap, greeting card messages, poetry, and verse of all kinds. In all of these, the sounds of rhyme can please and tickle our ears. This book helps you write verse that rhymes.

There are different kinds of rhymes: **perfect**, **imperfect**, and **slant**. Some poets use only perfect rhyme, but you can be more casual, especially if you're rhyming for fun.

Words that sound exactly the same, such as *wait* and *weight*, are not considered rhymes at all — even though the two words sound alike and are spelled differently.

A **perfect rhyme** is formed by two words which have different consonant sounds before identical rhyming sounds. *Cake* and *lake* form a perfect rhyme.

An **imperfect rhyme** has the same consonant before the rhyming sound, such as *therefore* and *before*. (The rhyming sound is *ore* and the consonant is *f*.)

A **slant rhyme** is one in which the sounds are pronounced alike even when they are technically different. For instance, the words *daddy* and *chatty* are frequently spoken with the same rhyming sound: *addy*. Slant rhymes are not true rhymes, but they often sound the same to our ears.

Locating a Rhyming Sound

Unlike other dictionaries which list words by the beginning letter of the word, a rhyming dictionary lists words by the beginning vowel of the rhyming sound.

RHYMING SOUNDS ALWAYS START WITH A VOWEL. The vowels are *A, E, I, O, U*, and sometimes *Y*. All rhyming sounds will start with one of these vowels. Therefore, the main part of this book is divided into six sections — one for each vowel. The sounds are listed alphabetically under the starting vowel.

There are two ways to locate a rhyme in this book. For instance, if you are looking for a rhyme for the word *self*, you can do one of two things:

1. Go directly to the *elf* sound in the rhyming dictionary.

2. Look up the word *self* in the **index** at the back of the book. There the words are listed alphabetically by the beginning letter of the word. There you will see: self/elf.

cake
snake

What is the rhyming sound of a word?

Which sound toward the end of the word is louder, or has more stress? One-syllable words have only one sound in them, like *snake* and *cake*. Their rhyming sound is *ake*. But, what if you wanted something to rhyme with a two-syllable word like *silly*? Listen to the sound that you stress the most in *silly — ill*. The rhyming sound includes the stressed syllable plus the rest of the word. So, to rhyme *silly*, you would look up the sound *illy* in the **I** section. There you would find words which end with the same sound, such as *chili*, *frilly*, and *hilly*.

One sound, different spellings

Sometimes you might look up a rhyming sound in the dictionary, but instead of finding a list of words that rhyme, you are sent to another sound. This is a **cross-reference**. For instance, if you are looking for words that rhyme with *jacks* and you go to *acks* in the dictionary, you won't find a list. Instead you'll find a cross-reference: - - - - - - - - - - - - -

acks as in jacks,
see ax

The *ax* list contains *jacks, tax, kayaks, lilacs*—all the words with different spellings of the same sound. Without cross-references, the dictionary would contain many duplicated lists. It would be a very heavy book!

One word, many sounds

Some words end in the same spelling but have totally different sounds. When this happens, the spelling may be listed two or three times, once for each pronunciation of the sound. Each sound will be marked with a number. For instance, you will find three listings for the spelling *ard*. Each stands for a different sound that **ard** makes:

ard 1 stands for sounds like *card* and *guard*.

ard 2 stands for sounds like *reward* and *cord*.

ard 3 stands for sounds like *backward* and *bird*.

The way you hear a word's sound may depend on the region of the country in which you live. That's why in this dictionary you may find some words on a list that don't seem to you to rhyme. The same word may appear on another list under the sound familiar to you.

The point of this book is that you can have fun writing rhymes. As you begin to write your own verse, you may think of rhymes that are not in this or any other book. We encourage you to use your imagination to its fullest.

One word, no rhyme

What if the word you want to rhyme with has no rhyme? *Orange* and *pint* don't have a rhyme. It would be very difficult to complete a two-line rhyme which began:

> *Every day I eat an orange*

If you wanted a rhyme, you could try instead:

> *I always eat an orange a day*
> *It's good for me, or so they say*

By not placing the hard-to-rhyme word at the end, you made it easier to find a rhyme.

Whether you want to write a rap or a sonnet, the world of verse is yours for the rhyming. Rhyming sounds, together with the melody of meter, ensure that what we write will be pleasing to the ear.

Sue Young

A

A

a 1 as in USA,
see **ay**

a 2 as in spa,
see **aw**

ab 1
blab
cab
crab
dab
drab
fab
flab
gab
grab
jab
lab
nab
scab
stab
tab

backstab
rehab
sand crab

taxicab

ab 2 as in swab,
see **ob**

abber
blabber
drabber
gabber
grabber

jabber
backstabber
money grabber

abble
babble
dabble
rabble
Scrabble

Tower of Babel

abby
abbey
blabby
cabby
crabby
drabby
flabby
gabby
grabby
shabby
tabby

Dear Abby

able
able
cable
fable
label
sable
stable
table

disable
enable
mislabel
times table
timetable

unable
unstable

Aesop's fable
Cain and Abel
warning label

willing and able

aby
baby
maybe

ac as in almanac,
see **ack**

ace
ace
base
bass
brace
case
chase
face
grace
lace
pace
place
race
space
trace
vase

birthplace
bookcase
briefcase
deface
disgrace
embrace

aced to ack

erase
fireplace
home base
horse race
misplace
neck brace
replace
retrace
sack race
shoelace
staircase
suitcase
unlace
workplace

anyplace
breathing space
change of pace
data base
double-space
everyplace
face to face
freckle face
human race
just in case
outer space
out of place
poker face
saving grace
wild-goose chase

aced as in laced,
see **aste**

ach as in attach,
see **atch** 1

ache 1 as in
headache,
see **ake**

ache 2 as in
moustache,
see **ash** 1

acial
facial
glacial
racial
spatial

interracial

acious
gracious
spacious

audacious
curvacious
flirtatious
Horatius
loquacious
tenacious
vivacious

ostentatious

acity
audacity
capacity
sagacity
tenacity
veracity

ack
back
black
crack
flack
hack
jack
knack
lack
pack
plaque
quack
rack
sack
shack
slack
smack
snack
stack
tack
track
whack
yak

attack
backpack
backtrack
blackjack
drawback
feedback
flapjack
flashback
fullback
haystack
hijack
icepack
Iraq
kayak
knapsack
laugh track

3

offtrack
one-track
racetrack
ransack
setback
sidetrack
six-pack
soundtrack
thumbtack
Tic Tac
unpack
wisecrack
wrong track

almanac
back to back
Cadillac
camelback
crackerjack
cul-de-sac
gunnysack
heart attack
hit the sack
jumping jack
lumberjack
maniac
paperback
piggyback
quarterback
railroad track

amnesiac
insomniac
panic attack
yakkity-yak

acked as in cracked, see **act**

ackle
cackle
crackle
jackal
shackle
spackle
tackle

debacle
ramshackle

fishing tackle
tabernacle

acks as in jacks, see **ax**

acs as in maniacs, see **ax**

act
act
backed
cracked
fact
lacked
packed
pact
quacked
sacked
smacked
snacked
stacked
tacked
tact
tracked
tract
whacked

yakked

abstract
attacked
attract
backpacked
compact
contract
distract
enact
exact
extract
hijacked
impact
in fact
jam-packed
ransacked
react
sidetracked
subtract
transact
unpacked
wisecracked

artifact
interact
overact
riot act
vacuum-packed

matter of fact
overreact

actical
practical
tactical

impractical

action
action
faction

fraction
traction

abstraction
attraction
contraction
distraction
extraction
inaction
infraction
reaction
subtraction
transaction

chain reaction
interaction
satisfaction
star attraction

dissatisfaction

affirmative action

active

active

attractive
inactive
reactive

hyperactive
overactive
retroactive

radioactive - - - - - -

acts as in facts,
see **ax**

acy

Casey
Gracie
lacy
spacey
Tracy

ad 1

ad
add
bad
cad
Chad
clad
dad
fad
grad
had
lad
mad
pad
plaid
sad
tad

comrade
doodad
egad
granddad
ink pad
nomad
Sinbad
too bad

Galahad
ironclad
launching pad
mom and dad
not so bad
shoulder pad
Trinidad

undergrad

Olympiad
stark raving mad

ad 2 as in squad,
see **awed**

ada

armada
cicada
Granada
piñata
regatta
tostada

enchilada

aficionada

adder as in ladder,
see **atter**

addle as in paddle,
see **attle**

addy as in daddy,
see **atty**

ade 1

aid
aide
blade
braid
fade
frayed
grade

5

grayed
jade
laid
made
maid
neighed
paid
played
prayed
raid
shade
spade
sprayed
stayed
suede
swayed
trade
wade
weighed

afraid
arcade
Band-aid
betrayed
blockade
bridesmaid
charade
crusade
decade
decayed
delayed
displayed
first aid
grenade
homemade
invade
Kool-Aid
lampshade
mermaid

nursemaid
obeyed
okayed
outweighed
parade
persuade
portrayed
repaid
surveyed
tirade
unmade
unpaid
upgrade
x-rayed

accolade
barricade
cavalcade
centigrade
custom-made
disobeyed
escapade
foreign aid
Gatorade
hearing aid
hit parade
lemonade
make the grade
marmalade
masquerade
overpaid
promenade
razor blade
ready-made
renegade
ricocheted
Rose Parade
serenade
shoulder blade

unafraid
underpaid

penny arcade
visual aid

ade 2 as in facade, see awed

ader

cater
crater
freighter
gator
greater
hater
later
nadir
raider
skater
straighter
trader
traitor
waiter

creator
crusader
debater
dictator
equator
ice skater
invader
narrator
persuader
spectator
tailgater
translator

agitator

alligator
animator
aviator
calculator
decorator
demonstrator
detonator
duplicator
educator
elevator
escalator
generator
illustrator
imitator
indicator
innovator
instigator
legislator
liberator
masquerader
mediator
moderator
navigator
operator
perpetrator
radiator
regulator
roller skater
see you later
serenader
speculator
terminator
ventilator

assassinator
coordinator
exaggerator
exterminator

facilitator
impersonator
investigator
manipulator
negotiator
procrastinator
refrigerator

sooner or later

ady
eighty
Haiti
Katie
lady
matey
shady
weighty

aff
calf
graph
half
laugh
staff

behalf
decaf
giraffe
riffraff

autograph
belly laugh
better half
chief of staff
paragraph
phonograph
photograph
telegraph

aft
craft
draft
graft
laughed
raft
shaft
staffed

aircraft
life raft
mine shaft
spacecraft
witchcraft

autographed
fore and aft
photographed

after
after
drafter
laughter
rafter

hereafter
thereafter

forever after

afty
crafty
drafty

7

ag

bag
brag
drag
flag
gag
jag
lag
nag
rag
sag
shag
snag
stag
tag
wag
zag

beanbag
dishrag
dog tag
grab bag
jet lag
mailbag
name tag
price tag
ragtag
sandbag
tea bag
trash bag
washrag
windbag
zigzag

doggie bag
litterbag
lollygag
saddlebag
sleeping bag

age 1

age
cage
gauge
page
rage
sage
stage
wage

backstage
bird cage
Bronze Age
engage
enrage
front page
Ice Age
offstage
old age
outrage
rampage
rib cage
space age
Stone Age
teenage
upstage

middle age
under age

minimum wage

age 2

barrage
collage
corsage
garage
massage
mirage

bon voyage
camouflage
entourage
sabotage

espionage

ageous

contagious
courageous
enrage us
outrageous
rampageous
upstage us

advantageous

aggy

baggy
draggy
Maggie
saggy
shaggy

ah as in hah, see **aw**

ai as in bonzai, see **y**

aid as in paid, see **ade** 1

aider as in raider, see **ader**

ail as in mail, see ale 1

aily

daily
gaily
scaly

Israeli
shillelagh
ukulele

Barnum and Bailey

aim

aim
blame
came
claim
fame
flame
frame
game
lame
maim
name
same
shame
tame

acclaim
aflame
ball game
became
defame
exclaim
for shame
inflame
nickname

reclaim
surname
take aim

claim to fame
Hall of Fame
Notre Dame
overcame
put to shame

ain

brain
cane
chain
crane
drain
gain
grain
Jane
lane
main
Maine
mane
pain
pane
plain
plane
rain
reign
rein
sane
slain
Spain
sprain
stain
strain
train
vain
vane
vein

wane
abstain
airplane
birdbrain
bloodstain
campaign
champagne
chow mein
complain
contain
disdain
domain
Elaine
explain
freight train
Great Dane
humane
insane
in vain
Lorraine
maintain
Mark Twain
migraine
mundane
obtain
profane
refrain
regain
remain
restrain
retain
sustain
tearstain
terrain
Ukraine
unchain

acid rain
ascertain

9

air to aire

candy cane
cellophane
down the drain
entertain
featherbrain
hurricane
inhumane
lovers' lane
Novocain
potty-train
scatterbrain
Solarcaine
wagon train
weathervane
windowpane

memory lane
no pain, no gain

air

air
bare
bear
blare
care
chair
dare
fair
fare
flair
flare
glare
hair
hare
heir
lair
mare
pair

pear
prayer
rare
scare
share
snare
spare
square
stair
stare
swear
tear
their
there
ware
wear
where

affair
airfare
aware
Bel-Air
beware
bus fare
child care
compare
declare
despair
elsewhere
fanfare
fresh air
health care
high chair
impair
midair
nightmare
no fair
nowhere
outwear

Pierre
prepare
repair
somewhere
threadbare
Times Square
unfair
warfare
welfare
wheelchair

anywhere
billionaire
county fair
debonair
Delaware
dentist chair
everywhere
fair and square
here and there
millionaire
not all there
on the air
over there
questionnaire
rocking chair
silverware
solitaire
teddy bear
unaware
underwear
wash and wear

electric chair
intensive care
Smokey the Bear

aire as in millionaire, see **air**

airy as in fairy,
see **ary**

aise as in praise,
see **aze**

ait as in bait,
see **ate**

ak as in yak,
see **ack**

ake
ache
bake
Blake
brake
break
cake
fake
flake
Jake
lake
make
quake
rake
sake
shake
snake
stake
steak
take
wake

awake
backache
beefsteak

cheesecake
clambake
cupcake
daybreak
earache
earthquake
fruitcake
handshake
headache
heartache
heartbreak
housebreak
intake
jailbreak
keepsake
milk shake
mistake
namesake
newsbreak
opaque
outbreak
pancake
remake
shortcake
snowflake
toothache

bellyache
birthday cake
coffee break
double take
give and take
make or break
overtake
pat-a-cake
rattlesnake
Shake 'n Bake
stomachache
take a break

wide-awake

for goodness' sake
for pity sake
gimme a break
jump in the lake

aks as in kayaks,
see **ax**

al
Al
gal
Hal
pal
shall

canal
chorale
corral
decal
locale
low-cal
morale
pen pal

musicale
rationale
root canal

ald as in bald,
see **alled**

ale 1
ail
ale
bail'
Braille

fail
frail
gale
hail
jail
mail
male
nail
pail
pale
quail
rail
sail
sale
scale
snail
stale
tail
tale
trail
veil
wail
whale
Yale

airmail
blackmail
cocktail
curtail
derail
detail
dovetail
exhale
fan mail
female
for sale
hangnail
impale
inhale

pigtail
prevail
retail
shirttail
telltale
thumbnail
toenail
unveil
upscale
wholesale

Abigail
cottontail
fairy tale
fingernail
garage sale
ginger ale
Holy Grail
killer whale
monorail
nature trail
nightingale
rummage sale
tattletale
without fail

ale 2 as in morale,
see **al**

ale 3 as in finale,
see **olly**

alf as in calf,
see **aff**

ality 1
brutality
fatality
finality
formality
legality
locality
mentality
morality
mortality
neutrality
normality
reality
totality
vitality

abnormality
hospitality
illegality
immorality
immortality
informality
joviality
nationality
personality
practicality
principality
punctuality
rationality
technicality
triviality

congeniality
municipality
originality
sentimentality

confidentiality
constitutionality
individuality

ality 2
quality
equality
frivolity
inequality

alk as in talk,
see ock

alker as in walker,
see ocker

alks as in walks,
see ox

all
all
ball
bawl
brawl
call
crawl
doll
drawl
fall
gall
hall
haul
loll
mall
maul
Paul
Saul
scrawl
shawl

small
sprawl
squall
stall
tall
wall

appall
baseball
birdcall
blackball
close call
downfall
enthrall
eyeball
football
free fall
goofball
gum ball
handball
install
meatball
nightfall
oddball
phone call
pinball
pitfall
rag doll
rainfall
recall
snowball
snowfall
spitball
stonewall
toll call

aerosol
alcohol
Barbie doll
basketball

butterball
cannonball
caterwaul
city hall
cotton ball
crystal ball
curtain call
free-for-all
know it all
Montreal
off-the-wall
overall
overhaul
paper doll
parasol
protocol
shopping mall
study hall
Taj Mahal
Tylenol
volleyball
wake-up call
wall-to-wall
waterfall

cholesterol
justice for all
Neanderthal

alled
bald
bawled
brawled
called
crawled
drawled
hauled
lolled
mauled

scald
scrawled
sprawled
squalled
stalled
walled

appalled
blackballed
enthralled
installed
recalled
snowballed
so-called

overhauled

aller
brawler
caller
collar
dollar
holler
scholar
smaller
squalor
taller

bird caller
blue-collar
flea collar
free-faller
installer
name-caller
white-collar

creepy crawler
hoot and holler
million-dollar ------>

alley
alley
Bali
dally
galley
rally
Sally
tally
valley

blind alley
Death Valley
pep rally

allow 1
aloe
hallow
shallow

marshmallow

allow 2
follow
hollow
swallow
wallow

Apollo

ally as in rally, see alley

alm
balm
calm
palm
psalm
qualm

embalm
napalm

alt
fault
halt
malt
salt
vault

asphalt
assault
default
exalt
pole-vault

somersault

alter
altar
alter
falter
halter
vaulter
Walter

assaulter
Gibraltar

alts
faults
halts
malts
salts

vaults
waltz

assaults
defaults

smelling salts
somersaults

am

am
clam
cram
dam
gram
ham
jam
lamb
ma'am
Pam
ram
Sam
scam
scram
sham
slam
swam
tram
wham
yam

exam
flimflam
grand slam
madame
outswam
program
toe jam

Abraham
Amsterdam

anagram
Birmingham
diagram
in a jam
leg of lamb
milligram
telegram
traffic jam
Uncle Sam

ama 1

comma
drama
llama
mama
Rama
trauma

pajama

cinerama
melodrama
Yokohama

ama 2

pajama

Alabama
cinerama
panorama

ame as in fame,
see **aim**

ami as in pastrami,
see **ommy**

ammy

clammy
Grammy
Tammy
whammy

Miami

amp

amp
camp
champ
clamp
cramp
damp
lamp
ramp
scamp
stamp
tramp
vamp

postage stamp
summer camp
writer's cramp

amper

camper
damper
hamper
pamper
scamper
tamper

an 1

an
Anne
ban
bran

can
clan
fan
Fran
Jan
man
Nan
pan
plan
ran
scan
span
Stan
tan
than
van

Batman
began
cancan
caveman
Chopin
deadpan
dishpan
dustpan
hangman
Japan
lawman
life span
madman
oat bran
outran
Pac-Man
sandman
sedan
Spokane
suntan
time span
trashcan

caravan
frying pan
handyman
man-to-man
moving van
overran
Pakistan
Peter Pan
spic-and-span
Superman

Afghanistan
attention span
catamaran
flash-in-the-pan
medicine man
orangutan

an 2 as in pecan, see awn

ana 1

Anna

banana
bandanna
Diana
Havana
Montana
Savannah
Susanna

Indiana
Pollyanna

Louisiana

ana 2 as in iguana, see onna

ance

ants
aunts
chance
chants
dance
France
glance
grants
lance
pants
plants
prance
stance
trance

advance
break dance
by chance
enchants
enhance
entrance
expanse
fat chance
finance
folk dance
free-lance
last chance
rain dance
romance
square dance
sweat pants
tap dance
transplants

circumstance
disenchants
fighting chance
song and dance
underpants

and

and
band
banned
bland
brand
canned
fanned
gland
grand
hand
land
panned
planned
sand
spanned
stand
strand
tanned

armband
backhand
bandstand
command
cowhand
crash-land
demand
disband
dreamland
expand
firsthand
grandstand
handstand
headband
homeland
kickstand
Lapland
longhand
name-brand

offhand
quicksand
shorthand
suntanned
Thailand
wasteland

baby grand
beforehand
close-at-hand
contraband
Disneyland
Dixieland
fairyland
hand-in-hand
helping hand
Holy Land
hot dog stand
no man's land
reprimand
Rio Grande
rubber band
secondhand
sleight of hand
understand

chain of command
fantasyland
law of the land
misunderstand

supply and demand

ane as in lane,
see **ain**

ang

bang
clang
dang

fang
gang
hang
rang
sang
slang
sprang
Tang
twang

chain gang
harangue
meringue
mustang

boomerang------
overhang

orangoutang

ange

change
range
strange

arrange
downrange
exchange
long-range
shortchange

interchange
prearrange
rearrange

ank

bank
blank
clank
crank
dank
drank

17

frank
plank
prank
rank
sank
shrank
spank
tank
thank
yank

blood bank
fish tank
gangplank
outrank
point-blank
think tank

data bank
draw a blank
savings bank
walk the plank

blankety-blank

military rank

anky
blanky
clanky
cranky
Frankie
hankie
lanky
swanky
Yankee

hanky-panky

anned as in banned, see and

anner
banner
manner
manor
planner
scanner
tanner

anny
Annie
Danny
granny
nanny

uncanny

ans as in swans, see ons

ant 1
ant - - - - - - - - - - - - -
aunt
can't
chant
grant
pant
plant
rant
scant
slant

eggplant
enchant

implant
Rembrandt
supplant
transplant

disenchant
gallivant
power plant

ant 2 as in want, see aunt

ante as in confidante, see aunt

antic
antic
frantic

Atlantic
gigantic
romantic

transatlantic
unromantic

ants as in pants, see ance

any as in many, see enny

ap
cap
chap
clap
flap

gap
lap
map
nap
rap
sap
scrap
slap
snap
strap
tap
trap
wrap
yap
zap

backslap
burlap
catnap
dunce cap
firetrap
giftwrap
hubcap
kidnap
kneecap
madcap
mishap
mousetrap
recap
road map
unwrap
wiretap

baseball cap
beat the rap
booby trap
bottlecap
gender gap
gingersnap
handicap

overlap
thinking cap
tourist trap

generation gap

ape

ape
cape
drape
gape
grape
scrape
shape
tape

agape
egg-shape
escape
go ape
landscape
red tape
reshape
shipshape

fire escape
out of shape
ticker tape

aph as in graph,
see **aff**

aphed as in
autographed,
see **aft**

aphic

graphic
traffic

geographic
one-way traffic
photographic

apple

apple
chapel
grapple

appy

happy
pappy
sappy
scrappy
snappy

grandpappy
slaphappy
unhappy

make it snappy
trigger-happy

ar

are
bar
car
czar
far
jar
mar
par
scar
spar
star
tar

19

ajar
all-star
bazaar
bizarre
boxcar
cigar
costar
disbar
guitar
jaguar
memoir
Renoir
snack bar
so far
streetcar

cable car
candy bar
caviar
cookie jar
CPR
falling star
handlebar
movie star
near and far
registrar
reservoir
salad bar
seminar
superstar
VCR
Zanzibar

ara
Clara
Sarah

mascara
Sahara

arch
arch
March
march
parch
starch

ard 1
bard
barred
card
charred
guard
hard
jarred
lard
marred
scarred
sparred
starred
tarred
yard

armed guard
backyard
barnyard
Bernard
blowhard
bombard
Coast Guard
costarred
cue card
diehard
discard
flash card
graveyard
junkyard
lifeguard
postcard

regard
safeguard
scorecard
shipyard
vanguard

avant-garde
baseball card
battle-scarred
birthday card
bodyguard
boulevard
credit card
crossing guard
disregard
leotard
report card
St. Bernard

ard 2 as in reward, see ord

ard 3 as in backward, see erd

arder as in harder, see arter

ardy
arty
hardy
hearty
Marty
party
smarty

tardy

foolhardy
search party
tea party

birthday party

are as in care,
see **air**

area
area

Bavaria
Bulgaria
hysteria
malaria

arent
parent

apparent
grandparent
inherent
transparent

unapparent

arer
barer
error
fairer
rarer
terror

pallbearer
seafarer
torchbearer
wayfarer

holy terror
trial and error

arf 1
arf
barf
scarf

arf 2
dwarf
wharf

arge
barge
charge
large
Marge
sarge

discharge
enlarge
recharge
take charge

overcharge

ari as in safari,
see **arry 2**

arious
various

Aquarius
gregarious
hilarious
precarious
vicarious

Sagittarius

arity
charity
clarity
rarity

barbarity
dexterity
disparity
hilarity
posterity
prosperity
severity
sincerity
vulgarity

insincerity
popularity
regularity
similarity
solidarity

familiarity
irregularity
peculiarity

ark
arc
ark
bark
Clark
dark
hark
lark
mark
park
shark
spark
stark

aardvark

arm to art

ballpark
birthmark
bookmark
check mark
Denmark
earmark
footmark
landmark
monarch
postmark
remark
skylark
theme park
trademark

baseball park
Central Park
disembark
double-park
Joan of Arc
Noah's ark
question mark

arm 1

arm
charm
farm
harm

alarm
disarm
firearm

arm in arm
false alarm
fire alarm
lucky charm
underarm

arm 2 as in warm, see orm

arn

barn
darn
yarn

aron

Aaron
baron
barren
heron
Karen
Sharon

arred as in barred, see ard 1

arrot

bear it
carat
carrot
dare it
ferret
merit
parrot
scare it
share it
swear it
wear it

demerit
inherit
prepare it
repair it

disinherit

arrow

arrow
marrow
narrow
pharaoh ➤
sparrow

bolero
bone marrow
Camaro
dinero
sombrero
wheelbarrow

bow and arrow
caballero
straight and narrow

Rio de Janeiro

arry 1 as in carry, see ary

arry 2

sari
sorry
starry

Ferrari
safari

calamari

art 1

art
cart
chart

dart
heart
mart
part
smart
start
tart

apart
depart
eye chart
false start
folk art
go cart
golf cart
head start
impart
jump-start
K Mart
Mozart
outsmart
Pop Tart
restart
street smart
sweetheart
upstart

à la carte
applecart
change of heart
counterpart
fall apart
heart to heart
lonely heart
martial art
minimart
Purple Heart
running start
shopping cart
work of art

art 2 as in wart,
see **ort**

arter

ardor
barter
charter
garter
harder
martyr
smarter
starter
Tartar
tarter

self-starter
slow starter

arty as in party,
see **ardy**

arve

carve
Marv
starve

ary

airy
Barry
berry
bury
Carrie
carry
cherry
dairy
fairy
ferry

Gary
hairy
Harry
Larry
marry
Mary
merry
prairie
scary
tarry
Terry
vary
very
wary

canary
contrary
library
primary
raspberry
remarry
Rosemary
strawberry
tooth fairy

adversary
arbitrary
aviary
cemetery
commentary
culinary
customary
dictionary
dietary
dignitary
dromedary
February
fragmentary
honorary
January

23

legendary
literary
mercenary
military
missionary
momentary
monastery
mortuary
necessary
ordinary
planetary
sanctuary
sanitary
secondary
secretary
sedentary
solitary
stationary
stationery
temporary
visionary
voluntary

contemporary
disciplinary
extraordinary
hereditary
imaginary
itinerary
obituary
precautionary
preliminary
sugarplum fairy
unnecessary
vocabulary

revolutionary

as as in has,
see **azz**

asco
fiasco
Tabasco

ase 1 as in case,
see **ace**

ase 2 as in phase,
see **aze**

ased as in chased,
see **aste**

ash 1
ash
bash
brash
cache
cash
clash
crash
dash
flash
gash
gnash
hash
lash
mash
rash
sash
slash
smash

splash
stash
thrash
trash

backlash
eyelash
mishmash
mustache
news flash
whiplash

balderdash
corned beef hash
diaper rash
succotash

ash 2 as in wash,
see **osh**

ashy
flashy
splashy
trashy

asion
Asian

abrasion
Caucasian
equation
Eurasian
evasion
invasion
occasion
persuasion

ask
ask
bask
cask
flask
mask --->
task

asket
basket
casket
gasket

asm
chasm
spasm

sarcasm

enthusiasm

ason
basin
chasten
hasten
Jason
mason

asp
clasp
gasp
grasp
rasp

ass
ass
bass
brass
class

crass
gas
glass
grass
lass
mass
pass
sass

amass
bypass
first class
harass
hourglass
impasse
spyglass
surpass
tear gas
trespass

boarding pass
bonny lass
laughing gas
looking glass
middle-class
out of gas
overpass
sassafras
smooth as glass

head of the class
snake in the grass

magnifying glass

assed as in passed, see ast

assy
brassy
chassis
classy
glassy
grassy
sassy

Tallahassee

ast
blast
cast
caste
fast
gassed
last
mast
passed
past
sassed
vast

aghast
amassed
at last
bombast
broadcast
contrast
downcast
forecast
full blast
gymnast
halfmast
harassed
miscast
newscast
outcast
outclassed
outlast

sandblast
steadfast
surpassed
typecast

all-star cast
flabbergast
overcast
telecast
unsurpassed

enthusiast
iconoclast

aste

aced
baste
braced
chased
chaste
faced
graced
haste
laced
paced
paste
placed
raced
spaced
taste
traced
waist
waste

bad taste
defaced
disgraced
displaced
distaste
embraced
erased

fast paced
good taste
misplaced
red-faced
replaced
retraced
straitlaced
toothpaste
two-faced
unlaced

aftertaste
baby-faced
cut-and-paste
freckle-faced
haste makes waste
interlaced
interspaced

hazardous waste

asten as in chasten, see ason

aster

blaster
faster
master
pastor
plaster
vaster

bandmaster
broadcaster
disaster
forecaster
headmaster
newscaster ----▸
postmaster
sandblaster

schoolmaster
scoutmaster

alabaster

astic

drastic
plastic
spastic

bombastic
elastic
fantastic
gymnastic
sarcastic
scholastic

ecclesiastic
enthusiastic
interscholastic

asty

hasty
tasty

at 1

at
bat
brat
cat
chat
fat

flat
gnat
hat
mat
pat
rat
sat
spat
splat
that
vat

chitchat
combat
dingbat
doormat
fat cat
format
hardhat
muskrat
nonfat
pack rat
place mat
tomcat
wildcat
wombat

acrobat
alley cat
army brat
baby fat
baby-sat
bureaucrat
copy cat
cowboy hat
democrat
diplomat
dirty rat
fraidy cat
habitat

laundromat
pussycat
smell a rat
thermostat
this and that
tit for tat
welcome mat

aristocrat
blind as a bat
calico cat

at 2 as in swat,
see **ot**

atch 1

batch
catch
hatch
latch
match
patch
scratch
snatch
thatch

arm patch
attach
detach
dispatch
knee patch
mismatch
unlatch

boxing match
cabbage patch
mix and match
reattach

atch 2 as in watch,
see **otch**

atchy

catchy
patchy
scratchy

Apache

ate

ate
bait
crate
date
eight
fate
freight
gait
gate
grate
great
hate
Kate
late
mate
plate
rate
skate
slate
state
straight
strait
trait
wait
weight

await
birthrate

blind date
cellmate
cheapskate
checkmate
classmate
Colgate
create
debate
deflate
donate
elate
equate
estate
first-rate
frustrate
gyrate
helpmate
ice skate
inflate
ingrate
inmate
innate
locate
mandate
migrate
narrate
ornate
playmate
primate
prom date
pulsate
rebate
relate
rotate
sedate
stagnate
stalemate
tailgate
translate

update
vacate
vibrate

activate
advocate
aggravate
agitate
allocate
amputate
animate
calculate
candidate
captivate
celebrate
chief of state
circulate
complicate
concentrate
confiscate
contemplate
cultivate
decorate
dedicate
delegate
demonstrate
detonate
devastate
deviate
dislocate
dominate
double-date
duplicate
educate
elevate
emigrate
escalate
estimate
excavate

fascinate
fluctuate
formulate
fumigate
generate
Golden Gate
graduate
gravitate
heavyweight
hesitate
hibernate
hyphenate
illustrate
imitate
immigrate
indicate
infiltrate
instigate
integrate
irrigate
irritate
isolate
legislate
liberate
liquidate
lubricate
medicate
meditate
motivate
mutilate
nauseate
navigate
nominate
operate
out-of-date
overate
overrate
overstate
overweight

paperweight
penetrate
percolate
populate
punctuate
radiate
real estate
regulate
roller skate
second-rate
segregate
separate
situate
speculate
stimulate
strangulate
suffocate
terminate
tolerate
underrate
underweight
up-to-date
vaccinate
validate
vindicate
violate

abbreviate
accelerate
accommodate
accumulate
alienate
alleviate
annihilate
anticipate
appreciate
asphyxiate
assassinate
associate

at any rate
carbohydrate
communicate
congratulate
contaminate
cooperate
coordinate
deliberate
discriminate
elaborate
eliminate
emancipate
evacuate
evaluate
evaporate
exaggerate
exasperate
exhilarate
exterminate
hallucinate
humiliate
illuminate
impersonate
initiate
inoculate
insinuate
interrogate
intimidate
intoxicate
investigate
invigorate
manipulate
officiate
participate
procrastinate
recuperate
reiterate
retaliate
reverberate

ater 1 as in later,
see **ader**

ater 2 as in water,
see **otter**

ath
bath
math
path
wrath

birdbath
steam bath
warpath

aftermath
bubble-bath
psychopath

ather 1
gather
lather
rather

ather 2
bother
father

godfather
grandfather
no bother

atial to ation

atial as in spatial, see acial

atic
attic
static

asthmatic
dramatic
ecstatic
erratic
fanatic
traumatic

acrobatic
Adriatic
aromatic
Asiatic
autocratic
automatic
bureaucratic
charismatic
democratic
diplomatic
Instamatic
mathematic
problematic
symptomatic
systematic

aristocratic
melodramatic
psychosomatic

idiosyncratic
semiautomatic

atin
fatten
flatten

Latin
satin

Manhattan
pig Latin

ation
nation
station

citation
creation
Dalmatian
dictation
donation
duration
elation
fire station
fixation
flirtation
formation
foundation
frustration
inflation
location
migration
ovation
plantation
probation
quotation
relation
rotation
starvation
summation
taxation
vacation
vibration

adaptation
admiration

aggravation
agitation
animation
application
aviation
calculation
cancellation
celebration
circulation
combination
complication
concentration
confirmation
congregation
consolation
conversation
corporation
declaration
decoration
dedication
dehydration
demonstration
desperation
destination
devastation
duplication
elevation
expectation
explanation
exploration
fabrication
fascination
generation
graduation
hesitation
illustration
imitation
immigration
inflammation

atious (to) atter

information
innovation
inspiration
integration
irritation
isolation
legislation
liberation
limitation
medication
meditation
moderation
motivation
mutilation
nomination
obligation
observation
occupation
operation
perspiration
population
preparation
presentation
preservation
punctuation
radiation
recreation
registration
regulation
relaxation
reputation
reservation
resignation
revelation
segregation
separation
situation
speculation
stimulation

transportation
variation
violation

abbreviation
acceleration
anticipation
appreciation
assassination
civilization
communication
consideration
cooperation
coordination
determination
discrimination
elimination
evaluation
exasperation
extermination
hallucination
humiliation
imagination
impersonation
initiation
interpretation
interrogation
intimidation
intoxication
investigation
justification
manipulation
multiplication
notification
organization
participation
procrastination
pronunciation
qualification
realization

recommendation
retaliation
sophistication
verification

atious as in flirtatious, see **acious**

ator as in narrator, see **ader**

atten as in flatten, see **atin**

atter
batter
bladder
chatter
clatter
fatter
flatter
gladder
ladder
latter
madder
matter
platter
sadder
scatter
shatter
splatter
tatter

gallbladder
gray matter
Mad Hatter

31

attery to ause

no matter

hook and ladder
pitter-patter

attery
battery
flattery

attle
battle
cattle
paddle
prattle
rattle
saddle
straddle
tattle

dog paddle
Seattle
sidesaddle
skedaddle

atty
batty
bratty
caddie
catty
chatty
daddy
faddy
fatty
patty
ratty

granddaddy
rice paddy

Cincinnati

aud as in fraud,
see awed

aught as in taught,
see ot

aughter as in
daughter,
see otter

aughty as in
naughty,
see ody

aul as in haul,
see all

auled as in hauled,
see alled

ault as in fault,
see alt

aulter as in vaulter,
see alter

aults as in faults,
see alts

aunch
conch
haunch

launch
paunch
staunch

aunder as in
launder,
see onder

aunt
aunt
daunt
flaunt
gaunt
haunt
jaunt
taunt
want

bouffant
Vermont

confidante
debutante
dilettante
nonchalant
restaurant

aur as in dinosaur,
see ore

ause
cause
clause
claws

flaws
gauze
jaws
laws
pause
paws
straws
vase

applause
because
jigsaws
lost cause
outlaws
seesaws

Santa Claus
Wizard of Oz

aust as in exhaust, see **ost 2**

aut as in taut, see **ot**

avage
ravage
savage

ave
brave
cave
crave
gave
grave
knave
pave
rave

save
shave
slave
waive
wave

behave
brainwave
engrave
forgave
heat wave
shockwave

aftershave
galley slave
microwave
misbehave
rant and rave
tidal wave

avel
gavel
gravel
travel

unravel

aver
braver
favor
flavor
savor
shaver
waiver
waver

disfavor
flag-waver
lifesaver
time-saver

avery
Avery
bravery
savory
slavery

unsavory

avity
cavity
gravity

depravity

law of gravity

avor as in favor, see **aver**

avy
gravy
navy
wavy

aw
ah
awe
blah
claw
draw
flaw
gnaw
hah
jaw
law
ma
pa
paw
raw

awed to awled

saw
spa
straw
thaw

ga-ga
grandma
grandpa
ha ha
hoopla
hurrah
jigsaw
last straw
outdraw
outlaw
seesaw
southpaw
Utah
withdraw

Arkansas
hem and haw
la de da
Mardi Gras
Omaha
Panama
Wichita

awed

awed
broad
Claude
clawed
clod
flawed
fraud
gnawed
God
mod
nod

odd
pawed
plod
pod
prod
quad
rod
sawed
squad
Todd
trod
wad

abroad
applaud
Cape Cod
facade
hot rod
outlawed
pea pod
seesawed
slipshod
spit-wad
tightwad
tripod
vice squad

act of God
cattle prod
firing squad
fishing rod
goldenrod
hemmed and hawed
land of Nod
lightning rod
promenade
riot squad

awful

awful
lawful
waffle

falafel
unlawful

awk as in hawk, see ock

awks as in hawks, see ox

awky

cocky
gawky
hockey
jockey
rocky
stocky

disc jockey
ice hockey
Milwaukee

Jabberwocky
teriyaki
walkie-talkie

awl as in crawl, see all

awled as in crawled, see alled

34 Scholastic Rhyming Dictionary

awler as in brawler, see **aller**

awly as in crawly, see **olly**

awn

con
dawn
don
drawn
fawn
gone
John
lawn
on
pawn
Ron
spawn
swan
yawn

Antoine
baton
bon-bon
Cézanne
chiffon
coupon
doggone
Don Juan
ex-con
Iran
long gone
pecan
python
run-on
Saigon
salon

Szechwan
Taiwan
Tucson
upon
withdrawn
won ton
Yukon
Yvonne

Amazon
Audubon
Avalon
Babylon
crack of dawn
decathlon
Genghis Khan
hanger-on
hexagon
leprechaun
liaison
marathon
Mazatlán
octagon
off and on
overdrawn
paragon
parmesan
pentagon
pro and con
silicon
talkathon
woebegone

phenomenon
Saskatchewan

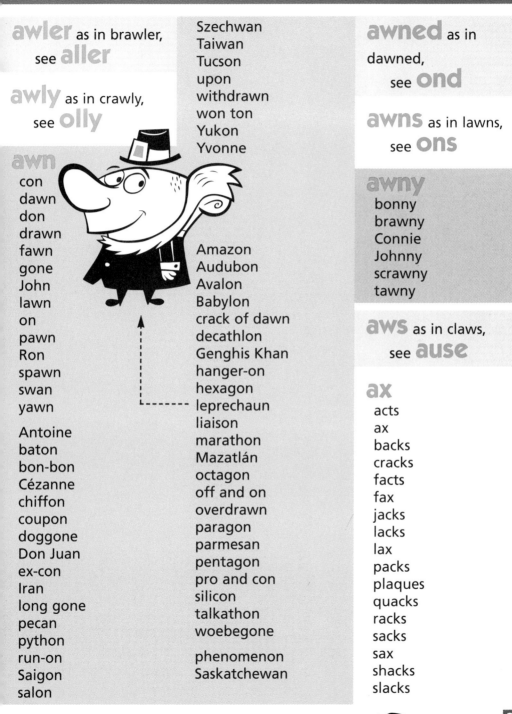

awned as in dawned, see **ond**

awns as in lawns, see **ons**

awny

bonny
brawny
Connie
Johnny
scrawny
tawny

aws as in claws, see **ause**

ax

acts
ax
backs
cracks
facts
fax
jacks
lacks
lax
packs
plaques
quacks
racks
sacks
sax
shacks
slacks

smacks
snacks
stacks
tax
tracks
wax
yaks

attacks
attracts
climax
contacts
distracts
drawbacks
earwax
haystacks
ice packs
kayaks
lilacs
reacts
relax
subtracts
thumbtacks
unpacks
wisecracks

artifacts
Cadillacs
candle wax
Cracker Jacks
heart attacks
income tax
interacts
jumping jacks
maniacs
overacts
railroad tracks

overreacts

axi

taxi
waxy

ay

bay
bray
clay
day
fray
gay
gray
hay
hey
lay
may
nay
neigh
pay
play
pray
prey
ray
say
slay
sleigh
spray
stay
stray
sway
they
tray
way
weigh

away
ballet
birthday
blue jay

bouquet
cafe
croquet
decay
delay
display
essay
gangway
halfway
hallway
headway
highway
ice tray
Norway
obey
okay
one-way
railway
relay
repay
role-play
runway
someway
stairway
stingray
subway
survey
Taipei
today
weekday
x-ray

by the way
day by day
disobey

everyday
faraway
holiday
matinee
Milky Way
night and day
play-by-play
protégé
PTA
right-of-way
runaway
San Jose
Santa Fe
stowaway
throwaway
tooth decay
underway
USA
yesterday

any which way
April Fools' Day
day after day
far and away
happy birthday
out of the way
rub the wrong way
St. Patrick's Day
vitamin A

TWA

ayed as in played,
see **ade** 1

ayer

grayer
layer
mayor

player
betrayer
conveyor
soothsayer
surveyor
taxpayer

ays as in days,
see **aze**

aze

bays
blaze
craze
days
daze
faze
gaze
glaze
graze
haze
laze
maze
nays
pays
phase
phrase
plays
praise
prays
raise
rays
slays
sprays
stays
strays
sways

trays
ways
weighs

ablaze
always
amaze
ballets
betrays
birthdays
blue jays
bouquets
cafes
decays
delays
displays
essays
hallways
obeys
okays
outweighs
portrays
railways
repays
rephrase
school days
sideways
stargaze
subways
surveys
trailblaze
x-rays

disobeys
gamma rays
holidays
mayonnaise
nowadays
paraphrase
runaways

azon
blazon
brazen
raisin

emblazon

azy
crazy
daisy
hazy
lazy

stir-crazy

upsy-daisy

azz
as
has
jazz
razz

pizzazz
topaz

Alcatraz
razzmatazz

azzy
jazzy
snazzy

e as in be,
see **ee**

ea as in flea,
see **ee**

each
beach
bleach
each
leech
peach
preach
reach
screech
speech
teach

free speech
impeach
outreach

figure of speech

eacher
bleacher
creature ------------
feature
preacher
screecher
teacher

ead 1 as in plead,
see **eed**

ead 2 as in bread,
see **ed**

eader 1 as in leader
see **eeder**

eader 2
as in deader,
see **etter**

eady as in ready,
see **etty**

eager
eager
meager

little leaguer
overeager

eagle as in beagle,
see **egal**

eague
league

big league
blitzkrieg
colleague
fatigue
intrigue

Little League

eak 1 as weak,
see **eek**

eak 2 as in break,
see **ake**

eaker
beaker
peeker
sneaker
speaker
weaker

loudspeaker

eaky
creaky
freaky
geeky
leaky
sneaky
squeaky

eal as in real,
see **eel**

ealed as in healed,
see **ield**

eally
freely
really
wheelie

ideally
Swahili

39

ealous to ease

ealous
jealous
tell us
zealous

expel us

overzealous

eam as in dream, see eem

eamy
creamy
dreamy
Mimi
preemie
steamy

sashimi

ean as in bean, see een

eap as in leap, see eep

eaper as in cheaper, see eeper

ear 1 as in pear, see air

ear 2 as in year, see eer

earch as in search, see urch

earer
clearer
dearer
mirror
nearer

severer
sincerer

interferer

earful
cheerful
earful
fearful
tearful

earl as in pearl, see url

early as in pearly, see urly

earn as in learn, see urn

earse as in hearse, see erse

earth as in earth, see irth

eary as in weary, see eery

eas as in fleas, see eeze

ease 1 as in please, see eeze

ease 2
cease
crease
fleece
geese
grease
Greece
lease
niece
peace
piece

apiece
caprice
Clarisse
Cochise
decease
decrease
hairpiece
increase
Matisse
Maurice
obese
police
release
timepiece
wild geese
world peace

centerpiece
elbow grease
Golden Fleece
masterpiece ------
piece by piece
press release
time-release

all in one piece
gaggle of geese
secret police

justice of the peace

eason
reason
season
treason

out of season
stands to reason

east
beast
ceased
creased
east
feast
greased
least
pieced
priest
yeast

deceased
decreased
Far East
increased
Near East
policed
released

Middle East
wildebeest

last but not least

beauty and the beast

easure
measure
pleasure
treasure

displeasure
tape measure

easy
breezy
cheesy
easy
queasy
sneezy

Parcheesi
uneasy
Zambezi

eat 1 as in beat, see eet

eat 2 as in great, see ate

eat 3 as in sweat, see et

eaten
beaten
cretin
eaten
neaten
sweeten

browbeaten
moth-eaten ------

weatherbeaten

eater as in heater, see eeder

eath 1
breath
death

bad breath
Macbeth

kiss of death
out of breath
scared to death
starve to death

Elizabeth
tickled to death

eath 2

Keith
teeth
wreath

beneath
bequeath
false teeth

underneath

eather

feather
Heather
leather
tether
weather
whether

fair-weather
together

altogether
get-together
tar and feather

birds of a feather
light as a feather
under the weather

eature as in

creature,
see **eacher**

eaty as in meaty,
see **eedy**

eave

eve
grieve
heave
leave
sleeve
Steve
weave
we've

achieve
believe
conceive
deceive
naive
perceive
pet peeve
receive
relieve
retrieve
shirtsleeve
sick leave

Christmas Eve
make believe
Tel Aviv

Adam and Eve

eaver

beaver - - - - - - - - - - -
cleaver
fever
weaver

achiever
believer
hay fever
meat cleaver
receiver

spring fever

basket weaver
eager beaver
nonbeliever
scarlet fever

golden retriever
overachiever
underachiever

ebble

pebble
rebel
treble

eck

check
Czech
deck
fleck
heck
neck
peck
speck
trek
wreck

Aztec
hi-tech
paycheck
Quebec
raincheck

roughneck
shipwreck
spot-check
Star Trek

bottleneck
discotheque
double-check
hit the deck
hunt and peck
leatherneck
neck and neck
rubberneck
turtleneck

pain in the neck

ecked as in

checked,

see ect

eckle

freckle
heckle
Jekyll

ecks as in decks,

see ex

ecord

checkered
record

ect

checked
decked
flecked

sect
trekked
wrecked

affect
collect
connect
correct
defect
detect
direct
dissect
effect
eject
elect
erect
expect
infect
inject
insect
inspect
neglect
object
perfect
project
prospect
protect
reflect
reject
respect
select
shipwrecked
subject
suspect

architect
disconnect
disinfect
disrespect
double-checked

incorrect
indirect
intellect
intersect
recollect
reelect
self-respect
sound effect

cause and effect

ection

section

affection
collection
complexion
conception
connection
correction
cross-section
dejection
direction
ejection
election
infection
inflection
injection
inspection
objection
perfection
protection
reflection
rejection
selection

imperfection
interjection
intersection
recollection

resurrection

house of correction
sense of direction

ective

defective
detective
effective
elective
objective
perspective
reflective
selective
subjective

ineffective
retrospective

overprotective

ector

Hector
nectar
specter

collector
connector
defector
detector
director
inspector
projector
protector
reflector

ects as in insects,
see **ex**

ed

bed
bled
bread
bred
dead
dread
Ed
fed
fled
head
lead
led
read
red
said
shed
shred
sled
sped
spread
Ted
thread
tread
wed

ahead
bald head
behead
biped
blockhead
bloodshed
bobsled
bonehead

bunkbed
Club Med
coed
deathbed
drop dead
egghead
forehead
French bread
hardhead
homestead
ill-bred
inbred
instead
misread
moped
proofread
purebred
redhead
sickbed
spoonfed
spearhead
unsaid
unwed
well-bred
well-fed
widespread

arrowhead
bottlefed
city-bred
figurehead
gingerbread
Grateful Dead
infrared
knucklehead
letterhead
newlywed
overfed
overhead

sleepyhead
straight ahead
Sudafed
thoroughbred
underfed
waterbed

early to bed
full speed ahead
hole in the head
out of your head

edal as in pedal,
see **eddle**

edder as in shredder,
see **etter**

eddle

Gretel
kettle
medal
meddle
metal
pedal
peddle
petal
settle

backpedal
gold medal
rose petal
teakettle
unsettle

heavy metal

Hansel and Gretel

ede as in proceed,
see **eed**

edge

dredge
edge
hedge
ledge
pledge
veg
wedge

allege
on edge

edic

comedic

orthopedic

edicate

dedicate
medicate

edo

Frito
neat-o
veto

bandito
Benito
burrito
Toledo
torpedo
tuxedo

incognito

ee

be
bee
fee
flea
flee
free
gee
glee
he
key
knee
me
pea
plea
sea
see
she
ski
spree
tea
tee
three
tree
we

agree
carefree
deep-sea
degree
emcee
home free
ID
M.D.
Marie
monkey
off-key
peewee
queen bee

eech to eeder

RV
sightsee
sweet pea
tax-free
tee hee
teepee

absentee
bumblebee
caffeine-free
chimpanzee
Christmas tree
disagree
employee
fancy free
guarantee
jamboree
nominee
oversee
pardon me
pedigree
Ph.D.
referee
refugee
Rosemarie
shopping spree
spelling bee
sugar-free
Tennessee
VIP
water ski
worry-free

college degree
family tree
fiddle-de-dee
land of the free

under lock and key
Washington, D.C.

eech as in speech, see **each**

eed

bead
bleed
breed
creed
deed
feed
freed
greed
heed
knead
kneed
lead
need
plead
read
reed
seed
skied
speed
steed
treed
tweed
weed

agreed
concede
exceed
force-feed
full speed
impede
indeed
lip-read
mislead
nosebleed

precede
proceed
proofread
recede
seaweed
speed-read
stampede
succeed

centipede
disagreed
guaranteed
overfeed
refereed
supersede
tumbleweed
up to speed

eeder

beater
bleeder
cedar
cheater
eater
feeder
heater
leader
liter
meter
neater
Peter
reader
speeder
sweeter
teeter
weeder

anteater
bandleader
born leader

cheerleader
fire eater
gang leader
impeder
mind-reader
proofreader
repeater
ringleader
Saint Peter
two-seater

centimeter
kilometer
meter reader
overeater
parking meter
trick-or-treater

eedle
beetle
needle
wheedle

eedy
beady
greedy
meaty
needy
seedy
speedy
sweetie
treaty
weedy

entreaty
graffiti
peace treaty
Tahiti

eef as in beef, see ief

eek
beak
bleak
cheek
creak
creek
freak
geek
Greek
leak
meek
peak
peek
pique
reek
seek
shriek
sleek
sneak
speak
squeak
streak
tweak
weak
week

antique
boutique
critique
midweek
misspeak
mystique
oblique
physique
pip-squeak

technique
unique

cheek-to-cheek
Chesapeake
hide-and-seek
so to speak
tongue in cheek

eeker as in peeker, see eaker

eel
deal
eel
feel
heal
heel
keel
kneel
meal
peel
real
reel
seal
squeal
steal
steel
teal
veal
wheel
zeal

appeal
bastille
big deal
cartwheel
chenille
conceal

congeal
fair deal
for real
genteel
high heel
ideal
misdeal
mobile
newsreel
oatmeal
ordeal
piecemeal
reveal
unreal

bookmobile
Ferris wheel
glockenspiel
no big deal
Oldsmobile

automobile

eeled as in peeled, see **ield**

eem
beam
cream
deem
dream
gleam
ream
scheme
scream
seam
seem
steam
stream

team
teem
theme

bloodstream
daydream
downstream
drill team
esteem
extreme
ice cream
mainstream
moonbeam
pipe dream
redeem
regime
sunbeam
supreme
whipped cream

color scheme
double-team
let off steam
self-esteem
sour cream

een
bean
clean
dean
gene
glean
green
Jean
keen
lean
mean
queen
scene
screen

seen
sheen
teen

Bactine
between
caffeine
canteen
chlorine
Colleen
convene
cuisine
Darlene
dry clean
eighteen
Eugene
fifteen
fourteen
green bean
hygiene
Irene
Kathleen
machine
marine
Marlene
Maxine
mob scene
obscene
preteen
prom queen
protein
ravine
routine
sardine
serene
sixteen
smokescreen
sunscreen
thirteen

unseen
vaccine

evergreen
fairy queen
gasoline
go-between
guillotine
Halloween
intervene
jelly bean
Josephine
kerosene
lean and mean
limousine
magazine
Maybelline
mezzanine
movie screen
nectarine
nicotine
quarantine
serpentine
seventeen
squeaky clean
submarine
sweet sixteen
tambourine
tangerine
trampoline
Vaseline

eep

beep
bleep
cheap
creep
deep
heap

jeep
keep
leap
peep
reap
seep
sheep
sleep
steep
sweep
weep

asleep
Bo Peep
junkheap
knee-deep
skin-deep

beauty sleep
oversleep

eeper

beeper
cheaper
creeper
deeper
keeper
reaper
sleeper
steeper
sweeper
weeper

housekeeper
timekeeper

eepy

creepy
sleepy
tepee
weepy

eer

beer
cheer
clear
dear
deer
ear
fear
gear
hear
here
jeer
leer
mere
near
peer
pier
rear
sheer
smear
sneer
spear
sphere
steer
tear
tier
veer
year

adhere
all clear
appear
career
cashier
cashmere
frontier
leap year
pierced ear
premier

49

reindeer
root beer
severe
Shakespeare
sincere
unclear

atmosphere
auctioneer
buccaneer
cavalier
chandelier
crystal-clear
disappear
engineer
far and near
free and clear
hemisphere
insincere
interfere
loud and clear
mouseketeer
musketeer
mutineer
never fear
overhear
Paul Revere
persevere
pioneer
racketeer
reappear
souvenir
stratosphere
volunteer

eery

cheery
dearie
dreary

eerie
leery
query
teary
theory
weary

hara-kiri

ees as in bees, see eeze

eese as in geese, see ease 2

eet

beat
beet
bleat
cheat
eat
feat
feet
fleet
greet
heat
meat
meet
neat
Pete
pleat
seat
sheet
sleet
street
suite
sweet
treat

tweet
wheat

athlete
backseat
browbeat
cold feet
compete
complete
conceit
concrete
deadbeat
deceit
defeat
delete
discreet
discrete
elite
excrete
flat feet
heartbeat
mistreat
off-beat
petite
receipt
repeat
retreat
secrete
upbeat
Wall Street

bittersweet
incomplete
indiscreet
overeat
parakeet
short and sweet
shredded wheat
stocking feet
trick or treat

two left feet

red as a beet
Sesame Street

eeter as in sweeter,
see **eeder**

eethe
breathe
seethe
teethe

eeve as in sleeve,
see **eave**

eeze
bees
breeze
cheese
ease
fees
fleas
flees
frees
freeze
keys
knees
peas
pleas
please
seas
sees
seize
skis
sneeze
sprees

teas
tease
these
trees
wheeze

agrees
big cheese
Chinese
cream cheese
deep freeze
degrees
disease
displease
foresees
high seas
Louise
monkeys
sea breeze
sweet peas
tepees
trapeze
TVs

ABCs
Androcles
antifreeze
bumblebees
chickadees
chimpanzees
cottage cheese
disagrees
dungarees
guarantees
Hercules
ill at ease
jamborees
Japanese
nominees
overseas

oversees
pedigrees
pretty please
referees
shopping sprees
Siamese
Socrates
water skis

eezer
Caesar
freezer
geezer
squeezer
tweezer

eezy as in breezy,
see **easy**

ef
chef
clef
deaf
Jeff
ref

eft
deft
left
theft

eg
beg
egg
Greg
keg
leg

Meg
peg

nest egg
renege

Winnipeg

egal
beagle
eagle
legal
regal

bald eagle
illegal

egion
legion
region

collegian
Norwegian

eigh as in sleigh,
see **ay**

eight as in weight,
see **ate**

eighty as in weighty,
see **ady**

eir as in their,
see **air**

eist as in heist,
see **iced**

eit as in conceit,
see **eet**

eive as in receive,
see **eave**

el as in hotel,
see **ell**

elch
belch
squelch
welch

eld
held
jelled
meld
quelled
shelled
spelled
weld
yelled

beheld
compelled
excelled
expelled
hand-held
misspelled
propelled
rebelled
repelled
upheld
withheld

unparalleled

elf
elf
self
shelf

bookshelf
herself
himself
itself
myself
yourself

ell
bell
belle
cell
dwell
fell
gel
hell
jell
Nell
sell
shell
smell
spell
swell
tell
well
yell

Adele
bombshell
compel
doorbell
dumbbell
eggshell
excel
expel

farewell
gazelle
hotel
inkwell
jail cell
lapel
Maxwell
misspell
motel
Noel
nutshell
pastel
propel
Raquel
rebel
repel
retell
schoolbell
sleighbell
unwell

carousel
clientele
dinner bell
Isabel
magic spell
NFL
oil well
parallel
personnel
Raphael
show and tell
Tinker Bell
very well
William Tell
wishing well

clear as a bell
mademoiselle

ella

Della
Ella
fella
Stella

umbrella

a cappella
Cinderella
Isabella
mozzarella

ellar as in stellar, see eller

elle as in belle, see ell

elled as in spelled, see eld

eller

cellar
dweller
feller
seller
speller
stellar
teller
yeller

cave dweller
propeller
storm cellar

fortune-teller - - - - - - - - - ->
interstellar
Rockefeller

ello as in cello, see ellow

ellow

bellow
cello
fellow
hello
Jell-O
mellow
yellow

Longfellow
marshmallow

elly

belly
deli
jelly
Kelly
Nellie
Shelley
smelly

New Delhi
potbelly

elp

help
kelp
yelp

elt
belt
Celt
dealt
felt
knelt
melt
pelt
svelte
welt

heartfelt
seat belt

elter
shelter
smelter
swelter

helter-skelter

elve
delve
shelve
twelve

em
gem
hem
stem
them

A.M.
condemn
FM
P.M.

ember
ember
member

December
gang member
November
remember
September

emble
tremble

assemble
resemble

eme as in theme, see eem

empt
dreamt
tempt

attempt
contempt
exempt

en
Ben
den
hen
men
pen
ten
than
then
when
yen

again
amen
bullpen
Cheyenne
hang ten
pigpen
playpen

Adrienne
lion's den
mother hen
now and then
poison pen

ena
Gina
Tina

arena
cantina
Christina
hyena
marina
subpoena

Argentina
ballerina
Pasadena

ence as in fence, see ense

ench

bench
clench
drench
French
quench
stench
trench
wrench

park bench
unclench

monkey wrench

encher as in quencher,
see enture

encil

pencil
stencil

utensil

end

bend
blend
end
friend
lend
mend
penned
send
spend
tend
trend

amend

ascend
attend
best friend
boyfriend
dead end
defend
depend
descend
extend
girlfriend
intend
offend
pretend
suspend
transcend
unbend
upend
wit's end

apprehend
bitter end
comprehend
dividend
end-to-end
man's best friend
overspend
recommend

fair-weather friend

ender

blender
fender
gender
lender
render
sender
slender
splendor
tender

vendor

bartender
contender
defender
goaltender
offender
pretender
surrender
suspender

endor as in splendor,
see ender

ene as in gene,
see een

ength

length
strength

enny

any
Benny
Denny
Jenny
Kenny
many
penny

ense
cents
dense
dents
fence
gents
scents
sense
tense
tents
vents

commence
condense
defense
dispense
expense
good sense
immense
incense
intense
make sense
nonsense
offense
percents
presents
pretense
resents
sixth sense
suspense

common sense
compliments
consequence
evidence
false pretense
no-nonsense
represents
self-defense

dollars and cents

ension as in
tension,
see ention

ensity
density

immensity
intensity

ensive
pensive

defensive
expensive
extensive
intensive
offensive

apprehensive
comprehensive
inexpensive

labor-intensive

ent
bent
cent
dent
gent
Lent
meant
rent
scent
sent
spent
tent
vent
went

air vent

cement
consent
content
descent
dissent
event
extent
for rent
frequent
indent
intent
invent
lament
misspent
percent
present
prevent
repent
resent
torment
well-spent

came and went
circus tent
compliment
discontent
evident
heaven sent
implement
malcontent
represent
underwent

blessed event
experiment - - - - - - -
misrepresent

ental
dental
gentle
lentil
mental
rental

judgmental
parental

accidental
continental
departmental
detrimental
elemental
fundamental
governmental
incidental
instrumental
monumental
ornamental
sentimental
temperamental
transcendental

coincidental
environmental
experimental

enter
center
enter
mentor

dissenter
inventor
off center
presenter
reenter
tormentor

civic center
do not enter
front and center
shopping center

ential
credential
essential
potential
torrential

confidential
deferential
influential
preferential
presidential
residential

ention
mention
pension
tension

attention
convention
detention
dimension
dissension
extension
intention
invention
pretension
prevention
suspension

apprehension
comprehension
hypertension
inattention
intervention

not to mention
three dimension

misapprehension
ounce of prevention

honorable mention

entive
attentive
incentive
inventive
preventive

ently
gently

contently
intently

consequently
evidently
incidentally

entor as in mentor, see enter

ents as in cents, see ense

enture
censure
denture
quencher
venture

adventure
fist clencher
joint venture
thirst quencher

57

ep

pep
prep
schlep
step
strep
yep

bicep
doorstep
sidestep

overstep

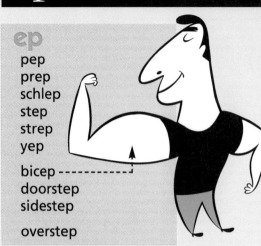

epped as in
stepped,
  see **ept**

ept

crept
kept
pepped
slept
stepped
swept
wept

accept
concept
except
inept
rainswept
sidestepped
windswept

intercept
overslept
overstepped

eption

conception
deception
exception
perception
reception

depth perception
interception
misconception

er

blur
burr
err
fir
fur
gr-r-r
her
per
purr
sir
slur
spur
stir
were

astir
Ben Hur
concur
confer
defer
demur
deter
infer
occur
prefer
refer
yes sir

emperor
him and her

erb as in verb,
  see **urb**

erce as in coerce,
  see **erse**

erd

bird
blurred
erred
heard
herd
purred
slurred
spurred
stirred
third
word

absurd
backward
Big Bird
blackbird

buzzword
code word
concurred
conferred
crossword
deferred
deterred
forward
inferred
jailbird
lovebird ------
occurred
one-third
password
preferred
referred
songbird
swearword
transferred
unheard
watchword

afterward
early bird
hummingbird
ladybird
massacred
mockingbird
overheard
reoccurred
self-assured
solemn word
word for word

four-letter word
free as a bird

ere 1 as in sphere,
see **eer**

ere 2 as in there,
see **air**

erer as in sincerer,
see **earer**

erge
merge
purge
splurge
surge
urge
verge

converge
diverge
emerge
submerge

ergent
urgent

detergent
divergent
emergent
insurgent

eria
Syria

Algeria
bacteria
diphtheria
Nigeria
Siberia

cafeteria

erious
serious

delirious
mysterious

erish
bearish
cherish
garish
perish

erit as in merit,
see **arrot**

erity as in sincerity,
see **arity**

erk
clerk
irk
jerk
Kirk
lurk
perk
quirk
shirk
smirk
Turk
work

berserk
brain-work
clockwork
footwork
framework
groundwork
guesswork

homework
housework
legwork
network
patchwork
schoolwork
teamwork
woodwork

dirty work
handiwork
out of work
overwork

erky

jerky
murky
perky
quirky
turkey

beef jerky
cold turkey

Albuquerque

erm

firm
germ
perm
squirm
term
worm

affirm
bookworm
confirm
earthworm
glowworm
long-term
midterm

silkworm

pachyderm
wiggle worm

ern as in stern, see urn

ernal

colonel
journal
kernel

eternal
external
fraternal
internal
maternal
nocturnal
paternal

ero 1

hero
Nero
zero

ero 2 as in sombrero, see arrow

erred as in transferred, see erd

error as in terror, see arer

erry as in cherry, see ary

erse

curse
hearse
nurse ---->
purse
terse
verse
worse

adverse
coerce
commerce
converse
disperse
diverse
immerse
inverse
rehearse
reverse
submerse
transverse

intersperse
reimburse
universe

ersed as in conversed, see irst

ersion

Persian
version

aversion

coercion
conversion
diversion
excursion
immersion
submersion

ersity

adversity
diversity

university

erson

person
worsen

layperson
spokesperson

ert

Bert
blurt
curt
dirt
flirt
hurt
pert
shirt
skirt
spurt
squirt

alert
assert
avert
convert
covert
desert
dessert

divert
exert
Frankfurt
insert
invert
nightshirt
overt
pay dirt
redshirt
stuffed shirt
subvert
unhurt

extrovert
hula skirt
introvert
miniskirt
smog alert
undershirt

overexert

erter

herder
murder
squirter

absurder
converter
deserter
frankfurter

erve

curve
nerve
serve
swerve
verve
conserve
deserve

hors d'oeuvre
observe
preserve
reserve
self-serve
unnerve

brown-and-serve

ery as in very, see ary

escent

crescent

fluorescent
incessant

adolescent
convalescent
effervescent
iridescent

esh

flesh
fresh
mesh

enmesh
gooseflesh
refresh

Bangladesh
in the flesh

esident

hesitant
president
resident

esque

desk

burlesque
grotesque

picturesque

ess

Bess
bless
chess
dress
guess
less
mess
press
stress
Tess
yes

access
address
bench-press
caress
confess
depress
digress
distress
duress
excess
express
finesse
impress
Loch Ness
oppress
outguess
possess
profess
progress

recess
regress
repress
success
suppress
undress
unless

air express
fancy dress
full-court press
more or less
nonetheless
overdress
printing press
repossess
second-guess
s.o.s.

change of address
nevertheless
pony express

anybody's guess
freedom of the press
Gettysburg Address

essed as in blessed, see est

esser as in lesser, see essor

essful

stressful

distressful
successful

ession

freshen
session

aggression
concession
confession
depression
discretion
expression
impression
jam session
obsession
oppression
possession
procession
profession
progression
rap session
recession
refreshen
repression
succession
suppression

indiscretion
self-expression
summer session

essive

aggressive
excessive
expressive
impressive

obsessive
oppressive
possessive
progressive

essor

dresser
guesser
lesser
yes sir

aggressor
assessor
compressor
confessor
hairdresser
oppressor
possessor
processor
professor
successor

fancy dresser
food processor
predecessor
second-guesser
word processor

essy

dressy
Jessie
messy

est

best
blessed
breast
chest
crest
dressed

guessed
guest
jest
messed
nest
pest
pressed
quest
rest
stressed
test
vest
west
zest

addressed
arrest
bird nest
blood test
caressed
Celeste
confessed
conquest
contest
crow's nest
depressed
detest
digressed
distressed
expressed
finessed
fun fest
hope chest
impressed
invest

life vest
next best
obsessed
oppressed
outguessed
possessed
professed
progressed
protest
recessed
repressed
request
screen test
suggest
suppressed
undressed
Wild West

beauty rest
day of rest
decongest
false arrest
hornet's nest
last request
level best
manifest
overdressed
second best
treasure chest
unimpressed

bulletproof vest
medicine chest
permanent-pressed
under arrest

ester

Chester
Esther
fester

63

jester
Lester
pester
tester

ancestor
court jester
investor
protestor
semester

polyester

estion

question

congestion
digestion
suggestion

decongestion
indigestion
pop the question

out of the question

estor as in investor, see ester

et

bet
debt
fret
get
jet
met
net
pet
set
sweat

threat
vet
wet
whet
yet

abet
all set
all wet
brunette
cadet
cold sweat
coquette
Corvette
dragnet
dudette
duet
forget
Jeanette
jet set
no sweat
not yet
Paulette
quartet
regret
reset
sunset
Tibet
upset

alphabet
Antoinette
bassinet
bayonet
Bernadette
better yet
cigarette
clarinet
dripping wet
Juliet

majorette
minuet
out of debt
pirouette
safety net
silhouette
Soviet
suffragette
teacher's pet

mosquito net
national debt
Russian roulette

etal as in metal, see eddle

etch

etch
fetch
retch
sketch
stretch
wretch

homestretch

ete as in athlete, see eet

eter as in meter, see eeder

ether as in together, see eather

etic
athletic
cosmetic
frenetic
genetic
magnetic
pathetic
phonetic
poetic
synthetic

anesthetic
diabetic
dietetic
energetic
sympathetic

apologetic

ette as in brunette, see et

etter
better
cheddar
deader
debtor
letter
redder
shredder
sweater
wetter

fan letter
forgetter
go-getter
jet setter
love letter
newsletter

trendsetter
doubleheader
paper shredder

etti as in confetti, see etty

ettle as in kettle, see eddle

etto
ghetto
meadow

falsetto
Gepetto
libretto
stiletto

etty
Betty
Eddie
Freddie
heady
petty
ready
steady
sweaty
Teddy

already
confetti
go steady
machete
spaghetti --------
unsteady

rough and ready

eur as in chauffeur, see ure

evel
bevel
devil
level
revel

daredevil
dishevel

even
Devon
heaven
Kevin
seven

eleven
thank heaven

ever
clever
ever
lever
never
sever
Trevor

endeavor
forever
however
whatever
whenever
wherever
whichever
whoever

ew

blew
blue
boo
brew
chew
clue
crew
cue
dew
do
drew
due
ewe
few
flew
flu
glue
gnu
goo
grew
hue
knew
mew
moo
new
pew
pooh
rue
screw
shoe
slew
stew
sue
threw
through
to
too

true
two
view
who
woo
you
zoo

ado
ah-choo
anew
bamboo
boo-boo
boohoo
brand-new
breakthrough
canoe
cashew
choo-choo
construe
corkscrew
cuckoo
curfew
debut
dog-doo
drive-through
goo-goo
hairdo
horseshoe
how-to
into
IQ
kazoo
kung fu
miscue
misdo
muumuu
on cue
on view

outdo
outgrew
past due
Peru
PU
pursue
redo
renew
review
revue
Says who?
see-through
shampoo
snafu
subdue
taboo
tattoo
thank you
true blue
tutu
undo
unscrew
unto
untrue
voodoo
who's who
withdrew
world-view
yoo-hoo

avenue
ballyhoo
barbecue
bird's-eye view
black-and-blue
book review
buckaroo
bugaboo
caribou

cockatoo
countersue
curlicue
I love you
impromptu
interview
Irish stew
jujitsu
kangaroo
Malibu
misconstrue
navy blue
no can do
Oahu
overdo
overdue
peek-a-boo
point of view
postage due
quite a few
rendezvous
residue
revenue
stinkaroo
Super Glue
switcheroo
through and through
Timbuktu
toodle-oo
tried and true
two by two
Waterloo
well-to-do
whoop-de-do

catch-22
hullabaloo
out of the blue
red, white, and blue

skeleton crew
Winnie the Pooh

cock-a-doodle-doo
panoramic view

ewd as in shrewd,
see **ude**

ewed as in brewed,
see **ude**

ews as in chews,
see **use** 2

ewy
buoy
chewy
dewy
gooey
phooey
screwy

chop suey
mildewy

ex
checks
decks
ex
flecks
flex
hex
necks
pecks
sex
treks

vex
wrecks

affects
annex
apex
collects
complex
connects
corrects
defects
detects
directs
duplex
effects
ejects
elects
erects
expects
index
infects
injects
insects
inspects
Kleenex
neglects
objects
perfects
perplex
projects
prospects
protects
reflects
reflex
rejects
respects
selects
subjects
suspects

architects
birth defects
dialects
disconnects
double-checks
intersects
reelects
rubbernecks
sound effects

eys as in keys,
see **eeze**

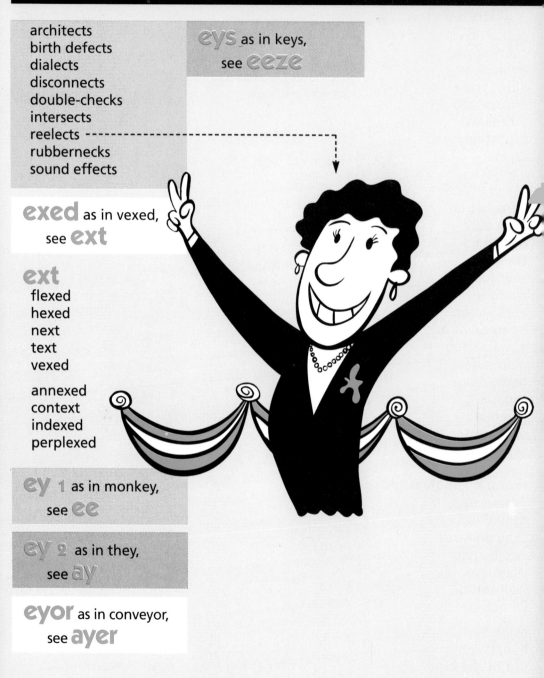

exed as in vexed,
see **ext**

ext
flexed
hexed
next
text
vexed

annexed
context
indexed
perplexed

ey 1 as in monkey,
see **ee**

ey 2 as in they,
see **ay**

eyor as in conveyor,
see **ayer**

i as in alibi, see y

iable

liable
pliable
viable

reliable

justifiable
undeniable
unreliable

ial as in trial, see ile 1

iance

clients
giants
science

alliance
appliance
defiance
reliance

iant

Bryant
client
giant
pliant

defiant
reliant

self-reliant

ib

bib
crib
fib
glib
nib
rib

ad lib
prime rib
sparerib

women's lib

ibble

dribble
kibble
nibble
quibble
scribble
Sibyl

ibe

bribe
gibe
scribe
tribe

describe
imbibe
inscribe
prescribe
subscribe
transcribe

diatribe

ibit

ad-lib it
exhibit
inhibit

prohibit
flibbertigibbet

ic as in picnic, see ick

ice 1

dice
ice
lice
mice
nice
price
rice
slice
spice
splice
twice
vice

advice
concise
device
entice
no dice
precise
sale price
suffice
think twice

merchandise
paradise
sacrifice
three blind mice

at any price
fool's paradise
legal advice
self-sacrifice
sugar and spice

ice to ick

ice 2 as in police,
see **ease** 2

iced
diced
heist
iced
priced
sliced
spiced

enticed
high-priced
sufficed

overpriced
poltergeist
sacrificed

ich as in rich,
see **itch**

icial
initial
judicial
official

artificial
beneficial
prejudicial
superficial
unofficial

ician as in
musician,
see **ition**

icient
deficient
efficient
omniscient
sufficient

inefficient
insufficient
self-sufficient

icious
vicious

ambitious
auspicious
delicious
fictitious
judicious
malicious
nutritious
suspicious

repetitious
superstitious

icit
kiss it
miss it

dismiss it
elicit
explicit
illicit
implicit
is this it?
solicit

icity
duplicity
ethnicity

publicity
simplicity
toxicity

authenticity
domesticity
eccentricity
elasticity
electricity - - - - - - -

ick
brick
chick
click
flick
kick
lick
nick
pick
prick
quick
sick
slick
stick
thick
tick
trick

airsick
beatnik
broomstick
card trick
Chap Stick
chopstick
drumstick
handpick
heartsick
homesick
lipstick
lovesick

nitpick
picnic
seasick
sidekick
slapstick
St. Nick
toothpick
yardstick

candlestick
dirty trick
heretic
lunatic
Moby Dick
nervous tic

icked as in licked,
see ict

icken
chicken
quicken
sicken
stricken
thicken

grief-stricken
spring chicken

panic-stricken
rubber chicken

icker
bicker
clicker
flicker
kicker
liquor
picker

quicker
sicker
slicker
sticker
thicker
ticker
wicker

nitpicker
picnicker

city slicker

icket
cricket
picket
thicket
ticket
wicket

ickle
fickle
nickel
pickle
sickle
tickle
trickle

bicycle
dill pickle
icicle
Popsicle
tricycle
vehicle

pumpernickel

hammer and sickle

ickly
prickly
quickly
sickly
thickly
tickly

icks
bricks
chicks
clicks
fix
flicks
kicks
licks
mix
nicks
nix
picks
pricks
six
sticks
ticks
tricks
wicks

cake mix
chopsticks
conflicts
drumsticks
evicts
lipsticks
nitpicks
picnics
pinpricks
predicts
quick fix
restricts
toothpicks

transfix

bag of tricks
contradicts
fiddlesticks
pick-up-sticks
politics
ton of bricks

icky
icky
Mickey
Nicky
picky
quickie
sticky
tricky
Vicki

icle as in vehicle, see ickle

ics as in politics, see icks

ict
clicked
flicked
kicked
licked
nicked
picked
pricked
slicked
strict
ticked
tricked

afflict
conflict
convict
evict
handpicked
inflict
nitpicked
picnicked
predict
restrict

contradict
derelict

iction
diction
fiction
friction

addiction
conviction
eviction
nonfiction
prediction
restriction

benediction
contradiction
drug addiction
jurisdiction
science fiction

ictor
stricter
tricked 'er
victor

constrictor
predictor

contradictor

icts as in conflicts, see icks

icy
icy
pricey
spicy

nicey-nicey

id
bid
did
grid
hid
id
kid
lid
rid
Sid
skid
slid
squid

amid
eyelid
forbid
hybrid
Madrid
outbid
outdid
redid
whiz kid

arachnid
overdid
pyramid

idal as in tidal, see **idle**

iddy as in giddy, see **itty**

idden

bidden
hidden

bedridden
forbidden

overridden

idder as in bidder, see **itter**

iddle

brittle
diddle
fiddle
griddle
little
middle
piddle
riddle
twiddle
whittle

acquittal
belittle
committal
hospital
transmittal

Chicken Little
noncommittal
peanut brittle
second fiddle

little by little

ide

bride
chide
cried
died
dried
dyed
eyed
fried
glide
guide
hide
lied
pride
pried
ride
shied
side
sighed
slide
snide
spied
stride
tide
tied
tried
vied
wide

applied
aside
bedside
beside
bright-eyed
chloride

cockeyed
collide
confide
cross-eyed
decide
deep-fried
defied
denied
divide
fireside
implied
inside
joyride
landslide
misguide
outside
provide
relied
replied
reside
riptide
roadside
subside
supplied
tongue-tied
untied
worldwide

clarified
coincide
dignified
eagle-eyed
far and wide
glorified
horrified
horseback ride
justified
magnified
modified

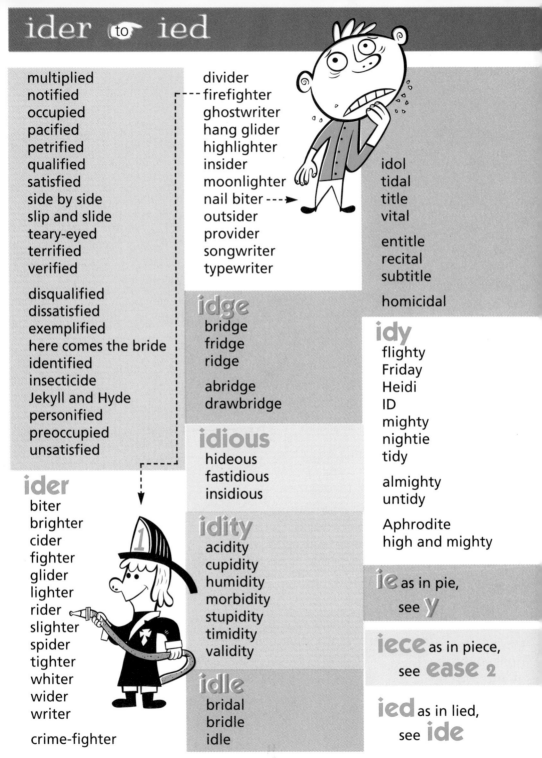

multiplied
notified
occupied
pacified
petrified
qualified
satisfied
side by side
slip and slide
teary-eyed
terrified
verified

disqualified
dissatisfied
exemplified
here comes the bride
identified
insecticide
Jekyll and Hyde
personified
preoccupied
unsatisfied

divider
firefighter
ghostwriter
hang glider
highlighter
insider
moonlighter
nail biter
outsider
provider
songwriter
typewriter

idge
bridge
fridge
ridge

abridge
drawbridge

idious
hideous
fastidious
insidious

idity
acidity
cupidity
humidity
morbidity
stupidity
timidity
validity

idle
bridal
bridle
idle

ider
biter
brighter
cider
fighter
glider
lighter
rider
slighter
spider
tighter
whiter
wider
writer

crime-fighter

idol
tidal
title
vital

entitle
recital
subtitle

homicidal

idy
flighty
Friday
Heidi
ID
mighty
nightie
tidy

almighty
untidy

Aphrodite
high and mighty

ie as in pie, see **y**

iece as in piece, see **ease** 2

ied as in lied, see **ide**

ief

beef
brief
chief
grief
leaf
reef
thief

belief
corned beef
debrief
fire chief
good grief
motif
relief
roast beef

cloverleaf
disbelief
handkerchief

commander-in-chief

ield

field
healed
peeled
reeled
sealed
shield
yield

appealed
concealed
four-wheeled
high-heeled
mine field
revealed
windshield

ier as in pier, see **eer**

ies as in lies, see **ize**

iet

buy it
diet
eye it
quiet
riot
try it

iety

piety

anxiety
propriety
society
variety

notoriety

ieve as in grieve, see **eave**

iever as in believer, see **eaver**

ife

knife
life

strife
wife

housewife
jackknife
nightlife
wildlife

husband and wife
larger-than-life

iff

cliff
if
miff
sniff
stiff
tiff
whiff

midriff
scared stiff

iffed as in sniffed, see **ift**

iffy

iffy
jiffy
spiffy

ific

horrific
Pacific
prolific
specific
terrific

scientific

ift

drift
gift
lift
miffed
rift
shift
sift
sniffed
swift
thrift
whiffed

airlift
face-lift
makeshift
night shift
shoplift
ski lift
snowdrift
spendthrift
uplift

ifty

fifty
nifty
shifty
thrifty

ig

big
dig
fig
gig
jig
pig
rig
swig
twig

wig
bigwig
oil rig
shindig

guinea pig

thingamajig

igger

bigger
digger
rigor
snigger
trigger
vigor

ditchdigger
gold digger
hair trigger

iggle

giggle
jiggle
squiggle
wiggle

iggly

giggly
jiggly
squiggly
wiggly

igh as in high,
see y

ighs as in sighs,
see ize

ight

bite
blight
bright
cite
Dwight
fight
flight
fright
height
kite
knight
light
might
night
plight
quite
right
rite
sight
site
slight
spite
sprite
tight
trite
white
write

airtight
all-night
all right
birthright
bullfight
catfight
daylight
delight
excite
eyesight

finite
firelight
fistfight
flashlight
foresight
forthright
frostbite
gang fight
good night
green light
handwrite
headlight
highlight
hindsight
ignite
incite
indict
insight
invite
limelight
midnight
moonlight
night-light
not quite
outright
playwright
polite
prizefight
recite
red light
searchlight
skintight
snakebite
Snow White
spotlight
stage fright
starlight
stoplight
sunlight

termite
tonight
twilight
unite
upright
uptight
white knight

appetite
black and white
civil right
copyright
day and night
dynamite
fahrenheit
gesundheit
impolite
neon light
neophyte
out-of-sight
overbite
overnight
oversight
parasite
pillow fight
reunite
satellite
socialite

meteorite
opening night
out like a light

ighten
brighten
frighten
heighten
lighten
tighten

whiten

enlighten

ighter as in fighter, see **ider**

ighty as in flighty, see **idy**

ign as in sign, see **ine**

igned as in signed, see **ind** 1

igor as in vigor, see **igger**

igue as in intrigue, see **eague**

ike
bike
hike
like
mic
pike
psych
spike
strike
tyke

alike
dislike

hitchhike
lifelike
unlike
warlike

childlike
hunger strike
ladylike
look-alike
motorbike

iker

biker
hiker
striker

hitchhiker

ild

child
dialed
filed
mild
piled
riled
smiled
styled
tiled
wild

brainchild
exiled
godchild
hogwild
misdialed
misfiled
moonchild
stepchild
stockpiled

ile 1

aisle
dial
file
I'll
isle
mile
Nile
pile
rile
smile
style
tile
trial
vile
while

argyle
awhile
exile
freestyle
high-style
life-style
meanwhile
nail file
profile
reptile
senile
stockpile
turnstile
woodpile
worthwhile

crocodile
domicile
family style
infantile
juvenile
out of style

rank and file
reconcile
single file

after a while
bibliophile
fingernail file
once in a while

ile 2 as in automobile, see eel

iled as in filed, see ild 1

ilian as in reptilian, see illion

ility

ability
agility
civility
facility
futility
hostility
humility
mobility
nobility
senility
stability
tranquillity
utility

capability
credibility
disability
durability

flexibility
gullibility
inability
liability
possibility
probability
sensibility
versatility

acceptability
adaptability
amiability
availability
compatibility
dependability
impossibility
responsibility

ilk

bilk
ilk
milk
silk

buttermilk
malted milk

ill

bill
chill
dill
drill
fill
frill
gill
grill
hill
ill
Jill
kill

mill
nil
Phil
pill
shrill
sill
skill
spill
still
thrill
till
trill
will

anthill
Brazil
downhill
dullsville
fire drill
freewill
fulfill
goodwill
ill will
instill
oil spill
refill
standstill
treadmill
until
uphill
vaudeville
windmill

chlorophyll
daffodil
dollar bill
game of skill
Jack and Jill
overkill
whippoorwill

windowsill

Buffalo Bill
Capitol Hill
king of the hill
run-of-the-mill

illa

villa

Attila
chinchilla
gorilla
guerilla
Manila
Priscilla
vanilla

ille as in bastille,
see eel

illed

billed
build
chilled
drilled
filled
frilled
grilled
guild
killed
milled
skilled
spilled
stilled
thrilled
tilled
trilled
willed

79

fulfilled
rebuild
strong-willed
unskilled

overbuild
unfulfilled

iller

chiller
filler
killer
pillar
thriller

pain killer

caterpillar
chiller-diller

illion

billion
million
trillion
zillion

Brazilian
civilian
cotillion
pavilion
reptilian
Sicilian

illow

pillow
willow

Amarillo
armadillo
pussy willow
weeping willow

illy

Billy
chili
chilly
filly
frilly
hilly
lily
Millie
shrilly
silly

water lily
willy-nilly

ilt

built
guilt
hilt
jilt
kilt
lilt
quilt
spilt
stilt
tilt
wilt

im

brim
dim
grim
him
hymn
Jim
Kim
limb
prim
rim

skim
slim
swim
Tim
trim
whim

antonym
homonym
pseudonym
sink or swim
synonym

imble

cymbal
nimble
symbol
thimble

imbo

limbo

akimbo

ime

chime
climb
crime
dime
grime
I'm
lime
mime
prime
rhyme
slime
thyme
time

bedtime
bigtime

daytime
enzyme
lifetime
meantime
nighttime
old-time
part-time
pastime
peacetime
prime time
showtime
small-time
sometime
springtime
sublime
wartime

anytime
curtain time
dinnertime
every time
Father Time
maritime
mountain climb
one more time
overtime
pantomime
party time
summertime

all in good time
nursery rhyme
one at a time
partners in crime

once in a lifetime
once upon a time

immer

dimmer
glimmer
grimmer
shimmer
simmer
slimmer
swimmer
trimmer

imp

blimp
chimp
crimp
imp
limp
primp
shrimp
skimp
wimp

imple

dimple
pimple
simple

impy

shrimpy
skimpy
wimpy

in

been
bin
chin
din
fin
grin

in
inn
kin
pin
shin
sin
skin
spin
thin
tin
twin
win

again
begin
Berlin
break-in
captain
cave-in
Corryn
drive-in
hairpin
has-been
pigskin
sheepskin
shoo-in
snakeskin
stand-in
tailspin
trash bin
unpin
within

bobby-pin
bowling pin
discipline
double chin
Gunga Din
mandolin
next of kin

play to win
Rin Tin Tin
rolling pin
safety pin
thick and thin
violin

fraternal twin
guilty as sin
Rumpelstiltskin
self-discipline

Huckleberry Finn
identical twin
time and time again

ina 1 as in ballerina, see ena

ina 2
China
Dinah

angina

North Carolina
South Carolina

ince
blintze
chintz
hints
mince
mints
prince
prints
rinse
since
sprints

tints
wince

blueprints
convince
footprints
imprints
misprints

inch
cinch
clinch
finch
flinch
inch
lynch
pinch

inch by inch

inct
blinked
clinked
inked
kinked
linked
winked

distinct
extinct
hoodwinked
instinct
precinct
succinct

ind 1
bind
blind
dined
find

fined
grind
kind
lined
mind
mined
pined
rind
signed
whined
wind

assigned
behind
combined
confined
declined
defined
designed
entwined
headlined
outlined
refined
remind
resigned
snow-blind
streamlined
unkind
unwind

change of mind
colorblind
humankind
intertwined
lemon rind
mastermind
never mind
one-track mind
peace of mind
underlined

undermined
unrefined

boggle the mind
one of a kind

ind 2 as in wind,
see inned

indle

dwindle
kindle
spindle
swindle

ine 1

dine
fine
line
mine
nine
pine
shine
shrine
sign
spine
swine
twine
vine
whine
wine

airline
alpine
assign
baseline

beeline
benign
canine
chow line
clothesline
cloud nine
coal mine
coastline
combine
confine
cosign
deadline
decline
define
design
divine
Einstein
entwine
feline
goal line
gold mine
grapevine
guideline
hairline
headline
hemline
hot line
incline
lifeline
neckline
outline
outshine
peace sign
pipeline
punch line
recline
refine
resign
shoeshine

sideline
skyline
stop sign
streamline
sunshine

borderline
checkout line
clinging vine
danger sign
dollar sign
draw the line
drop a line
first in line
Frankenstein
intertwine
iodine
out of line
Palestine
picket line
porcupine
rain or shine
rise and shine
storyline
toe the line
traffic fine
underline
undermine
valentine
warning sign

ine 2 as in routine,
see een

ined as in dined,
see ind 1

iner

diner
miner
minor
shiner
whiner

airliner
coal miner
designer
eyeliner
headliner
jetliner
one-liner
recliner
shoeshiner

Asia Minor
forty-niner
hair designer

ing

bring
cling
ding
fling
king
ping
ring
sing
sling
spring
sting
string
swing
thing
wing
wring
zing

bee sting
Beijing
class ring
drawstring
earring
first-string
offspring
plaything
porch swing
shoestring
Sing Sing
something
wingding

anything
bathtub ring
boxing ring
diamond ring
ding-a-ling
everything
rite of spring
static cling
teething ring

puppet on a string

inge

binge
cringe
fringe
hinge
singe
tinge
twinge

infringe
syringe

inger 1

finger
linger
ringer
singer
stinger
zinger

bee stinger
folk singer
gunslinger
humdinger
mud slinger
wingdinger

inger 2

binger
ginger
injure

ingle

jingle
mingle
shingle
single
tingle

commingle
Kriss Kringle

ingo

bingo
dingo
gringo
lingo
Ringo

flamingo

ingy to inned

ingy 1
clingy
dinghy
springy
zingy

ingy 2
dingy
fringy
stingy

ini
beanie
genie
Jeanie
meany
teeny
wienie

bikini
Houdini
linguine
martini
zucchini

eeny meeny
fettucine
teeny weeny
tortellini

inister
minister
sinister

administer
prime minister

inity
trinity

affinity
divinity
infinity
vicinity

femininity
masculinity

ink
blink
brink
clink
drink ----▶
fink
ink
kink
link
mink
pink
rink
shrink
sink
slink
stink
think
wink
zinc

cuff link
hoodwink
hot pink
lip sync
rethink
soft drink

missing link
on the blink
pen and ink

rinky-dink
roller rink
tickled pink

inked as in blinked, see inct

inkle
crinkle
sprinkle
twinkle
wrinkle

periwinkle
Rip Van Winkle

inky
blinky
dinky
pinkie
slinky
stinky
Twinkie

Helsinki

rinky-dinky

inned
grinned
pinned
sinned
skinned
thinned
wind

downwind
tailwind
thick-skinned

whirlwind
woodwind

bag of wind
disciplined

inner

dinner
grinner
inner
sinner
spinner
thinner
winner

beginner
Berliner
prizewinner

inny

any
Ginny
many
mini
Minnie
ninny
skinny
tinny
whinny

New Guinea

ino 1

rhino

albino

ino 2

Reno

bambino

casino
Latino

Angeleno
cappuccino
Filipino
palomino

int

flint
glint
hint
lint
mint
print
splint
sprint
squint
stint
tint

blueprint
fine print
footprint
imprint
misprint
newsprint
shin splint
spearmint

fingerprint
peppermint
U.S. Mint

inter

printer
splinter
sprinter
winter

midwinter

ints as in hints, see ince

inus

dryness
Linus
minus
shyness
sinus
slyness
spryness

Your Highness

plus or minus

iny

shiny
spiny
tiny
whiny

ion

Brian
lion
Ryan

Hawaiian
Orion
O'Brien
sea lion

dandelion

ip

blip
chip
clip
dip
drip

flip
grip
gyp
hip
lip
nip
pip
quip
rip
ship
sip
skip
slip
snip
strip
tip
trip
whip
zip

bean dip
catnip
courtship
drag strip
equip
fat lip
field trip
friendship
guilt trip
hardship
hot tip
kinship
Q-Tip
round trip
spaceship
unzip

battleship
censorship
chips and dip

chocolate chip
comic strip
crack the whip
double-dip
ego trip
fellowship
fingertip
Gaza Strip
internship
leadership
membership
ownership
paper clip
penmanship
pirate ship
poker chip
salesmanship
scholarship
skinny-dip
sportsmanship
Sunset Strip

apprenticeship
bargaining chip
championship
citizenship
companionship
dictatorship
Freudian slip
good sportsmanship
guardianship
one-upmanship
postnasal drip
potato chip
stiff upper lip

ipe
gripe
hype
pipe
ripe
stripe
swipe
type
wipe

bagpipe
peace pipe
pinstripe
pitch pipe
sideswipe
tailpipe
unripe
windpipe

guttersnipe
overripe
prototype

media hype
stereotype

iper
diaper
griper
hyper
piper
sniper
viper
wiper

bagpiper
pied piper
sandpiper

ipped

chipped
clipped
crypt
dipped
dripped
flipped
gypped
nipped
quipped
ripped
script
shipped
sipped
skipped
slipped
snipped
stripped
tipped
tripped
whipped
zipped

equipped
postscript
tight-lipped
transcript

manuscript
nondescript

ipper

chipper
clipper
dipper
dripper
flipper
shipper
sipper

skipper
slipper
tipper
tripper
zipper

Big Dipper
glass slipper

ipple

cripple
ripple
triple

ippy

dippy
drippy
hippie
lippy
nippy
Skippy
snippy
yippee
zippy

Mississippi

ipsy

gypsy
tipsy

ipt as in script, see ipped

iption

conniption
description

Egyptian
inscription
prescription
subscription

ique as in unique, see eek

ir as in stir, see er

ird as in third, see erd

ire

choir
dire
fire
hire
sire
spire
squire
tire
wire

acquire
admire
afire
aspire
attire
backfire
barbed wire
bonfire
campfire
cease-fire
church choir
conspire

crossfire
desire
entire
expire
flat tire
haywire
hot-wire
inquire
inspire
live wire
on fire
perspire
require
retire
sapphire
satire
spitfire
surefire
transpire
umpire
vampire

ball of fire
overtire
rapid-fire

irk as in smirk,
see **erk**

irl as in twirl,
see **url**

irly as in swirly,
see **urly**

irm as in firm,
see **erm**

irred as in stirred,
see **erd**

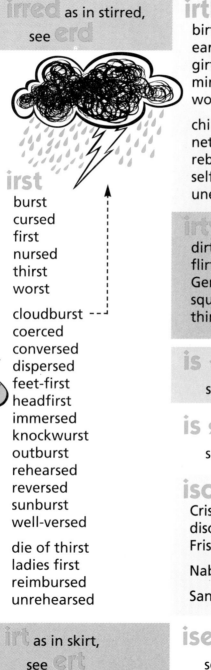

irst

burst
cursed
first
nursed
thirst
worst

cloudburst
coerced
conversed
dispersed
feet-first
headfirst
immersed
knockwurst
outburst
rehearsed
reversed
sunburst
well-versed

die of thirst
ladies first
reimbursed
unrehearsed

irt as in skirt,
see **ert**

irth

birth
earth
girth
mirth
worth

childbirth
net worth
rebirth
self-worth
unearth

irty

dirty
flirty
Gertie
squirty
thirty

is 1 as in this,
see **iss**

is 2 as in his,
see **iz**

isco

Crisco
disco
Frisco

Nabisco

San Francisco

ise 1 as in paradise,
see **ice 1**

ise 2 as in rise,
see **ize**

iser as in wiser,
see **izer**

ish

dish
fish
squish
swish
wish

cold fish
death wish
goldfish

jellyfish

ision

vision

collision
decision
division
envision
incision
Parisian
precision
provision
revision

double vision
indecision
split decision
supervision
television
tunnel vision

landmark decision

isk

brisk
disc
disk
frisk
risk
whisk

high risk
slipped disk
tsk tsk

asterisk
floppy disk

isky

frisky
risky
whiskey

ism

prism
quiz 'em
schism

baptism
fascism
racism
realism
truism

activism
atheism
barbarism
chauvinism
communism

criticism
cynicism
egotism
heroism
hypnotism
idealism
journalism
magnetism
mannerism
mysticism
optimism
organism
pacifism
pessimism
plagiarism
skepticism
socialism
symbolism
terrorism
vandalism
witticism

antagonism
cannibalism
capitalism
commercialism
favoritism
patriotism
romanticism
volunteerism

colloquialism
industrialism
materialism
professionalism
sensationalism
spiritualism

individualism
vegetarianism

isor as in visor, see izer

isp
crisp
lisp
wisp

isper
crisper
lisper
whisper

iss
bliss
hiss
kiss
miss
sis
Swiss
this

amiss
dismiss
near miss

hit or miss

issed as in kissed, see ist

ission as in mission, see ition

issive
missive

admissive
permissive
submissive

issue
issue
kiss you
miss you
tissue

scar tissue

issy
hissy
kissy
missy
prissy
sissy

ist
cyst
fist
gist
hissed
kissed
list
missed
mist
twist
wrist

assist

blacklist
checklist
consist
dismissed
enlist
exist
gymnast
insist
persist
price list
resist
tongue twist

coexist
reminisced
shopping list

enthusiast

istance
distance

assistance
consistence
existence
insistence
long-distance
persistence
resistance

istence as in existence, see istance

ister
blister
Mister
sister
twister

stepsister
transistor

istic

mystic

artistic
holistic
linguistic
simplistic
statistic

altruistic
fatalistic
futuristic
optimistic
realistic

animalistic
antagonistic
characteristic
idealistic
opportunistic
ritualistic
unrealistic
vital statistic

istle

bristle
gristle
missile
thistle
whistle

dismissal

istory

blistery
history
mystery

it

bit
fit
flit
get
grit
hit
it
kit
knit
lit
mitt
pit
quit
sit
skit
slit
spit
split
wit
zit

acquit
admit
armpit
close-knit
cockpit
commit
forget
helmet
legit
mess kit
misfit
moonlit
nitwit
omit
outfit
outwit
permit

pinch-hit
smash hit
snake pit
submit
sunlit
switch-hit
tar pit
tight fit
tool kit
transmit
unfit

advocate
baby-sit
benefit
bit by bit
counterfeit
estimate
first aid kit
graduate
hypocrite
perfect fit
separate
throw a fit
banana split
bottomless pit
conniption fit
deliberate
lickety-split

ita

cheetah
pita
Rita

fajita
Juanita

señorita

Santa Anita

ital as in vital,
see **idle**

itch

ditch
glitch
hitch
itch
niche
pitch
rich
snitch
stitch
switch
twitch
which
witch

bewitch
enrich
light switch
unhitch

fever pitch
master switch
strike it rich

ite 1 as in bite,
see **ight**

ite 2 as in petite,
see **eet**

iter as in writer,
see **ider**

ith

myth
smith
with
blacksmith
gunsmith
herewith
locksmith

ither

dither
hither
slither
wither
zither

itic

critic

arthritic

analytic
movie critic
parasitic

itical

critical

political

analytical
hypocritical

ition

mission

addition
admission
ambition
audition
beautician

commission
condition
edition
ignition
magician
musician
nutrition
optician
permission
petition
physician
position
rendition
submission
suspicion
technician
tradition
transition
transmission
tuition

abolition
acquisition
air-condition
ammunition
apparition
coalition
competition
composition
definition
demolition
dietician
disposition
electrician
exhibition
expedition
imposition
inhibition
inquisition

93

intermission
intuition
malnutrition
obstetrician
politician
premonition
preposition
prohibition
proposition
recognition
repetition
superstition

decomposition
mathematician
out of commission
pediatrician

itious as in

ambitious,
see **icious**

itis

arthritis
bronchitis
delight us
despite us
excite us
gastritis
invite us

laryngitis
reunite us
tonsillitis

appendicitis

ito as in bandito,
see **edo**

its

bits
blitz
fits
flits
gets
grits
hits
its
kits
knits ------
mitts
pits
quits
sits
skits
slits
spits
splits
spritz
wits
zits

admits
armpits
cockpits
commits
misfits
nitwits
outfits
outwits
permits
tar pits
tidbits
transmits

baby-sits
counterfeits
hypocrites

on the fritz
banana splits
hominy grits

ittal as in acquittal,
see **iddle**

itten

bitten
kitten
mitten
smitten
written

frostbitten
Great Britain
handwritten
typewritten
unwritten

itter

bidder
bitter
critter
fritter
glitter
hitter
kidder
knitter
litter
quitter
sitter
spitter
titter
twitter

consider
low bidder
baby-sitter
kitty litter
reconsider

ittery
glittery
jittery
skittery

ittle as in little, see iddle

itty
biddy
bitty
city
ditty
flitty
giddy
gritty
kiddie
kitty
pity
pretty
witty

committee
self-pity

inner city
itty-bitty
nitty-gritty
Salt Lake City

itz as in blitz, see its

itzy
ditzy
glitzy
Mitzi
ritzy

itsy-bitsy

iva
Godiva
saliva

ival
rival

archrival
arrival
revival
survival

ive 1
dive
drive
five
hive
I've
jive
live
strive
thrive

alive
archive
arrive
beehive
connive
contrive
crash-dive
deprive

high dive
high five
nosedive
revive
skydive
survive
take five
test drive

deep-sea dive
nine-to-five

ive 2
give
live
sieve

forgive
outlive
relive

ivel
civil
drivel
shrivel
snivel
swivel

uncivil

iven
driven
given
striven

forgiven
God-given

power-driven

iver 1
diver
driver

cabdriver
conniver
screwdriver
skydiver
slave driver
survivor

racecar driver - - - - -

iver 2
giver
liver
quiver
river
shiver
sliver

chopped liver
deliver
downriver
forgive her

ivity
activity
captivity
festivity
nativity

creativity
objectivity
productivity
relativity
sensitivity

insensitivity
radioactivity

ix as in fix, see icks

iz
fizz
frizz
his
is
Liz
Ms.
quiz
'tis
whiz

as is
gee whiz
pop quiz
showbiz

izard
blizzard
gizzard
lizard
wizard

ize
buys
cries
dies
dries
dyes

eyes
flies
fries
guise
guys
highs
lies
pies
prize
rise
shies
sighs
size
skies
spies
thighs
ties
tries
vise
wise

advise
applies
arise
baptize
capsize
chastise
clockwise
comprise
defies
denies
despise
devise
disguise
door prize
drip-dries
first prize
franchise
French fries

hi-fis
high-rise
implies
king-size
Levi's
likewise
mud pies
neckties
outcries
pigsties
relies
replies
revise
snake eyes
sunrise
supplies
surprise
unties
unwise
wise guys

advertise
agonize
alibis
analyze
authorize
beautifies
booby prize
burglarize
butterflies
certifies
civilize
clarifies
colonize
compromise
criticize
dragonflies
dramatize
eagle eyes

emphasize
energize
enterprise
exercise
family ties
fantasize
fertilize
glorifies
goo-goo eyes
gratifies
harmonize
horrifies
hypnotize
idolize
improvise
jeopardize
justifies
legalize
lullabies
magnifies
memorize
mesmerize
mobilize
modernize
modifies
mortifies
multiplies
mystifies
neutralize
Nobel Prize
notifies
occupies
organize
ostracize
otherwise

pacifies
paralyze
pasteurize
patronize
penalize
plagiarize
publicize
qualifies
ratifies
realize
recognize
satirize
satisfies
scrutinize
sensitize
signifies
simplifies
socialize
specialize
specifies
stabilize
sterilize
stupefies
summarize
supervise
sympathize
take the prize
tantalize
televise
tenderize
terrifies
terrorize
theorize
tranquilize
traumatize
unifies
utilize
verbalize
verifies

izer to izzy

victimize
vitalize
vocalize

alphabetize
antagonize
apologize
capitalize
categorize
characterize
commercialize
demoralize
demystifies
deodorize
disqualifies
dissatisfies
economize
exemplifies
familiarize
family ties

idealize
identifies
intensifies
little white lies
monopolize
nationalize
personifies
popularize
preoccupies
reorganize
revitalize
romanticize
solidifies
take by surprise
visualize

riser
visor
wiser

advisor
incisor

advertiser
atomizer
energizer
exerciser
fertilizer
improviser
organizer
supervisor
vaporizer

deodorizer

izer
geyser
miser - - - -

izz as in frizz,
see **iz**

izzard as in blizzard,
see **izard**

izzle
chisel
drizzle
fizzle
sizzle

izzy
busy
dizzy
fizzy
frizzy
is he?
tizzy

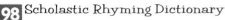

O

O 1

beau
blow
bow
crow
doe
dough
flow
foe
go
glow
grow
Joe
know
low
mow
no
oh
owe
pro
row
sew
show
slow
snow
so
stow
though
throw
toe
tow
whoa
woe

aglow
ago
although
below
death row

game show
golf pro
gung ho
heave-ho
hello
info
John Doe
low blow
no-go
no-no
no show
outgrow
pueblo
rainbow
scarecrow
sideshow
skid row
so so
talk show
tiptoe
yo-yo
Alamo
apropos
blow by blow
buffalo
calico
cookie dough
cupid's bow
do-si-do
dynamo
ebb and flow
even though
fashion show
fatal blow
friend or foe
heel-and-toe
high and low
Idaho

Ivanhoe
Jacques Cousteau
long ago
Mary Jo
Mexico
mistletoe
Navajo
Oreo
overflow
piccolo
picture show
radio
ratio
right to know
rodeo
Romeo
Sloppy Joe
sourdough
status quo
stereo
stop and go
studio
talent show
tale of woe
tic tac toe
tippytoe
to and fro
Tokyo
touch and go
TV show
undertow
video
yes and no

Geronimo
get-up-and-go
New Mexico
pay as you go
Pinocchio

pistachio
portfolio
ready, set, go

o 2 as in do,
see **ew**

oach
broach
coach
poach
roach

approach
cockroach
reproach
stagecoach

oad 1 as in toad,
see **ode**

oad 2 as in broad,
see **awed**

oaf
loaf
oaf

oak as in soak,
see **oke**

oaks as in cloaks,
see **okes**

oal as in coal,
see **ole**

oam as in foam,
see **ome 1**

oan as in loan,
see **one 1**

oar as in soar,
see **ore**

oard as in board,
see **ord 1**

oarder as in boarder,
see **order**

oared as in roared,
see **ord 1**

oarse as in coarse,
see **orse**

oast as in coast,
see **ost 1**

oat as in coat,
see **ote**

oax as in coax,
see **okes**

ob
blob
bob
daub
glob
gob
job
knob
lob
mob
rob
slob ---
snob
sob
swab
throb

con job
corncob
doorknob
heartthrob
hobnob
snow job

cotton swab
inside job
shish kebab

corn on the cob
thingamabob

obber
clobber
robber
slobber
sobber

grave-robber
macabre

obble
bauble
bobble
gobble
hobble
squabble
wobble

obbler
cobbler
gobbler
hobbler
squabbler
wobbler

cherry cobbler

obby
Bobby
hobby
knobby
lobby
snobby

obe
globe
Job
lobe
probe
robe

bathrobe
disrobe
earlobe
space probe
wardrobe

oble
global
Mobil
mobile
noble

Chernobyl
immobile

ocal
focal
local
vocal
yokel

bifocal

ocious
atrocious
ferocious
precocious

supercalifragilistic-
 expialidotious

ocity
atrocity
ferocity
monstrosity
velocity

animosity
curiosity
generosity
reciprocity

ock
Bach
block
chalk

clock
crock
doc
dock
flock
frock
gawk
hawk
Jacques
jock
knock
lock
mock
rock
shock
smock
sock
squawk
stock
talk
walk
wok

back talk
Bangkok
beanstalk
boardwalk
cell block
crosswalk
deadlock
fast-talk
girl talk
gridlock
hard rock
headlock
Hitchcock
jaywalk
jive talk
knock knock

livestock
Mohawk
o'clock
outtalk
padlock
peacock
pep talk
punk rock
roadblock
shamrock
shell shock
Sherlock
sidewalk
sleepwalk
small talk
space walk
sunblock
sweet talk
ticktock
unlock
woodblock

aftershock
alarm clock
auction block
baby talk
butcher block
chopping block
cuckoo clock
culture shock
double talk
laughingstock
mental block
nature walk
out of stock
poppycock
round-the-clock
stumbling block
tomahawk

"What's up, Doc?"
writer's block

ocker

blocker
knocker
locker
rocker
shocker
soccer
talker
walker

fast talker
footlocker
jaywalker
night stalker
sleepwalker

ocket

docket
locket
pocket
rocket
socket

light socket
pickpocket
skyrocket

Davy Crockett

ocks as in rocks, see OX

ockey as in hockey, see awky

ocky as in rocky, see awky

oco

cocoa
loco

ocracy

autocracy
bureaucracy
democracy
hypocrisy

aristocracy

od as in nod, see awed

oda as in soda, see ota

oddle

bottle
coddle
dawdle
model
throttle
toddle
waddle

Aristotle

ode

bowed
code
crowed
flowed
glowed
goad
load
mode
mowed
ode
owed
road
rode
rowed
showed
slowed
snowed
stowed
strode
toad
towed

abode
carload
crossroad
decode
dress code
erode
explode
freeload
implode
Morse Code
railroad
tiptoed
truckload
unload
workload
zip code

à la mode
electrode
episode
hit the road
overflowed
overload
penal code
pigeon-toed

area code

odge

dodge
lodge

dislodge
hodgepodge

odious

odious

commodious
melodious

ody

Audi
bawdy
body
Dotty
gaudy
haughty
knotty
naughty
potty
Saudi
Scottie
shoddy
snotty
spotty

embody
homebody
karate
nobody
somebody

antibody
anybody
busybody
student body

everybody
heavenly body

oe 1 as in doe,
see **o**

oe 2 as in shoe,
see **ew**

oes 1 as in shoes,
see **use**

oes 2 as in goes,
see **ose 2**

off

coif
cough
off
scoff
trough

blast off
brush-off

103

cutoff
kickoff
liftoff
payoff
play-off
rip-off
show-off
trade-off
well-off

on and off
stroganoff

often
coffin
often
soften

og
bog
clog
dog
flog
fog
frog
grog
hog
jog
log

bulldog
bullfrog
groundhog
hounddog
leapfrog
prologue
road hog
ship's log
top dog

watchdog

catalog
chili dog
dialogue
monologue
synagogue
travelogue
underdog

oggle
boggle
goggle
joggle
ogle

boondoggle

oggy
doggie
foggy
froggy
groggy
smoggy
soggy

ogical
logical

illogical

astrological
biological
chronological
geological
mythological
psychological

ography
biography
demography
geography
photography

bibliography
choreography
oceanography

autobiography

ogue 1
brogue
rogue
vogue

ogue 2 as in
dialogue,
see og

oic
stoic

heroic

oice
choice
Joyce
voice

first choice
no choice
one voice
rejoice
Rolls-Royce
turquoise

oid

Floyd
Freud
Lloyd
toyed
void

annoyed
avoid
destroyed
devoid
employed
enjoyed
tabloid

asteroid
celluloid
null and void
overjoyed
paranoid
Polaroid
self-employed
unemployed

oil

boil
broil
coil
foil
loyal
oil
royal
soil
spoil
toil

disloyal
gargoyle
hard-boil
recoil

tinfoil
turmoil

oin

coin
groin
join
loin

Des Moines
purloin
rejoin
sirloin

flip a coin
tenderloin

oing as in going, see owing

oint

joint
point

appoint
ballpoint
checkpoint
high point
pinpoint
viewpoint
West Point

disappoint
focal point
needlepoint
out of joint
starting point

oir as in memoir, see ar

oise as in noise, see oys

oke

broke
choke
Coke
croak
folk
joke
oak
poke
smoke
soak
spoke
stoke
stroke
woke
yolk

awoke
cowpoke
dead broke
egg yolk
heatstroke
kinfolk
provoke
slowpoke
sunstroke

artichoke
cloud of smoke
Diet Coke
go for broke
holy smoke

okey-doke
poison oak

oken

broken
oaken
spoken
token

awoken
heartbroken
Hoboken
housebroken
love token
misspoken
outspoken
plainspoken
soft-spoken
unbroken
unspoken

oker

broker
choker
joker
poker
smoker

pawnbroker
provoker
stockbroker

mediocre

okes

chokes
cloaks
coax
Cokes
croaks
folks

hoax
jokes
oaks
pokes
smokes
spokes
stokes
strokes
yolks

provokes

artichokes
Diet Cokes

ol 1 as in alcohol, see **all**

ol 2 as in control, see **ole**

ola

cola
Lola

Crayola
Loyola
payola
viola

ayatollah
Coca-Cola
gladiola
Pepsi-Cola

olar

bowler
molar
polar
roller
solar
stroller

controller
high roller
patroller
steamroller

old

bold
bowled
cold
doled
fold
gold
hold
mold
old
polled
rolled
scold
sold
strolled
told

age-old
behold
billfold
blindfold
cajoled
catch cold
choke hold
consoled
controlled
enfold

enrolled
extolled
foothold
household
ice-cold
out cold
paroled
patrolled
retold
steamrolled
stronghold
threshold
toehold
unfold
untold
withhold

common cold
days of old
good as gold
heart of gold
hot and cold
pigeonholed
pot of gold
rock-and-rolled
self-controlled
solid gold
stranglehold
uncontrolled

out in the cold

older

bolder
boulder
colder
older
shoulder
smolder

cold shoulder
pot holder
shareholder

ole

bowl
coal
dole
foal
goal
hole
Joel
knoll
Lowell
mole
pole
poll
role
roll
scroll
sole
soul
stole
stroll
toll
troll
whole

cajole
charcoal
console
control
Creole
drum roll
egg roll
enroll
extol
fishbowl
flagpole

foxhole
keyhole
loophole
manhole
mudhole
North Pole
parole
patrol
payroll
peephole
porthole
pothole
Rose Bowl
steamroll
tadpole
unroll

buttonhole
camisole
casserole
cruise control
cubbyhole
fishing pole
heart and soul
Old King Cole
pigeonhole
rock and roll
self-control
starring role
sugar bowl
swimming hole
toilet bowl
Tootsie Roll
totem pole

ace in the hole
body and soul
Hollywood Bowl
out of control
remote control

oled to ology

oled as in cajoled, see **old**

olen
colon
Nolan
stolen
swollen

semicolon

olic
colic
frolic

hydraulic
symbolic

chocoholic
diabolic
foodaholic
fun and frolic
sleepaholic
workaholic

olish
polish
smallish
tallish

abolish
demolish

apple-polish
spit-and-polish

olk as in yolk, see **oke**

olks as in folks, see **okes**

oll 1 as in roll, see **ole**

oll 2 as in doll, see **all**

ollar as in dollar, see **aller**

oller as in roller, see **olar**

olley as in trolley, see **olly**

ollow as in follow, see **allow 2**

olly
Ali
collie
crawly
dolly
folly
golly
holly
jolly
Molly
Polly
trolley

volley
Wally

by golly
finale
Svengali
tamale

creepy-crawly
grand finale
hot tamale
melancholy

olo
polo
solo

ologist
biologist
ecologist
geologist
psychologist
zoologist

archaeologist
dermatologist
sociologist

ology
anthology
apology
astrology
biology
chronology
ecology
geology
mythology
pathology
psychology

108 Scholastic Rhyming Dictionary

technology
zoology

archaeology
criminology
dermatology
sociology
terminology

meteorology

olster

bolster
holster
oldster
pollster

olt

bolt
colt
dolt
jolt

deadbolt
revolt

lightning bolt

olve

solve

dissolve
evolve
involve
resolve
revolve

oly

goalie
holey
holy

slowly
solely
wholly

parolee
unholy

guacamole
ravioli
roly-poly

om

balm
bomb
calm
Guam
mom
palm
prom
psalm
qualm
tom

A-bomb
dive-bomb
embalm
fire bomb
pompom
sitcom
time bomb
tom-tom
wigwam

intercom
peeping Tom
supermom
Vietnam

oma

coma

aroma
diploma

Oklahoma

omb 1 as in comb, see ome 1

omb 2 as in tomb, see oom

ome 1

chrome
comb
dome
foam
gnome
home
poem
roam
Rome

Stockholm
syndrome

Astrodome
broken home
foster home
home sweet home
honeycomb
metronome
mobile home
palindrome
shaving foam
Superdome

ome to one

ome 2 as in come, see **um**

ometer
barometer
kilometer
odometer
speedometer
thermometer

omic
comic

atomic

astronomic
economic
stand-up comic

omination
domination
nomination

abomination
denomination

ommy
mommy
swami
Tommy

pastrami
tsunami

origami

omp
chomp
clomp

romp
stomp
swamp
tromp
whomp

on 1 as in con, see **awn**

on 2 as in ton, see **un**

ona
Jonah
Mona

kimono

Arizona
Barcelona

oncho
honcho
poncho

ond
blond
bond
conned
dawned
donned
fawned
fond
pawned
pond
wand
yawned

beyond
doggoned
fishpond
James Bond
respond

correspond
magic wand
vagabond

onder
blonder
condor
fonder
launder
ponder
squander
wander
yonder

onds as in bonds, see **ons**

one 1
blown
bone
clone
cone
drone
flown
groan
grown
hone
Joan
known
loan
lone
moan

own
phone
prone
sewn
shone
shown
stone
throne
thrown
tone
zone

alone
backbone
birthstone
car phone
cologne
condone
cyclone
dethrone
dial tone
disown
end zone
full-blown
full-grown
grindstone
headphone
headstone
homegrown
hormone
jawbone
milestone
outshone
ozone
pay phone
pinecone
postpone
Ramon
rhinestone
sno-cone

T-bone
time zone
tombstone
trombone
unknown
war zone
well-known
windblown
wishbone

baritone
buffer zone
chaperon
cobblestone
combat zone
crazy bone
doggie bone
funny bone
ice cream cone
microphone
moan and groan
monotone
overgrown
rolling stone
saxophone
stepping-stone
telephone
twilight zone
xylophone
Yellowstone

accident-prone

one 2 as in gone,
see **awn**

one 3 as in done,
see **un**

one 4 as in
minestrone,
see **ony**

oney as in money,
see **unny**

ong
dong
gong
long
song
strong
thong
throng
wrong

along
belong
ding-dong
folk song
headlong
headstrong
Hong Kong
King Kong
lifelong
love song
oblong
Ping-Pong
prolong
sarong
so long
swan song

all along
dinner gong
get along
hop-a-long

right or wrong
sing-along
tagalong

oni as in macaroni,
see **ony**

onia
Sonia

ammonia
begonia
Bologna
pneumonia

onial
colonial

ceremonial
matrimonial
testimonial

onic
chronic
phonic
sonic
tonic

bionic
demonic
harmonic
ironic
moronic
Platonic
symphonic
catatonic
electronic
Panasonic

supersonic
telephonic

stereophonic

onica
Hanukkah
harmonica
Veronica

Santa Monica

onical
chronicle
conical
monocle

ironical

onish
admonish
astonish

onk
bonk
honk
konk
zonk

only
lonely
only

one and only
sad and lonely

onna
Donna
Ghana
gonna
sauna
wanna

Chicana
iguana
mañana
piranha

prima donna
Tijuana

Americana
flora and fauna

onned as in conned
see **ond**

onomy
astronomy
autonomy
economy

onor
goner
honor
yawner

dishonor

ons
blondes
bonds
bronze
cons
dawns
dons
fawns
Hans
lawns
pawns
ponds
swans
wands
yawns

batons
ex-cons
icons
long johns
morons
neutrons
pecans
pythons
responds

Amazons
corresponds
leprechauns
marathons
paragons
pros and cons
vagabonds

ont as in front, see unt

onto
pronto
Tonto

Toronto

ony
bony
crony
phony
pony
Sony
stony
Tony

baloney
Shoshone

abalone
alimony
ceremony
macaroni
matrimony
minestrone
pepperoni
rigatoni
sanctimony
testimony

phony-baloney

oo as in zoo, see ew

ooch
mooch
pooch
smooch

ood 1 as in food, see ude

ood 2 as in blood, see ud

ood 3
could
good
hood
should
stood
wood
would

childhood
deadwood
driftwood
falsehood
no-good
redwood
sainthood

brotherhood
fatherhood
Hollywood
likelihood
livelihood
motherhood
neighborhood
pretty good
Robin Hood
sisterhood
understood

misunderstood
Red Riding Hood
so far so good

finger-licking good

oodle
brutal
doodle
feudal
futile
noodle
poodle
strudel

apple strudel
Yankee Doodle

oody
beauty
bootie
booty
cootie
cutie
duty
fruity
Judy
moody
snooty
Trudy

off duty

bathing beauty
double-duty
heavy duty
Howdy Doody
Sleeping Beauty
tutti-frutti

ooed as in
shampooed,
see ude

ooey as in gooey,
see ewy

oof 1
goof
poof
proof
roof
spoof

aloof
childproof
fireproof
foolproof
soundproof

oof 2
hoof
roof
woof

oofy
goofy
poofy
spoofy

ook 1 as in spook,
see uke

ook 2
book
brook
cook
crook
hook
look
nook

rook
shook
took

checkbook
fishhook
handbook
mistook
notebook
outlook
scrapbook
textbook
unhook

Captain Cook
comic book
dirty look
donnybrook
overlook

gobbledygook

ookie
bookie
cookie
hooky
rookie

ool
cool
drool
fool
fuel
ghoul
mule
pool
rule
school
spool
stool

tool
yule

barstool
car pool
cesspool
gag rule
high school
home rule
mob rule
module
preschool
tidepool
toadstool
whirlpool

April fool
as a rule
golden rule
Liverpool
miniscule
molecule
overrule
ridicule
Sunday School
supercool
swimming pool
nobody's fool
nursery school

majority rule

ooler

cooler
crueler
drooler
jeweler
ruler

car pooler
preschooler

oom

bloom
boom
broom
doom
fume
gloom
groom
loom
plume
room
tomb
whom
womb
zoom

assume
bathroom
bridegroom
classroom
consume
costume
courtroom
entomb
exhume
heirloom
homeroom
leg room
mushroom
perfume
presume
rest room

baby boom
bride and groom
elbow room
gloom and doom
locker room
love in bloom

powder room
smoke-filled room
sonic boom

oomer as in

groomer,
see umor

oomy

gloomy
roomy

perfumy

oon

croon
dune
goon
June
loon
moon
noon
prune
soon
spoon
strewn
swoon
tune

baboon
balloon
bassoon
buffoon
cartoon
cocoon
commune
fine tune
full moon

ooner to oos

harpoon
high noon
immune
lagoon
lampoon
maroon
monsoon
Neptune
platoon
pontoon
raccoon
Rangoon
saloon
spittoon
too soon
twelve noon
tycoon
typhoon

afternoon
Cameroon
Daniel Boone
honeymoon
loony tune
macaroon
opportune
out of tune
pretty soon
trial balloon

hot-air balloon
man in the moon

ooner
crooner
lunar
schooner
sooner
tuner

honeymooner

oop
bloop
coop
coupe
droop
dupe
goop
group
hoop
loop
poop
scoop
sloop
snoop
soup
stoop
swoop
troop
troupe
whoop

in-group
peer group
regroup
scout troop

alley oop
chicken soup
hula hoop

inside scoop
nincompoop
pressure group

ooper
blooper
drooper
pooper
scooper
snooper
stupor
super
trooper
trouper

state trooper

paratrooper
party pooper
pooper-scooper
super-duper

oopy
droopy
goopy
snoopy
soupy
whoopee

oor 1 as in poor, see **ure**

oor 2 as in door, see **ore**

oos as in tattoos, see **use** 2

oose 1 as in choose, see **use** 2

oose 2 as in moose, see **use** 1

oost as in roost, see **uced**

ooster

booster
rooster

oot 1 as in hoot, see **ute**

oot 2

foot
put
root
soot

afoot
barefoot
Big Foot
hotfoot
input
kaput
output
shotput

pussyfoot
tenderfoot
underfoot

ooter as in scooter, see **uter**

ooth

booth
couth
Ruth
sleuth
tooth
truth
youth

Babe Ruth
half-truth
phone booth
sweet tooth
uncouth
untruth

kissing booth
naked truth
snaggletooth
voting booth

fountain of youth
moment of truth

ootie as in cootie, see **oody**

ooty as is snooty, see **oody**

ooze as in snooze, see **use** 2

op

bop
chop
clop
cop
crop
drop
flop
hop
lop
mop
plop
pop
prop
shop
slop
stop
swap
top

Aesop
bebop
bellhop
big top
blacktop
box top
bus stop
cough drop
doorstop
eavesdrop
flattop
flip-flop
gumdrop
hilltop
hip hop
kerplop
name-drop
nonstop
pawnshop

pit stop
pork chop
raindrop
rooftop
shortstop
sock hop
teardrop
tiptop
treetop
truck stop
workshop

barbershop
belly flop --------
body shop
coffee shop
curly top
lemon drop
lollipop
mom and pop
mountaintop
party-hop
traffic-stop
window shop

cream of the crop
karate chop

ope
cope
dope
grope
hope
lope
mope
nope
pope
rope
scope
slope

soap
taupe

elope
jump rope
no hope
tightrope
towrope

antelope
bar of soap
cantaloupe
envelope
horoscope
microscope
periscope
stethoscope
telescope

opey
dopey
Hopi
mopey
soapy

opia
utopia

cornucopia
Ethiopia

opic
topic
tropic

subtopic

microscopic
telescopic

opper
chopper

copper
dropper
pauper
popper
proper
shopper
stopper
topper
whopper

clodhopper
eavesdropper
eyedropper
eye-popper
grasshopper
heartstopper
improper
name-dropper
sharecropper
show-stopper
woodchopper

teenybopper
window-shopper

oppy
choppy
copy
floppy
poppy
sloppy

jalopy
serape

carbon copy

option
option

adoption

opy as in copy,
see **oppy**

or as is for,
see **ore**

ora

aura
Dora
Nora

angora
fedora
menorah
señora

oral

choral
coral
floral
laurel
moral
oral
quarrel

amoral
immoral
pastoral

orce as in force,
see **orse**

orch

porch
scorch
torch

ord 1

board
bored
chord
cord
floored
Ford
gourd
hoard
lord
poured
roared
scored
snored
soared
stored
sword
ward
warred

abhorred
aboard
adored
afford
award
backboard
billboard
blackboard
cardboard
chalkboard
dashboard
discord
explored
fjord
ignored
keyboard
landlord
outscored
record

restored
reward
rip cord
scoreboard
skateboard
slumlord
surfboard
toward
washboard

all aboard
boogieboard
checkerboard
diving board
drawing board
harpsichord
overboard
room and board
smorgasbord
sounding board
spinal chord
tape-record
unexplored

across the board
bulletin board
stiff as a board

ord 2 as in word,
see **erd**

order

boarder
border
courter
hoarder
mortar
order
porter

119

quarter
shorter

cavorter
court order
exporter
gag order
importer
recorder
reporter
supporter
transporter

flight recorder
law and order
made-to-order
out of order
tape recorder

ore

boar
bore
chore
core
corps
door
drawer
floor
for
four
gore
lore
more
nor
oar
or
poor
pore
pour
roar

snore
soar
score
shore
sore
store
swore
tore
war
wore
your

abhor
adore
ashore
before
cold sore
cold war
condor
decor
downpour
drugstore
encore
explore
eyesore
folklore
galore
hard-core
hoped-for
ignore
indoor
mentor
next-door
no more
outdoor
outscore
Peace Corps
postwar
rapport
restore

seashore
señor
ten-four
therefore
trapdoor
uproar

all ashore
antiwar
anymore
apple core
Baltimore
blood and gore
carnivore
civil war
corridor
dinosaur
door-to-door
Ecuador
evermore
furthermore
Marine Corps
matador
metaphor
nevermore
por favor
reservoir
rich or poor
saddle sore
ship-to-shore
Singapore
sophomore
Theodore
troubadour
tug of war
two-by-four
underscore

forevermore
titanosaur

ored as in bored,
see **ord** 1

orge
forge
George
gorge
engorge
Valley Forge

orial
oriole
censorial
memorial
pictorial
tutorial
dictatorial
editorial
territorial

oric
caloric
euphoric
historic
prehistoric
sophomoric

orify
glorify
horrify

orious
glorious
laborious
notorious
uproarious
victorious

ority
authority
majority
minority
priority
seniority
sorority
inferiority
moral majority
silent majority
superiority

orium
emporium
auditorium
crematorium
moratorium

ork 1
cork
dork
fork
pork
stork
New York
pitchfork

ork 2 as in work,
see **erk**

orm 1
dorm
form
norm
storm
swarm
warm
barnstorm
brainstorm
conform
deform
duststorm
free-form
inform
lukewarm
perform
platform
reform
snowstorm
transform
co-ed dorm
misinform
thunderstorm
uniform

orm 2 as in worm,
see **erm**

ormal
formal
normal
abnormal
informal
semiformal

ormer to ort

ormer
former
warmer

barnstormer
benchwarmer
chairwarmer
conformer
informer
performer
reformer
transformer

orn
born
corn
horn
morn
mourn
scorn
sworn
thorn
torn
warn
worn

acorn
adorn
airborne
bullhorn
first-born
foghorn
forewarn
forlorn
greenhorn
inborn
lovelorn
newborn
outworn

popcorn
reborn
shoehorn
timeworn
unborn
well-worn

Capricorn
ear of corn
foreign-born
Matterhorn
native-born
unicorn
weatherworn

orning
morning
mourning
warning

flood warning
good morning

tornado warning

orse
coarse
course
force
hoarse
horse
source

air force
brute force
clotheshorse
crash course
dark horse
divorce
endorse
enforce

golf course
main course
of course
racehorse
remorse
resource
task force
work force

charley horse
driving force
reinforce
rocking horse
show of force

collision course
matter of course
obstacle course

ort
court
fort
forte
port
quart
short
snort
sort
sport
thwart
wart

airport
bad sport
cavort
cohort
contort
deport
distort
escort

orter to ose

export
good sport
import
Newport
night court
passport
report
resort
seaport
spoilsport
support
transport

child support
heliport
last resort
Supreme Court
tennis court
traffic court
worrywart

orter as in shorter, see **order**

orth
fourth
north

come forth

back and forth
July Fourth

so on and so forth

ortify
fortify
mortify

ortion
portion

contortion
distortion
proportion

orty
forty
shorty
sporty
warty

ory
glory
gory
Laurie
quarry
story

love story
Old Glory
rock quarry

allegory
bedtime story
category
hunky-dory
laboratory
lavatory
mandatory
morning glory
purgatory
territory

conservatory
derogatory
explanatory
obligatory
observatory
reformatory

os 1 as in cosmos, see ose 1

os 2 as in videos, see ose 2

osal
disposal
proposal

ose 1
close
dose
gross

cosmos
engross
Laos
morose
up close
verbose

adios
comatose
diagnose
grandiose

ose 2
beaux
blows
bows
chose
close
clothes
crows
doze
flows
foes

123

froze
glows
goes
grows
hose
knows
lows
mows
nose
owes
pose
pros
prose
rose
rows
sews
shows
slows
snows
those
throws
toes
tows
woes

bozos
bulldoze
dispose
enclose
expose
fire hose
impose
low blows
no-nos
no-shows
oppose
propose
pug nose
rainbows

scarecrows
sideshows
suppose
tiptoes
yo-yos

buffaloes
bungalows
Cheerios
come to blows
decompose
dominoes
dynamos
Eskimos
heaven knows
nose-to-nose
Oreos
overflows
panty hose
radios
rodeos
runny nose
stereos
twinkle toes
videos

anything goes
open and close
overexpose

osh
gosh
josh
nosh
posh
quash
slosh
squash
wash

brainwash
carwash
hogwash
mouthwash
my gosh
whitewash

osion
corrosion
erosion
explosion
implosion

osity as in curiosity, see ocity

osive
corrosive
erosive
explosive

oss 1 as in gross, see ose 1

oss 2
boss
cross
floss
gloss
loss
moss
Ross
sauce
toss

across

crisscross
hot sauce ----→
lip gloss
Red Cross
ring toss
soy sauce

applesauce
at a loss
dental floss
double-cross
hearing loss

memory loss
profit and loss
sign of the cross

ost 1

boast
coast
ghost
grossed
host
most
post
roast
toast ------------

almost
bedpost
engrossed
goalpost
guidepost
outgrossed
outpost
pot roast
signpost
topmost
utmost

coast-to-coast
diagnosed
hitching post
innermost
parcel post
trading post
whipping post

ost 2

bossed
cost
crossed
flossed
frost
glossed
lost

tossed

crisscrossed
defrost
exhaust
low-cost

double-crossed
holocaust

at any cost

oster

foster
roster

defroster
impostor

osure

closure

composure
enclosure
exposure

osy

cozy
mosey
nosy
Rosie
rosy

ot

blot
bought
brought
caught
clot
cot
dot

ossed 1 as in

grossed,
　see ost 1

ossed as in bossed,
　see ost 2

ossum

awesome
blossom
possum

opossum
play possum

ossy

Aussie
bossy
glossy
mossy
posse
saucy

fought
got
hot
jot
knot
lot
not
ought
plot
pot
rot
Scot
shot
slot
snot
sought
spot
squat
swat
taught
taut
thought
tot
trot
what
yacht

big shot
blind spot
bloodshot
boycott
cannot
cheap shot
crackpot
distraught
dogtrot
flowerpot
forgot
gunshot

hot shot
inkblot
jackpot
long shot
mascot
mug shot
red-hot
robot
self-taught
slingshot
snapshot
somewhat
so what?
store-bought
teapot
tight spot
whatnot

afterthought
apricot
astronaut
beauty spot
boiling hot
booster shot
Camelot
coffee-pot
diddly-squat
food for thought
hit the spot
hot to trot
Lancelot
melting pot
not so hot
on the dot
on the spot
parking lot
polka dot
thanks a lot
tie the knot

forget-me-not
like it or not

ota

quota
soda

iota
pagoda
ricotta
Toyota

Minnesota
North Dakota
South Dakota

otch

blotch
botch
notch
Scotch
swatch
watch

birdwatch
hopscotch
stopwatch
topnotch
weight-watch
wristwatch

ote

bloat
boat
coat
dote
float
gloat
goat

moat
note
oat
quote
throat
tote
vote
wrote

afloat
cutthroat
devote
dreamboat
footnote
keynote
lifeboat
love note
misquote
outvote
promote
raincoat
remote
rewrote
rowboat
scapegoat
sore throat
steamboat
turncoat

anecdote
antidote
miss the boat
overcoat
petticoat
right to vote
rock the boat
root beer float
sugarcoat

one man, one vote

oth 1

both
growth
oath

regrowth

overgrowth
under oath

oth 2

broth
cloth
froth
moth
sloth

chicken broth
three-toed sloth

other

brother
mother
other
smother

another
each other
godmother
grandmother
none other
Oh, brother!
stepmother

one another

fairy godmother

otic

aquatic
chaotic
exotic

hypnotic
melodic
narcotic
neurotic
psychotic

idiotic
patriotic

antibiotic

otion

lotion
motion
notion
ocean
potion

commotion
devotion
emotion
love potion
promotion
slow motion

locomotion
magic potion

otional

devotional
emotional
promotional

unemotional

otten

cotton
gotten
rotten

forgotten
spoiled rotten

127

otter to ough

otter
broader
daughter
fodder
hotter
odder
otter
plotter
potter
prodder
slaughter
tauter
totter
trotter
water

bathwater
dishwater
floodwater
fly swatter
globetrotter
hot rodder
manslaughter
step-daughter

alma mater
bread and water
holy water
teeter-totter
underwater
walk on water

ottery
lottery
pottery
watery

ottle as in bottle,
see **oddle**

otto
auto
grotto
lotto
motto

otty as in knotty,
see **ody**

ou as in you,
see **ew**

ouble
bubble
double
rubble
stubble
trouble

car trouble
see double
soap bubble

double trouble
on the double

ouch
couch
crouch
grouch
ouch
pouch
slouch
vouch

oud
bowed
cloud
crowd
loud
plowed
proud
shroud
vowed
wowed

allowed
aloud
in-crowd
kowtowed
meowed
outloud
rain cloud
war cloud

bushy-browed
overcrowd
thundercloud

ouder as in louder,
see **owder**

ough 1 as in rough,
see **uff**

ough 2 as in cough,
see **off**

128 Scholastic Rhyming Dictionary

ough 3 as in through, see **ew**

ough 4 as in dough, see **o**

ougher as in tougher, see **uffer**

ought as in bought, see **ot**

ould as in would, see **ood** 3

oulder as in boulder, see **older**

ounce

bounce
counts
flounce
mounts
ounce
pounce
trounce

accounts
amounts
announce
discounts
pronounce

renounce
bank accounts
mispronounce
ounce for ounce

ound

bound
browned
clowned
crowned
downed
drowned
found
frowned
ground
hound
mound
pound
round
sound
wound

abound
aground
around
astound
background
bloodhound
campground
chowhound
compound
dog pound
dumbfound
earthbound
foreground
greyhound
inbound
newfound
outbound

playground
profound
rebound
renowned
snowbound
spellbound
surround
year-round

all around
battleground
fool around
homeward bound
honorbound
lost and found
musclebound
neutral ground
outward bound
pitcher's mound
round and round
runaround
solid ground
underground

merry-go-round
up and around

happy hunting ground

ount

count
mount

account
amount
discount
head count

bank account
paramount
tantamount

129

ounts 👉 out

ounts as in accounts, see **ounce**

oup as in soup, see **oop**

our 1
cower
flour
flower
hour
our
power
scour
shower
sour
tower

devour
empower
horsepower
lunch hour
Mayflower
noon hour
rain shower
rush hour
wallflower
wildflower
willpower

cauliflower
dinner hour
Eiffel Tower ----
overpower
superpower
sweet and sour
veto power

ivory tower

our 2 as in tour, see **ure**

our 3 as in four, see **ore**

oured as in devoured, see **owered**

ourn as in adjourn, see **urn**

ourse as in course, see **orse**

ouse
blouse
douse
house
louse
mouse
spouse

bird house
church mouse
clubhouse
courthouse
doghouse
firehouse
full house
lighthouse
madhouse
outhouse
penthouse

powerhouse
roughhouse
warehouse
White House

cat and mouse
haunted house
house-to-house
Mickey Mouse
on the house

oust
doused
joust
oust
roust

out
bout
clout
doubt
drought
out
pout
rout
route
scout
shout
snout
spout
sprout
stout
trout

about
blackout
blowout
Boy Scout
campout
cookout

devout
dropout
dugout
fade-out
fallout
far out
Girl Scout
handout
hangout
holdout
knockout
lookout
no doubt
pass out
psych-out
sauerkraut
shoot-out
sold-out
stakeout
standout
take-out
throughout
tryout
without
workout

beyond doubt
Brussels sprout
do without
down and out
falling-out
go without
in and out
inside out
knockabout
odd man out
roundabout
runabout
talent scout

day in, day out
knock-down-drag-out
over and out
up and about

outer as in stouter, see owder

outh 1

mouth
south

big mouth
Deep South
loudmouth

blabbermouth
hand-to-mouth
word of mouth

outh 2 as in youth, see ooth

ove 1

clove
cove
dove
drove
grove
mauve
stove
wove

alcove
by jove

ove 2

dove
glove
love
of
shove

above
self-love
sort of

boxing glove
puppy love
turtledove

brotherly love
labor of love
tunnel of love

none of the above

ove 3

groove
move
prove
you've

approve
disprove
false move
improve
remove

disapprove
on the move

over

clover
over
rover

bowl over

ow to owing

changeover
hangover
Land Rover
layover
leftover
once-over
pushover
sleep over
spillover
turnover
warmed-over

Cliffs of Dover
four-leaf clover

ow 1
bough
bow
brow
chow
cow
how
now
ow
plow
pow
row
sow
vow
wow

allow
bowwow
eyebrow
know-how
kowtow
luau
meow
Moscow
powwow

snowplow
somehow

anyhow
cat's meow
here and now
holy cow
solemn vow
take a bow

ow 2 as in blow, see o 1

owder
chowder
doubter
louder
pouter
powder
prouder
shouter
stouter

clam chowder
gun powder

owed 1 as in snowed, see ode

owed 2 as in vowed, see oud

owel as in towel, see owl

ower as in power, see our 1

owered
coward
cowered
flowered
Howard
powered
scoured
showered
soured
towered

devoured
empowered

overpowered

owing
blowing
crowing
flowing
glowing
going
growing
knowing
mowing
rowing
sewing
showing
snowing
throwing
towing

all-knowing
churchgoing
free-flowing
mind-blowing
ongoing
outgoing
tiptoeing

easygoing
overflowing
partygoing

owl

bowel
foul
growl
howl
owl
prowl
scowl
towel
vowel

on the prowl
wise old owl

owledge

college
knowledge

acknowledge

own 1 as in flown,
see one 1

own 2

brown
clown
crown
down

drown
frown
gown
noun
town

ballgown
breakdown
countdown
crackdown
crosstown
downtown
face-down
ghost town
hoedown
hometown
knockdown
letdown
lowdown
meltdown
nightgown
pronoun
put-down
renown
slowdown
small-town
splashdown
sundown
touchdown

broken-down
cap and gown
Chinatown
circus clown - - - -
hand-me-down
out-of-town
trickle-down
up and down
upside down
wedding gown

owned as in
drowned,
see ound

ows as in blows,
see ose 2

owy

blowy
Chloe
doughy
Joey
showy
snowy

ox

blocks
box
clocks
docks
flocks
fox
gawks
hawks
jocks
knocks
locks
mocks
ox
pox
rocks
shocks
smocks

socks
sox
squawks
stocks
talks
walks
woks

cashbox
crosswalks
deadlocks
detox
Fort Knox
jaywalks
knee socks
lunchbox
mailbox
Mohawks
outfox
peacocks
Reeboks
roadblocks
sandbox
shamrocks
sleepwalks
soap box
sweat socks
ticktocks
toy box
unlocks
Xerox

aftershocks
chatterbox
chickenpox
Goldilocks
music box
orthodox
paradox
shadowbox

stumbling blocks
tomahawks

jack-in-the-box
Pandora's box
unorthodox

oxy
boxy
foxy
proxy

oy
boy
buoy
coy
joy
ploy
Roy
soy
toy
Troy

ahoy
annoy
destroy
employ
enjoy
killjoy
life buoy
oh boy

corduroy
Illinois
overjoy
pride and joy
real McCoy

oyal as in royal,
see oil

oyed as in employed,
see oid

oys
boys
joys
noise
ploys
poise
toys

annoys
cowboys
decoys
destroys
enjoys
killjoys
turquoise

Tinkertoys
traffic noise

oze as in doze,
see ose 2

ozen
chosen
frozen -------

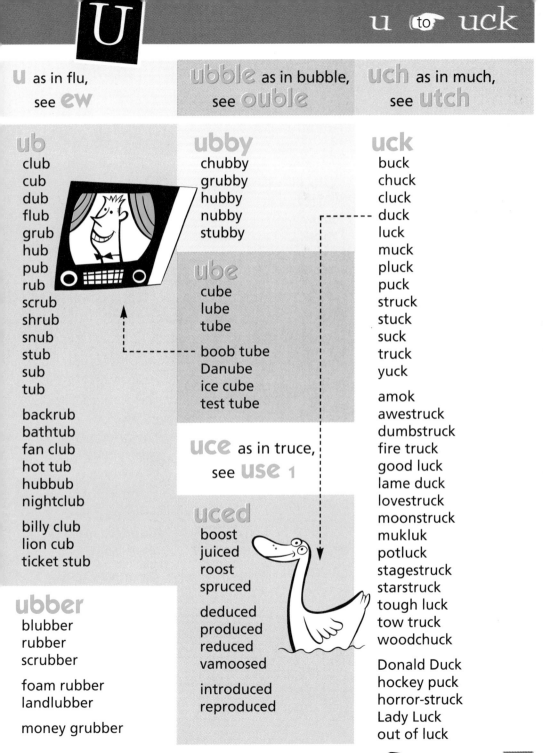

u as in flu,
see **ew**

ubble as in bubble,
see **ouble**

uch as in much,
see **utch**

ub

club
cub
dub
flub
grub
hub
pub
rub
scrub
shrub
snub
stub
sub
tub

backrub
bathtub
fan club
hot tub
hubbub
nightclub

billy club
lion cub
ticket stub

ubber

blubber
rubber
scrubber

foam rubber
landlubber

money grubber

ubby

chubby
grubby
hubby
nubby
stubby

ube

cube
lube
tube

boob tube
Danube
ice cube
test tube

uce as in truce,
see **use** 1

uced

boost
juiced
roost
spruced

deduced
produced
reduced
vamoosed

introduced
reproduced

uck

buck
chuck
cluck
duck
luck
muck
pluck
puck
struck
stuck
suck
truck
yuck

amok
awestruck
dumbstruck
fire truck
good luck
lame duck
lovestruck
moonstruck
mukluk
potluck
stagestruck
starstruck
tough luck
tow truck
woodchuck

Donald Duck
hockey puck
horror-struck
Lady Luck
out of luck

ucked to uctor

pass the buck
sitting duck
thunderstruck

beginner's luck

ucked as in plucked, see **uct**

ucker
clucker
pucker
sucker
trucker

bloodsucker

uckle
buckle
chuckle
knuckle

pinochle
swashbuckle
white-knuckle

honeysuckle

ucks
bucks
clucks
crux
ducks
flux
plucks
pucks
shucks
sucks
trucks

tux
aw, shucks
deluxe
dump trucks

ucky
Chuckie
ducky
lucky
mucky
plucky
yucky

Kentucky
unlucky

rubber ducky

happy-go-lucky

uct
bucked
chucked
clucked
ducked
duct
plucked
sucked
trucked
tucked

abduct
conduct
construct
deduct
destruct
instruct
obstruct
tear duct

aqueduct
reconstruct
self-destruct

uction
suction

abduction
construction
deduction
destruction
instruction
obstruction
production
reduction

introduction
reconstruction
reproduction

uctive
constructive
destructive
instructive
productive

reproductive
self-destructive
unproductive

counterproductive

uctor
abductor
conductor
instructor

ud
blood
bud
crud
dud
flood
mud
scud
spud
thud

blue blood
flash flood
Milk Dud
rosebud
taste bud

creeping crud
flesh and blood

stick in the mud

uda
Judah
Buddha

Bermuda

barracuda

udder as in rudder, see utter

uddle
cuddle - - - - - - - - - - - - - - - ->
huddle
muddle
puddle
scuttle

shuttle
subtle

befuddle
mud puddle
space shuttle

uddy
bloody
buddy
cruddy
muddy
nutty
putty
study

good buddy
peanutty

fuddy-duddy
nature study
Silly Putty
understudy

ude
booed
brewed
brood
chewed
crewed
crude

cued
dude
feud
food
glued
hued
mewed
mood
mooed
nude
poohed
prude
rude
rued
shrewd
spewed
stewed
sued
viewed
wooed

allude
boo-hooed
conclude
construed
delude
dog food
elude
exclude
exude
fast food
include
intrude
protrude
pursued
renewed
reviewed
Saint Jude
seafood

seclude
shampooed
soul food
subdued
tattooed
unglued

altitude
aptitude
attitude
baby food
ballyhooed
barbecued
family feud
gratitude
interlude
interviewed
in the mood
latitude
longitude
misconstrued
multitude
rendezvoused
solitude

udent
prudent
student

udge
budge
drudge
fudge
grudge
judge
nudge
sludge
smudge

trudge
hot fudge
misjudge
prejudge

ue as in blue,
see **ew**

ued as in glued,
see **ude**

uel
cruel
dual
duel
fuel
gruel
jewel ------------

renewal

ues as in blues,
see **use** 2

uff
bluff
buff
cuff
fluff
gruff
huff
muff
puff
rough
scruff

scuff
snuff
stuff
tough

cream puff
enough
handcuff
kid stuff
rebuff

blindman's bluff
fair enough
huff and puff
overstuff
powder puff
rough and tough
sure enough

uffer
bluffer
buffer
gruffer
rougher
suffer
tougher

stocking stuffer

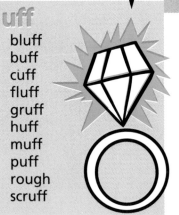

uffle
duffel
muffle
ruffle
scuffle
shuffle
snuffle
truffle

dust ruffle

uffy

fluffy
huffy
puffy
stuffy
toughie

ug

bug
chug
drug
dug
glug
hug
jug
lug
mug
plug
pug
rug
shrug
slug
smug
snug
thug
tug
ugh

bear hug
bedbug
beer mug
earplug
fireplug
humbug
unplug

chugalug
doodlebug

jitterbug
ladybug
litterbug
wonder drug

uge

huge
rouge
Scrooge
stooge

deluge
refuge

Baton Rouge
subterfuge

uggle

juggle
smuggle
snuggle
struggle

uggler

juggler
smuggler
snuggler
struggler

uild as in build, see illed

uise as in bruise, see use 2

uiser as in cruiser, see user

uit as in suit, see ute

uke

duke
fluke
kook
Luke
nuke
puke
spook

rebuke

antinuke

goobledygook

ule as in rule, see ool

ulge

bulge

divulge
indulge

overindulge

ulk

bulk
hulk
skulk
sulk

ull 1
cull
dull
gull
hull
lull
null
skull

annul
numskull
sea gull

ull 2
bull
full
pull
wool

chock-full
pit bull
push-pull
steel wool

Istanbul
Sitting Bull

ully
bully
fully
pulley
woolly

wild and woolly

ulp
gulp
pulp

ulsive
compulsive
impulsive
repulsive

ult
cult

adult
consult
exult
insult
occult
result
tumult

catapult
difficult
young adult

ulture
culture
vulture

agriculture
counterculture
horticulture

uly
coolly
cruelly
drooly
newly
stoolie
truly

unruly

um
bum
chum
come
crumb
drum
dumb
from
glum
gum
hum
mum
numb
plum
rum
scum
slum
some
strum
sum
thumb
yum

beach bum
become
eardrum
green thumb
ho-hum
humdrum
outcome
succumb
Tom Thumb
yum-yum

bubble gum
chewing gum
cookie crumb
deaf and dumb
overcome

rule of thumb

chrysanthemum
fee-fie-fo-fum

umb as in crumb, see um

umber 1
lumber
number
slumber

cucumber
outnumber

umber 2 as in plumber, see ummer

umble
crumble
fumble
grumble
humble
jumble
mumble
rumble
stumble
tumble

rough-and-tumble

umbling
bumbling
fumbling
grumbling
humbling
jumbling
mumbling
rumbling
stumbling
tumbling

ume as in assume, see oom

umer as in consumer, see umor

ummer
bummer
drummer
dumber
hummer
plumber
strummer
summer

latecomer
midsummer
newcomer
nose-thumber

up-and-comer

Indian summer

ummy
chummy
crummy
dummy
gummy
mummy
rummy
scummy
tummy
yummy

gin rummy

umor
bloomer
groomer
humor
rumor
tumor

consumer
costumer
good humor
late bloomer

baby boomer

umorous
humorous
numerous

ump
bump
chump
clump
dump
grump
hump

jump
lump
plump
pump
rump
slump
stump
thump
trump
ump

broad jump
goose bump
ski jump
speed bump
trash dump
tree stump

city dump
stomach pump
sugar lump
triple jump

umpkin
bumpkin
pumpkin

umption
gumption

assumption
consumption
presumption

umpy
bumpy
clumpy
dumpy
frumpy

jumpy
lumpy
stumpy

un
bun
done
fun
gun
hon
Hun
none
nun
one
pun
run
shun
son
spun
stun
sun
ton
won

all done
begun
blowgun
dog run
grandson
hired gun
home run
homespun
no one
outdone
outrun
redone
rerun
shotgun

someone
top gun
trial run
undone
well done

Air Force One
all or none
anyone
everyone
hit-and-run
hole in one
honeybun
hot dog bun
jump the gun
native son
9-1-1
number one
one by one
overdone
underdone

fun in the sun
hamburger bun
over and done
prodigal son

Attila the Hun

unch
brunch
bunch
crunch
hunch
lunch
munch
punch
scrunch

fruit punch

school lunch
whole bunch

honeybunch
out to lunch
pleased as punch

unction
function
junction

conjunction
dysfunction
malfunction

und
fund
gunned
punned
shunned
stunned
sunned

refund
trust fund

cummerbund

under
blunder
plunder
thunder
under
wonder

boy wonder
down under
no wonder

blood and thunder
loot and plunder

une as in tune, see oon

ung
clung
flung
hung
lung
rung
sprung
stung
sung
swung
tongue
wrung
young

among
far-flung
forked tongue
high-strung
unsung

egg foo yung
iron lung
mother tongue

slip of the tongue

unge
lunge
plunge
sponge

unger
hunger
younger

fishmonger
warmonger

rumormonger

ungle
bungle
jungle

concrete jungle

union
union

communion
reunion

unity
unity

community
immunity
impunity

opportunity

equal opportunity

diplomatic immunity

unk
bunk
chunk
clunk
drunk
dunk
flunk
funk

hunk
junk
monk
plunk
punk
shrunk
skunk
slunk
spunk
stunk
sunk
trunk

chipmunk
kerplunk
preshrunk
slam dunk

unken
drunken
Duncan
shrunken
sunken

unker
bunker
clunker
drunker
hunker
punker

slam-dunker

Archie Bunker

unky
chunky
clunky
funky

junky
monkey
punky
spunky

grease monkey

junk-food junky

unned as in punned, see und

unnel
funnel
tunnel

unner
gunner
punner
runner
stunner

front-runner
roadrunner
tail gunner

unny
bunny
funny
honey
money
runny
sonny
sunny

Bugs Bunny
hush money

Easter bunny
even money

unt
blunt
brunt
bunt
front
grunt
hunt
punt
runt
stunt

confront
forefront
homefront
manhunt
witch hunt

elephant
treasure hunt

unter
hunter
punter

headhunter
manhunter

unts
bunts
dunce
fronts
grunts
hunts
months
once
punts
runts
stunts

at once
witch hunts

all at once

up
cup
pup
up

backup
blowup
breakup
buildup
checkup
close-up
crackup
cutup
dress up
foul-up
grown-up
hang-up
hiccup
lineup
makeup
mix-up
pickup
roundup
setup
shut up
stickup
teacup
throw up
toss-up
touch-up
washed-up

all shook up
buckle up

buttercup
coffee cup
cover-up
cuddle up
giddy-up
paper cup
pick-me-up
runner-up
7-up

uper as in super,
see **ooper**

upid
cupid
stupid

upiter
Jupiter
stupider

uple
pupil
scruple

quadruple

upped as in
hiccupped,
see **upt**

upper
supper
hiccupper
picker-upper

uppy
guppy
puppy
yuppie

upt
cupped
upped

abrupt
bankrupt
corrupt
disrupt
erupt
hiccupped

interrupt

uption
corruption
disruption
eruption

interruption

ur as in fur,
see **er**

urable
curable
durable

endurable
incurable
securable

ural
mural
plural
rural

intramural

urance
assurance
endurance
insurance

reassurance
self-assurance

urb
blurb
curb
herb
verb

adverb
disturb
news blurb
perturb
proverb
suburb
superb

do not disturb

urch
birch
church
lurch
perch
search

research
soul-search

urder as in murder, see erter

urdle
curdle
fertile
girdle
hurdle
hurtle
turtle

urdy
birdy
nerdy
sturdy
wordy

ure
boor
cure
lure
poor
pure
sure
tour
your
you're

amour
assure
brochure
chauffeur
contour
demure
detour
endure
ensure

fer sure
impure
insure
liqueur
masseur
mature
obscure
secure
unsure
velour

amateur
aperture
connoisseur
curvature
immature
insecure
manicure
overture
pedicure
premature
reassure
saboteur

urf
serf
Smurf
surf
turf

urge as in surge, see erge

urgency
urgency

emergency
insurgency

urgent to urry

urgent as in insurgent, see **ergent**

urious
curious
furious

injurious
luxurious

urity
purity
surety

impurity
maturity
obscurity
security

immaturity
insecurity

urk as in lurk, see **erk**

url
curl
earl
girl
hurl
pearl
squirrel
swirl
twirl
whirl

awhirl

dream girl
unfurl

cover girl

mother of pearl

urly
burly
curly
early
pearly
Shirley
surly
swirly
twirly

hurly-burly

urn
burn
churn
earn
fern
learn
stern
turn
urn
yearn

adjourn
concern
downturn
heartburn
intern
Jules Verne
nocturne
return
slow burn
sojourn

sunburn
upturn
U-turn

live and learn
out of turn
overturn
tax return
toss and turn

urp
burp
chirp
slurp

syrup
usurp

Wyatt Earp

urr as in blur, see **er**

urred as in occurred, see **erd**

urry
blurry
curry
flurry
furry
hurry
scurry
worry

Missouri

not to worry

147

urse to use

urse as in nurse, see **erse**

ursed as in nursed, see **irst**

urst as in burst, see **irst**

urt as in blurt, see **ert**

urtle as in turtle, see **urdle**

ury
fury
jury

grand jury
Missouri

us
bus
cuss
fuss
muss
plus
pus
thus
us

discuss
nonplus
school bus

gloomy Gus
make a fuss

no fuss, no muss

usable
bruisable
usable

excusable
reusable
unusable

inexcusable

use 1
Bruce
deuce
goose
juice
loose
moose
mousse
noose
spruce
truce
use
Zeus

abuse
caboose
chartreuse
deduce
excuse
footloose
hang loose
induce
masseuse
misuse
mongoose

no use
papoose
produce
recluse
reduce
refuse
vamoose

child abuse
Dr. Seuss
hangman's noose
introduce
Mother Goose
no excuse
on the loose
out of use
reproduce
silly goose
what's the use?

chocolate mousse

use 2
blues
boos
bruise
chews
choose
clues
cruise
dues
fuse
glues
hues
lose
mews
moos
muse
news

148 Scholastic Rhyming Dictionary

ooze
ruse
screws
shoes --------
snooze
stews
sues
use
views
whose
zoos

abuse
accuse
amuse
bad news
boo-boos
boohoos
canoes
cashews
confuse
construes
corkscrews
cuckoos
curfews
defuse
effuse
enthuse
excuse
gumshoes
infuse
kazoos
miscues
misuse
muumuus
peruse
pursues
refuse
reviews

shampoos
short fuse
subdues
taboos
tattoos

avenues
baby shoes
barbecues ------
blow a fuse
born to lose
buckaroos
high-heeled shoes
interviews
kangaroos
pick and choose
revenues
win or lose

rhythm and blues

user

bruiser
chooser
cruiser
loser
muser
snoozer

user

abuser
accuser
bad loser
nonuser

child abuser
two-time loser

ush 1

blush
brush
crush
flush
gush
hush
lush
mush
plush
rush
shush
slush

bum's rush
cheek blush
gold rush
hairbrush
hush-hush
toothbrush

ush 2

bush
push
whoosh

ambush
rosebush

ushy
bushy
cushy
gushy
pushy

usion
fusion

collusion
conclusion
confusion
delusion
exclusion
illusion
inclusion
intrusion
protrusion
seclusion
transfusion

blood transfusion
disillusion

optical illusion

usive
abusive
conclusive
conducive
elusive
exclusive
illusive
intrusive
obtrusive
reclusive
seclusive

inconclusive
unobtrusive

usk
brusque
dusk
husk
musk
tusk

uss 1
puss
schuss

octopus - - - - - - - ┐
Oedipus
platypus
sourpuss

uss 2 as in fuss,
see us

ussed as in
discussed,
see ust

ussion
Russian

concussion
discussion
percussion

repercussion

ust
bussed
bust
crust
cussed

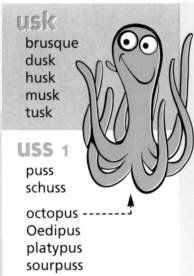

dust
fussed
gust
just
mussed
must
rust
thrust
trust

adjust
brain trust
coal dust
combust
crop dust
discussed
disgust
distrust
drug bust
entrust
gold dust
mistrust
nonplussed
pie crust
robust
sawdust
stardust
tongue-thrust
unjust

bite the dust
wanderlust

usted
busted
dusted
rusted
trusted

disgusted
mistrusted

uster

cluster
duster
fluster
luster
muster

blockbuster
crimebuster
lackluster

filibuster

ustle

bustle
hustle
muscle
mussel
Russell
rustle
tussle

hustle and bustle

usty

crusty
dusty
gusty
musty
rusty
trustee

ut 1

but
butt
cut
glut
gut
hut

jut
mutt
nut
putt
rut
shut
smut
strut
what

catgut
chestnut
clear-cut
haircut
King Tut
precut
rebut
shortcut
somewhat
so what
uncut

coconut
halibut
in a rut
Lilliput
scuttlebutt
undercut
uppercut

cigarette butt
emerald cut
open and shut

ut 2 as in put, see oot 2

utch

clutch
crutch
Dutch
hutch
much
such
touch

not much
retouch
soft touch

final touch
Midas touch
overmuch
pretty much
rabbit hutch
such and such

ute

beaut
boot
brute
Butte
chute
coot
cute
flute
fruit
hoot
loot
lute
moot
mute

151

newt
root
route
scoot
shoot
snoot
suit
toot

acute
astute
Beirut
commute
compute
deaf mute
dilute
dispute
en route
grapefruit
lawsuit
minute
outshoot
pollute
pursuit
recruit
refute
repute
salute
space suit
square root
tribute
uproot
zoot suit

absolute
attribute
birthday suit
constitute
destitute

execute
hot pursuit
ill repute
institute
monkey suit
overshoot
parachute
persecute
prosecute
resolute
substitute
troubleshoot

electrocute
forbidden fruit

Trivial Pursuit

uter
cuter
looter
neuter
pewter
rooter
scooter
shooter
suitor
tutor

commuter
computer
peashooter
polluter
recruiter
sharpshooter

motor scooter
persecutor
prosecutor
troubleshooter

uth as in truth, see ooth

ution
pollution
solution

absolution
air pollution
constitution
contribution
destitution
dissolution
distribution
evolution
execution
institution
persecution
prosecution
resolution
retribution
revolution
substitution

electrocution

utor as in tutor, see uter

utt as in mutt, see ut 1

utter
butter
clutter
cutter

flutter
gutter
mutter
putter
rudder
shudder
shutter
sputter
stutter
udder
utter

rain gutter
woodcutter

bread and butter
cookie cutter
paper cutter
peanut butter - - - - - - - - -

uys as in buys,
see **ize**

uzz
buzz
does
fuzz
was

abuzz

uzzle
guzzle
muzzle
nuzzle
puzzle

uttle as in scuttle,
see **uddle**

utty as in nutty,
see **uddy**

uture
future
moocher
suture

ux as in flux,
see **ucks**

uy as in guy,
see **y**

153

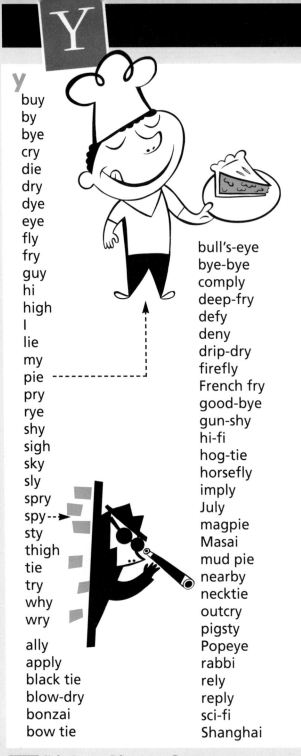

y

buy
by
bye
cry
die
dry
dye
eye
fly
fry
guy
hi
high
I
lie
my
pie
pry
rye
shy
sigh
sky
sly
spry
spy
sty
thigh
tie
try
why
wry

ally
apply
black tie
blow-dry
bonzai
bow tie

bull's-eye
bye-bye
comply
deep-fry
defy
deny
drip-dry
firefly
French fry
good-bye
gun-shy
hi-fi
hog-tie
horsefly
imply
July
magpie
Masai
mud pie
nearby
necktie
outcry
pigsty
Popeye
rabbi
rely
reply
sci-fi
Shanghai

shut-eye
sky-high
small fry
standby
supply
tongue-tie
untie
war cry
wise guy

alibi
amplify
apple pie
battle cry
beautify
beddy-bye
butterfly
camera-shy
certify
clarify
classify
crucify
cutie pie
dignify
do or die
dragonfly
evil eye
eye to eye
falsify
FBI
fortify
glorify
gratify
high and dry
horrify
hushaby
justify
lullaby
magnify

modify
mortify
multiply
mummify
mystify
notify
nullify
occupy
pacify
Paraguay
passerby
petrify
pizza pie
private eye
purify
qualify
ratify
rectify
rockaby
samurai
satisfy
signify
simplify
specify
stupefy
terrify
testify
tsetse fly
underlie
unify
Uruguay
verify
you and I

demystify
disqualify
dissatisfy
electrify
Eskimo Pie

exemplify
Fourth of July
identify
intensify
little white lie
personify
preoccupy
solidify

ycle as in bicycle,
see ickle

ye as in bye,
see y

yle as in style,
see ile 1

ym as in synonym,
see im

yme as in rhyme,
see ime

ype as in type,
see ipe

Index

ahead/ed	allocate/ate	amount/ount	antic/antic
ahoy/oy	allow/ow 1	amounts/ounce	anticipate/ate
aid/ade 1	allowed/oud	amour/ure	anticipation/ation
aide/ade 1	allude/ude	amp/amp	antidote/ote
ail/ale 1	ally/y	amplify/y	antifreeze/eeze
aim/aim	alma mater/otter	amputate/ate	antinuke/uke
air/air	almanac/ack	Amsterdam/am	antique/eek
airborne/orn	almighty/idy	amuse/use 2	antiwar/ore
aircraft/aft	almost/ost 1	an/an	Antoine/awn
airfare/air	aloe/allow 1	anagram/am	Antoinette/et
airlift/ift	alone/one 1	analytic/itic	antonym/im
airline/ine 1	along/ong	analytical/itical	ants/ance
airliner/iner	aloof/oof 1	analyze/ize	anxiety/iety
airmail/ale 1	aloud/oud	ancestor/ester	any/enny, inny
airplane/ain	alphabet/et	and/and	anybody/ody
airport/ort	alphabetize/ize	Androcles/eeze	anyhow/ow 1
airsick/ick	alpine/ine 1	anecdote/ote	anymore/ore
airtight/ight	already/etty	anesthetic/etic	anyone/un
airy/ary	altar/alter	anew/ew	anyplace/ace
aisle/ile 1	alter/alter	Angeleno/ino 2	anything/ing
ajar/ar	although/o	angina/ina 2	anytime/ime
akimbo/imbo	altitude/ude	angora/ora	anywhere/air
Al/al	altogether/eather	animalistic/istic	Apache/atchy
Alabama/ama 2	altruistic/istic	animate/ate	apart/art 1
alabaster/aster	always/aze	animation/ation	ape/ape
Alamo/o	am/am	animator/ader	aperture/ure
alarm/arm 1	A.M./em	animosity/ocity	apex/ex
albino/ino 1	Amarillo/illow	Anna/ana 1	Aphrodite/idy
Albuquerque/erky	amass/ass	Anne/an	apiece/ease 2
Alcatraz/azz	amassed/ast	annex/ex	Apollo/allow 2
alcohol/all	amateur/ure	annexed/ext	apologetic/etic
alcove/ove 1	amaze/aze	Annie/anny	apologize/ize
ale/ale 1	Amazon/awn	annihilate/ate	apology/ology
alert/ert	Amazons/ons	announce/ounce	appall/all
Algeria/eria	ambition/ition	annoy/oy	appalled/alled
Ali/olly	ambitious/icious	annoyed/oid	apparent/arent
alibi/y	ambush/ush 2	annoys/oys	apparition/ition
alibis/ize	amen/en	annul/ull 1	appeal/eel
alienate/ate	amend/end	another/other	appealed/ield
alike/ike	Americana/onna	ant/ant 1	appear/eer
alimony/ony	amiability/ility	antagonism/ism	appendicitis/itis
alive/ive 1	amid/id	antagonistic/istic	appetite/ight
all/all	amiss/iss	antagonize/ize	applaud/awed
allege/edge	ammonia/onia	anteater/eeder	applause/ause
allegory/ory	ammunition/ition	antelope/ope	apple/apple
alleviate/ate	amnesiac/ack	anthill/ill	applecart/art 1
alley/alley	amok/uck	anthology/ology	applesauce/oss 2
alliance/iance	among/ung	antibiotic/otic	appliance/iance
alligator/ader	amoral/oral	antibody/ody	application/ation

applied/ide	armpit/it	assume/oom	audition/ition
applies/ize	armpits/its	assumption/umption	auditorium/orium
apply/y	aroma/oma	assurance/urance	Audubon/awn
appoint/oint	aromatic/atic	assure/ure	aunt/ant 1, aunt
appreciate/ate	around/ound	asterisk/isk	aunts/ance
appreciation/ation	arrange/ange	asteroid/oid	aura/ora
apprehend/end	arrest/est	asthmatic/atic	auspicious/icious
apprehension/ention	arrival/ival	astir/er	Aussie/ossy
apprehensive/ensive	arrive/ive 1	astonish/onish	authenticity/icity
apprenticeship/ip	arrow/arrow	astound/ound	authority/ority
approach/oach	arrowhead/ed	Astrodome/ome 1	authorize/ize
approve/ove 3	art/art 1	astrological/ogical	auto/otto
apricot/ot	arthritic/itic	astrology/ology	autobiography/
apropos/o	arthritis/itis	astronaut/ot	ography
aptitude/ude	artichoke/oke	astronomic/omic	autocracy/ocracy
Aquarius/arious	artichokes/okes	astronomy/onomy	autocratic/atic
aquatic/otic	artifact/act	astute/ute	autograph/aff
aqueduct/uct	artifacts/ax	at/at 1	autographed/aft
arachnid/id	artificial/icial	ate/ate	automatic/atic
arbitrary/ary	artistic/istic	atheism/ism	automobile/eel
arc/ark	arty/ardy	athlete/eet	autonomy/onomy
arcade/ade 1	as/azz	athletic/etic	availability/ility
arch/arch	ascend/end	Atlantic/antic	Avalon/awn
archaeologist/ologist	ascertain/ain	atmosphere/eer	avant-garde/ard 1
archaeology/ology	ash/ash 1	atomic/omic	avenue/ew
Archie Bunker/unker	ashore/ore	atomizer/izer	avenues/use 2
architect/ect	Asian/asion	atrocious/ocious	aversion/ersion
architects/ex	Asiatic/atic	atrocity/ocity	avert/ert
archive/ive 1	aside/ide	attach/atch 1	Avery/avery
archrival/ival	ask/ask	attack/ack	aviary/ary
ardor/arter	asleep/eep	attacked/act	aviation/ation
are/ar	asphalt/alt	attacks/ax	aviator/ader
area/area	asphyxiate/ate	attempt/empt	avoid/oid
arena/ena	aspire/ire	attend/end	await/ate
arf/arf 1	ass/ass	attention/ention	awake/ake
Argentina/ena	assassinate/ate	attentive/entive	award/ord 1
argyle/ile 1	assassination/ation	attic/atic	aware/air
arise/ize	assassinator/ader	Attila/illa	away/ay
aristocracy/ocracy	assault/alt	attire/ire	awe/aw
aristocrat/at 1	assaulter/alter	attitude/ude	awed/awed
aristocratic/atic	assaults/alts	attract/act	awesome/ossum
Aristotle/oddle	assemble/emble	attraction/action	awestruck/uck
Arizona/ona	assert/ert	attractive/active	awful/awful
ark/ark	assessor/essor	attracts/ax	awhile/ile 1
Arkansas/aw	assign/ine 1	attribute/ute	awhirl/url
arm/arm 1	assigned/ind 1	auctioneer/eer	awoke/oke
armada/ada	assist/ist	audacious/acious	awoken/oken
armadillo/illow	assistance/istance	audacity/acity	ax/ax
armband/and	associate/ate	Audi/ody	ayatollah/ola

Aztec/eck

B

babble/abble
Babe Ruth/ooth
baboon/oon
baby/aby
baby-faced/aste
Babylon/awn
baby-sat/at 1
baby-sit/it
baby-sits/its
baby-sitter/itter
Bach/ock
back/ack
backache/ake
backboard/ord 1
backbone/one 1
backed/act
backfire/ire
background/ound
backhand/and
backlash/ash 1
backpack/ack
backpacked/act
backpedal/eddle
backrub/ub
backs/ax
backseat/eet
backslap/ap
backstab/ab 1
backstabber/abber
backstage/age 1
backtrack/ack
backup/up
backward/erd
backyard/ard 1
bacteria/eria
bactine/een
bad/ad 1
bag/ag
baggy/aggy
bagpipe/ipe
bagpiper/iper
bail/ale 1
bait/ate
bake/ake
bald/alled

balderdash/ash 1
Bali/alley
ball/all
ballerina/ena
ballet/ay
ballets/aze
ballgown/own 2
balloon/oon
ballpark/ark
ballpoint/oint
ballyhoo/ew
ballyhooed/ude
balm/alm, om
baloney/ony
Baltimore/ore
bambino/ino 2
bamboo/ew
ban/an
banana/ana 1
band/and
Band-Aid/ade 1
bandanna/ana 1
bandito/edo
bandleader/eeder
bandmaster/aster
bandstand/and
bang/ang
Bangkok/ock
Bangladesh/esh
bank/ank
bankrupt/upt
banned/and
banner/anner
baptism/ism
baptize/ize
bar/ar
barbarism/ism
barbarity/arity
barbecue/ew
barbecued/ude
barbecues/use 2
barbershop/op
Barcelona/ona
bard/ard 1
bare/air
barefoot/oot 2
barer/arer
barf/arf 1
barge/arge

baritone/one 1
bark/ark
barn/arn
barnstorm/orm 1
barnstormer/ormer
barnyard/ard 1
barometer/ometer
baron/aron
barracuda/uda
barrage/age
barred/ard
barren/aron
barricade/ade 1
Barry/ary
barstool/ool
bartender/ender
barter/arter 1
base/ace
baseball/all
baseline/ine 1
bash/ash 1
basin/ason
bask/ask
basket/asket
basketball/all
bass/ace, ass
bassinet/et
bassoon/oon
baste/aste
bastille/eel
bat/at 1
batch/atch 1
bath/ath
bathrobe/obe
bathroom/oom
bathtub/ub
bathwater/otter
Batman/an
baton/awn
Baton Rouge/uge
batons/ons
batter/atter
battery/attery
battle/attle
battleground/ound
battleship/ip
batty/atty
bauble/obble
Bavaria/area

bawdy/ody
bawl/all
bawled/alled
bay/ay
bayonet/et
bays/aze
bazaar/ar
be/ee
beach/each
bead/eed
beady/eedy
beagle/egal
beak/eek
beaker/eaker
beam/eem
bean/een
beanbag/ag
beanie/ini
beanstalk/ock
bear/air
bearish/erish
beast/east
beat/eet
beaten/eaten
beater/eeder
beatnik/ick
beau/o
beaut/ute
beautician/ition
beautifies/ize
beautify/y
beauty/oody
beaver/eaver
beaux/ose 2
bebop/op
became/aim
because/ause
become/um
bed/ed
bedbug/ug
bedpost/ost 1
bedridden/idden
bedside/ide
bedtime/ime
bee/ee
beef/ief
beefsteak/ake
beehive/ive 1
beeline/ine 1

been/in
beep/eep
beeper/eeper
beer/eer
bees/eeze
beet/eet
beetle/eedle
before/ore
beforehand/and
befuddle/uddle
beg/eg
began/an
begin/in
beginner/inner
begonia/onia
begun/un
behalf/aff
behave/ave
behead/ed
beheld/eld
behind/ind 1
behold/old
Beijing/ing
Beirut/ute
belch/elch
belief/ief
believe/eave
believer/eaver
belittle/iddle
bell/ell
belle/ell
bellhop/op
bellow/ellow
belly/elly
bellyache/ake
belong/ong
below/o
belt/elt
Ben/en
bench/ench
bend/end
beneath/eath 2
benediction/iction
beneficial/icial
benefit/it
Ben Hur/er
benign/ine 1
Benito/edo
Benny/enny

bent/ent
bequeath/eath 2
Berlin/in
Berliner/inner
Bermuda/uda
Bernadette/et
Bernard/ard 1
berry/ary
berserk/erk
Bert/ert
beside/ide
Bess/ess
best/est
bet/et
betrayed/ade 1
betrayer/ayer
betrays/aze
better/etter
Betty/etty
between/een
bevel/evel
beware/air
bewitch/itch
beyond/ond
bib/ib
bibliography/
  ography
bibliophile/ile 1
bicep/ep
bicker/icker
bicycle/ickle
bid/id
bidden/idden
bidder/itter
biddy/itty
bifocal/ocal
big/ig
Big Bird/erd
Big Foot/oot 2
bigger/igger
bigtime/ime
bigwig/ig
bike/ike
biker/iker
bikini/ini
bilk/ilk
bill/ill
billboard/ord 1
billed/illed

billfold/old
billion/illion
billionaire/air
Billy/illy
bin/in
bind/ind 1
binge/inge
binger/inger 2
bingo/ingo
biography/ography
biological/ogical
biologist/ologist
biology/ology
bionic/onic
biped/ed
birch/urch
bird/erd
birdbath/ath
birdbrain/ain
birdcall/all
birdwatch/otch
birdy/urdy
Birmingham/am
birth/irth
birthday/ay
birthdays/aze
birthmark/ark
birthplace/ace
birthrate/ate
birthright/ight
birthstone/one 1
bit/it
bite/ight
biter/ider
bits/its
bitten/itten
bitter/itter
bittersweet/eet
bitty/itty
bizarre/ar
blab/ab 1
blabber/abber
blabbermouth/
  outh 1
blabby/abby
black/ack
blackball/all
blackballed/alled
blackbird/erd

blackboard/ord 1
blackjack/ack
blacklist/ist
blackmail/ale 1
blackout/out
blacksmith/ith
blacktop/op
bladder/atter
blade/ade 1
blah/aw
Blake/ake
blame/aim
bland/and
blank/ank
blanky/anky
blare/air
blast/ast
blaster/aster
blaze/aze
blazon/azon
bleach/each
bleacher/eacher
bleak/eek
bleat/eet
bled/ed
bleed/eed
bleeder/eeder
bleep/eep
blend/end
blender/ender
bless/ess
blessed/est
blew/ew
blight/ight
blimp/imp
blind/ind 1
blindfold/old
blink/ink
blinked/inct
blinky/inky
blintze/ince
blip/ip
bliss/iss
blister/ister
blistery/istory
blitz/its
blitzkrieg/eague
blizzard/izard
bloat/ote

lob/ob	blurt/ert	bookmobile/eel	bows/ose 2
lock/ock	blush/ush 1	bookshelf/elf	bowwow/ow 1
lockade/ade 1	boar/ore	bookworm/erm	box/ox
lockbuster/uster	board/ord 1	boom/oom	boxcar/ar
locker/ocker	boarder/order	boomerang/ang	boxy/oxy
lockhead/ed	boardwalk/ock	boondoggle/oggle	boy/oy
locks/ox	boast/ost 1	Boone, Daniel/oon	boycott/ot
lond/ond	boat/ote	boor/ure	boyfriend/end
londer/onder	bob/ob	boos/use 2	boys/oys
londes/ons	bobble/obble	boost/uced	bozos/ose 2
lood/ud	Bobby/obby	booster/ooster	brace/ace
loodhound/ound	bobsled/ed	boot/ute	braced/aste
loodshed/ed	body/ody	booth/ooth	brag/ag
loodshot/ot	bodyguard/ard 1	bootie/oody	braid/ade 1
loodstain/ain	bog/og	booty/oody	Braille/ale 1
loodstream/eem	boggle/oggle	bop/op	brain/ain
loodsucker/ucker	boil/oil	Bo Peep/eep	brainchild/ild
loody/uddy	bold/old	border/order	brainstorm/orm 1
loomer/umor	bolder/older	borderline/ine 1	brainwash/osh
loop/oop	bolero/arrow	bore/ore	brainwave/ave
looper/ooper	Bologna/onia	bored/ord 1	brake/ake
lossom/ossum	bolster/olster	born/orn	bran/an
lot/ot	bolt/olt	boss/oss 2	brand/and
lotch/otch	bomb/om	bossed/ost 2	brand-new/ew
louse/ouse	bombard/ard 1	bossy/ossy	brash/ash 1
low/o	bombast/ast	botch/otch	brass/ass
lowgun/un	bombastic/astic	both/oth	brassy/assy
lowhard/ard 1	bombshell/ell	bother/ather	brat/at 1
lowing/owing	bon-bon/awn	bottle/oddle	bratty/atty
lown/one 1	bond/ond	bottlecap/ap	brave/ave
lowout/out	Bond, James/ond	bottlefed/ed	braver/aver
lows/ose 2	bonds/ons	bottleneck/eck	bravery/avery
lowup/up	bone/one 1	bouffant/aunt	brawl/all
lowy/owy	bonehead/ed	bough/ow 1	brawled/alled
ubber/ubber	bonfire/ire	bought/ot	brawler/aller
ue/ew	bonk/onk	boulder/older	brawny/awny
uejay/ay	bonny/awny	boulevard/ard 1	bray/ay
uejays/aze	bon voyage/age 2	bounce/ounce	brazen/azon
ueprint/int	bony/ony	bound/ound	Brazil/ill
ueprints/ince	bonzai/y	bouquet/ay	Brazilian/illion
ues/use 2	boo/ew	bouquets/aze	bread/ed
uff/uff	booed/ude	bout/out	break/ake
uffer/uffer	boogieboard/ord 1	boutique/eek	breakdown/own 2
under/under	boo-hooed/ude	bow/o, ow 1	breakthrough/ew
unt/unt	boo-hoos/use 2	bowed/ode, oud	breakup/up
ur/er	book/ook 2	bowel/owl	breast/est
urb/urb	bookcase/ace	bowl/ole	breath/eath 1
urred/erd	bookie/ookie	bowled/old	breathe/eethe
urry/urry	bookmark/ark	bowler/olar	bred/ed

breed/eed
breeze/eeze
breezy/easy
brew/ew
brewed/ude
Brian/ion
bribe/ibe
brick/ick
bricks/icks
bridal/idle
bride/ide
bridegroom/oom
bridesmaid/ade 1
bridge/idge
bridle/idle
brief/ief
briefcase/ace
bright/ight
brighten/ighten
brighter/ider
brim/im
bring/ing
brink/ink
brisk/isk
bristle/istle
brittle/iddle
broach/oach
broad/awed
broadcast/ast
broadcaster/aster
broader/otter
brochure/ure
brogue/ogue 1
broil/oil
broke/oke
broken/oken
broker/oker
bronchitis/itis
bronze/ons
brood/ude
brook/ook 2
broom/oom
broomstick/ick
broth/oth 2
brother/other
brotherhood/ood 3
brought/ot
brow/ow 1
browbeat/eet

browbeaten/eaten
brown/own 2
browned/ound
Bruce/use 1
bruisable/usable
bruise/use 2
bruiser/user
brunch/unch
brunette/et
brunt/unt
brush/ush 1
brush-off/off
brusque/usk
brutal/oodle
brutality/ality 1
brute/ute
Bryant/iant
bubble/ouble
buccaneer/eer
buck/uck
buckaroo/ew 2
buckaroos/use
bucked/uct
buckle/uckle
bucks/ucks
bud/ud
Buddha/uda
buddy/uddy
budge/udge
buff/uff
buffalo/o
Buffalo Bill/ill
buffaloes/ose 2
buffer/uffer
buffoon/oon
bug/ug
bugaboo/ew
build/illed
buildup/up
built/ilt
Bulgaria/area
bulge/ulge
bulk/ulk
bull/ull 2
bulldog/og
bulldoze/ose 2
bullfight/ight
bullfrog/og
bullhorn/orn

bullpen/en
bully/ully
bum/um
bumblebee/ee
bumblebees/eeze
bumbling/umbling
bummer/ummer
bump/ump
bumpkin/umpkin
bumpy/umpy
bun/un
bunch/unch
bungalows/ose 2
bungle/ungle
bunk/unk
bunkbed/ed
bunker/unker
Bunker, Archie/unker
bunny/unny
bunt/unt
bunts/unts
buoy/ewy, oy
bureaucracy/ocracy
bureaucrat/at 1
bureaucratic/atic
burglarize/ize
burlap/ap
burlesque/esque
burly/urly
burn/urn
burp/urp
burr/er
burrito/edo
burst/irst
bury/ary
bus/us
bush/ush 2
bushy/ushy
bussed/ust
bust/ust
busted/usted
bustle/ustle
busy/izzy
busybody/ody
but/ut 1
butt/ut 1
Butte/ute
butter/utter
butterball/all

buttercup/up
butterflies/ize
butterfly/y
buttermilk/ilk
buttonhole/ole
buy/y
buys/ize
buzz/uzz
buzzword/erd
by/y
bye/y
bypass/ass

C

cab/ab 1
caballero/arrow
cabby/abby
cabdriver/iver 1
cable/able
caboose/use 1
cache/ash 1
cackle/ackle
cad/ad 1
caddie/atty
cadet/et
Cadillac/ack
Cadillacs/ax
Caesar/eezer
cafe/ay
cafes/aze
cafeteria/eria
caffeine/een
cage/age 1
cajole/ole
cajoled/old
cake/ake
calamari/arry 2
calculate/ate
calculation/ation
calculator/ader
calf/aff
calico/o
call/all
called/alled
caller/aller
calm/alm, om
caloric/oric
Camaro/arrow

ame/aim
amelback/ack
Camelot/ot
Cameroon/oon
amisole/ole
amouflage/age 2
amp/amp
ampaign/ain
amper/amper
ampfire/ire
ampground/ound
an/an
anal/al
anary/ary
ancan/an
ancellation/ation
andidate/ate
andlestick/ick
ane/ain
anine/ine 1
anned/and
annibalism/ism
annonball/all
annot/ot
anoe/ew
anoes/use 2
an't/ant 1
antaloupe/ope
anteen/een
antina/ena
ap/ap
apability/ility
apacity/acity
ape/ape
Cape Cod/awed
apitalism/ism
apitalize/ize
appuccino/ino 2
aprice/ease 2
Capricorn/orn
apsize/ize
aptain/in
aptivate/ate
aptivity/ivity
ar/ar
arat/arrot
aravan/an
arbohydrate/ate
ard/ard 1

cardboard/ord 1
care/air
career/eer
carefree/ee
caress/ess
caressed/est
caribou/ew
carload/ode
carnivore/ore
carousel/ell
Carrie/ary
carrot/arrot
carry/ary
cart/art 1
cartoon/oon
cartwheel/eel
carve/arve
carwash/osh
case/ace
Casey/acy
cash/ash 1
cashbox/ox
cashew/ew
cashews/use 2
cashier/eer
cashmere/eer
casino/ino 2
cask/ask
casket/asket
casserole/ole
cast/ast
caste/ast
cat/at 1
catalog/og
catalytic/itic
catamaran/an
catapult/ult
catatonic/onic
catch/atch 1
catch-22/ew
catchy/atchy
categorize/ize
category/ory
cater/ader
caterpillar/iller
caterwaul/all
catfight/ight
catgut/ut 1
catnap/ap

catnip/ip
cattle/attle
catty/atty
Caucasian/asion
caught/ot
cauliflower/our 1
cause/ause
cavalcade/ade 1
cavalier/eer
cave/ave
caveman/an 1
caviar/ar
cavity/avity
cavort/ort
cavorter/order
cease/ease 2
ceased/east
cease-fire/ire
cedar/eeder
celebrate/ate
celebration/ation
Celeste/est
cell/ell
cellar/eller
cellmate/ate
cello/ellow
cellophane/ain
celluloid/oid
Celt/elt
cement/ent
cemetery/ary
censorial/orial
censorship/ip
censure/enture
cent/ent
center/enter
centerpiece/ease 2
centigrade/ade 1
centimeter/eeder
centipede/eed
cents/ense
ceremonial/onial
ceremony/ony
certifies/ize
certify/y
cesspool/ool
Cézanne/awn
Chad/ad 1
chain/ain

chair/air
chalk/ock
chalkboard/ord 1
champ/amp
champagne/ain
championship/ip
chance/ance
chandelier/eer
change/ange
changeover/over
chant/ant 1
chants/ance
chaotic/otic
chap/ap
chapel/apple
chaperon/one 1
characteristic/istic
characterize/ize
charade/ade 1
charcoal/ole
charge/arge
charismatic/atic
charity/arity
charm/arm 1
charred/ard 1
chart/art 1
charter/arter
chartreuse/use 1
chase/ace
chased/aste
chasm/asm
chassis/assy
chaste/aste
chasten/ason
chastise/ize
chat/at 1
chatter/atter
chatterbox/ox
chatty/atty
chauffeur/ure
chauvinism/ism
cheap/eep
cheaper/eeper
cheapskate/ate
cheat/eet
cheater/eeder
check/eck
checkbook/ook 2
checked/ect

checkerboard/ord 1
checkered/ecord
checklist/ist
checkmate/ate
checkpoint/oint
checks/ex
checkup/up
cheddar/etter
cheek/eek
cheer/eer
cheerful/earful
Cheerios/ose 2
cheerleader/eeder
cheery/eery
cheese/eeze
cheesecake/ake
cheesy/easy
cheetah/ita
chef/ef
chenille/eel
cherish/erish
Chernobyl/oble
cherry/ary
Chesapeake/eek
chess/ess
chest/est
Chester/ester
chestnut/ut 1
chew/ew
chewed/ude
chews/use 2
chewy/ewy
Cheyenne/en
Chicana/onna
chick/ick
chickadees/eeze
chicken/icken
chickenpox/ox
chicks/icks
chide/ide
chief/ief
chiffon/awn
child/ild
childbirth/irth
childhood/ood 3
childlike/ike
childproof/oof 1
chili/illy
chill/ill

chilled/illed
chiller/iller
chilly/illy
chime/ime
chimp/imp
chimpanzee/ee
chimpanzees/eeze
chin/in
China/ina 2
Chinatown/own 2
chinchilla/illa
Chinese/eeze
chintz/ince
chip/ip
chipmunk/unk
chipped/ipped
chipper/ipper
chirp/urp
chisel/izzle
chitchat/at 1
Chloe/owy
chloride/ide
chlorine/een
chlorophyll/ill
chocoholic/olic
choice/oice
choir/ire
choke/oke
choker/oker
chokes/okes
cholesterol/all
chomp/omp
choose/use 2
chooser/user
chop/op
Chopin/an
chopper/opper
choppy/oppy
chopstick/ick
chopsticks/icks
chop suey/ewy
choral/oral
chorale/al
chord/ord
chore/ore
choreography/
    ography
chose/ose 2
chosen/ozen

chow/ow 1
chowder/owder
chowhound/ound
chow mein/ain
Christina/ena
chrome/ome 1
chronic/onic
chronicle/onical
chronological/ogical
chronology/ology
chrysanthemum/um
chubby/ubby
chuck/uck
chucked/uct
Chuckie/ucky
chuckle/uckle
chug/ug
chugalug/ug
chum/um
chummy/ummy
chump/ump
chunk/unk
chunky/unky
church/urch
churchgoing/owing
churn/urn
chute/ute
cicada/ada
cider/ider
cigar/ar
cigarette/et
cinch/inch
Cincinnati/atty
Cinderella/ella
cinerama/
    ama 1, ama 2
circulate/ate
circulation/ation
circumstance/ance
citation/ation
cite/ight
citizenship/ip
city/itty
civil/ivel
civilian/illion
civility/ility
civilization/ation
civilize/ize
clad/ad 1

claim/aim
clam/am
clambake/ake
clammy/ammy
clamp/amp
clan/an
clang/ang
clank/ank
clanky/anky
clap/ap
Clara/ara
clarified/ide
clarifies/ize
clarify/y
clarinet/et
Clarisse/ease 2
clarity/arity
Clark/ark
clash/ash 1
clasp/asp
class/ass
classify/y
classmate/ate
classroom/oom
classy/assy
clatter/atter
Claude/awed
clause/ause
claw/aw
clawed/awed
claws/ause
clay/ay
clean/een
clear/eer
clearer/earer
cleaver/eaver
clef/ef
clench/ench
clerk/erk
clever/ever
click/ick
clicked/ict
clicker/icker
clicks/icks
client/iant
clientele/ell
clients/iance
cliff/iff
Cliffs of Dover/over

limax/ax	clunk/unk	collar/aller	communication/ation
limb/ime	clunker/unker	colleague/eague	communion/union
linch/inch	clunky/unky	collect/ect	communism/ism
ling/ing	cluster/uster	collection/ection	community/unity
lingy/ingy 1	clutch/utch	collector/ector	commute/ute
link/ink	clutter/utter	collects/ex	commuter/uter
linked/inct	coach/oach	Colleen/een	compact/act
lip/ip	coal/ole	college/owledge	companionship/ip
lipped/ipped	coalition/ition	collegian/egion	compare/air
lipper/ipper	coarse/orse	collide/ide	compatibility/ility
loaks/okes	coast/ost 1	collie/olly	compel/ell
lobber/obber	coastline/ine 1	collision/ision	compelled/eld
lock/ock	coat/ote	colloquialism/ism	compete/eet
locks/ox	coax/okes	collusion/usion	competition/ition
lockwise/ize	cobbler/obbler	cologne/one 1	complain/ain
lockwork/erk	cobblestone/one 1	colon/olen	complete/eet
lod/awed	Cochise/ease 1	colonel/ernal	complex/ex
lodhopper/opper	cockatoo/ew	colonial/onial	complexion/ection
log/og	cockeyed/ide	colonize/ize	complicate/ate
lomp/omp	cockpit/it	colorblind/ind 1	complication/ation
lone/one 1	cockpits/its	colt/olt	compliment/ent
lop/op	cockroach/oach	coma/oma	compliments/ense
lose/ose 1, ose 2	cocktail/ale 1	comatose/ose 1	comply/y
losure/osure	cocky/awky	comb/ome 1	composition/ition
lot/ot	cocoa/oco	combat/at 1	composure/osure
loth/oth 2	coconut/ut 1	combination/ation	compound/ound
lothes/ose 2	cocoon/oon	combine/ine 1	comprehend/end
lotheshorse/orse	coddle/oddle	combined/ind 1	comprehension/ention
lothesline/ine 1	code/ode	combust/ust	comprehensive/ensive
loud/oud	coed/ed	come/um	compressor/essor
loudburst/irst	coerce/erse	comedic/edic	comprise/ize
lout/out	coerced/irst	comic/omic	compromise/ize
love/ove 1	coercion/ersion	comma/ama 1	compulsive/ulsive
lover/over	coexist/ist	command/and	compute/ute
loverleaf/ief	coffeepot/ot	commence/ense	computer/uter
lown/own 2	cohort/ort	commentary/ary	comrade/ad 1
lowned/ound	coif/off	commerce/erse	con/awn
lub/ub	coil/oil	commercialism/ism	conceal/eel
lubhouse/ouse	coin/oin	commercialize/ize	concealed/ield
lub Med/ed	coincide/ide	commingle/ingle	concede/eed
luck/uck	coincidental/ental	commission/ition	conceit/eet
lucked/uct	Coke/oke	commit/it	conceive/eave
lucker/ucker	Cokes/okes	commits/its	concentrate/ate
lucks/ucks	cola/ola	committal/iddle	concentration/ation
lue/ew	cold/old	committee/itty	concept/ept
lues/use 2	colder/older	commodious/odious	conception/eption
lump/ump	Colgate/ate	commotion/otion	concern/urn
lumpy/umpy	colic/olic	commune/oon	
lung/ung	collage/age 2	communicate/ate	

concession/ession
conch/aunch
concise/ice 1
conclude/ude
conclusion/usion
conclusive/usive
concrete/eet
concur/er
concurred/erd
concussion/ussion
condemn/em
condense/ense
condition/ition
condone/one 1
condor/onder, ore
conducive/usive
conduct/uct
conductor/uctor
cone/one 1
confer/er
conferred/erd
confess/ess
confessed/est
confession/ession
confessor/essor
confetti/etty
confidante/aunt
confide/ide
confidential/ential
confidentiality/
    ality 1
confine/ine 1
confined/ind 1
confirm/erm
confirmation/ation
confiscate/ate
conflict/ict
conflicts/icks
conform/orm 1
conformer/ormer
confront/unt
confuse/use 2
confusion/usion
congeal/eel
congeniality/ality 1
congestion/estion
congratulate/ate
congregation/ation
conical/onical

conjunction/unction
connect/ect
connection/ection
connector/ector
connects/ex
conned/ond
Connie/awny
conniption/iption
connive/ive 1
conniver/iver 1
connoisseur/ure
conquest/est
cons/ons
consent/ent
consequence/ense
consequently/ently
conservatory/ory
conserve/erve
consider/itter
consideration/ation
cosign/ine 1
consist/ist
consistence/istance
consolation/ation
console/ole
consoled/old
conspire/ire
constitute/ute
constitution/ution
constitutionality/
    ality 1
constrictor/ictor
construct/uct
construction/uction
constructive/uctive
construe/ew
construed/ude
construes/use 2
consult/ult
consume/oom
consumer/umor
consumption/
    umption
contacts/ax
contagious/ageous
contain/ain
contaminate/ate
contemplate/ate
contemporary/ary

contempt/empt
contender/ender
content/ent
contently/ently
contest/est
context/ext
continental/ental
contort/ort
contortion/ortion
contour/ure
contraband/and
contract/act
contraction/action
contradict/ict
contradiction/iction
contradictor/ictor
contradicts/icks
contrary/ary
contrast/ast
contribution/ution
contrive/ive 1
control/ole
controlled/old
controller/olar
convalescent/escent
convene/een
convention/ention
converge/erge
conversation/ation
converse/erse
conversed/irst
conversion/ersion
convert/ert
converter/erter
conveyor/ayer
convict/ict
conviction/iction
convince/ince
cook/ook 2
cookie/ookie
cookout/out
cool/ool
cooler/ooler
coolly/uly
coop/oop
cooperate/ate
cooperation/ation
coordinate/ate
coordination/ation

coordinator/ader
coot/ute
cootie/oody
cop/op
cope/ope
copper/opper
copy/oppy
copyright/ight
coquette/et
coral/oral
cord/ord 1
corduroy/oy
core/ore
cork/ork 1
corkscrew/ew
corkscrews/use 2
corn/orn
corncob/ob
cornucopia/opia
corporation/ation
corps/ore
corral/al
correct/ect
correction/ection
corrects/ex
correspond/ond
corresponds/ons
corridor/ore
corrosion/osion
corrosive/osive
corrupt/upt
corruption/uption
Corryn/in
corsage/age 2
Corvette/et
cosmetic/etic
cosmos/ose 1
cost/ost 2
costar/ar
costarred/ard 1
costume/oom
costumer/umor
cot/ot
cotillion/illion
cotton/otten
cottontail/ale 1
couch/ouch
cough/off
could/ood 3

count/ount
countdown/own 2
counterculture/ulture
counterfeit/it
counterfeits/its
counterpart/art 1
counterproductive/uctive
countersue/ew
counts/ounce
coupe/oop
coupon/awn
courageous/ageous
course/orse
court/ort
courter/order
courthouse/ouse
courtroom/oom
courtship/ip
Cousteau, Jacques/o
couth/ooth
cove/ove 1
covert/ert
cow/ow 1
coward/owered
cowboys/oys
cower/our 1
cowered/owered
cowhand/and
cowpoke/oke
coy/oy
cozy/osy
CPR/ar
crab/ab 1
crabby/abby
crack/ack
crackdown/own 2
cracked/act
crackerjack/ack
crackle/ackle
crackpot/ot
cracks/ax
crackup/up
craft/aft
crafty/afty
cram/am
cramp/amp
crane/ain

crank/ank
cranky/anky
crash/ash 1
crass/ass
crate/ate
crater/ader
crave/ave
crawl/all
crawled/alled
crawly/olly
Crayola/ola
craze/aze
crazy/azy
creak/eek
creaky/eaky
cream/eem
creamy/eamy
crease/ease 2
creased/east
create/ate
creation/ation 1
creativity/ivity
creator/ader
creature/eacher
credential/ential
credibility/ility
creed/eed
creek/eek
creep/eep
creeper/eeper
creepy/eepy
crematorium/orium
Creole/ole
crept/ept
crescent/escent
crest/est
cretin/eaten
crew/ew
crewed/ude
crib/ib
cricket/icket
cried/ide
cries/ize
crime/ime
criminology/ology
crimp/imp
cringe/inge
crinkle/inkle
cripple/ipple

Crisco/isco
crisp/isp
crisper/isper
crisscross/oss 2
crisscrossed/ost 2
critic/itic
critical/itical
criticism/ism
criticize/ize
critique/eek
critter/itter
croak/oke
croaks/okes
crock/ock
Crockett, Davy/ocket
crocodile/ile 1
crony/ony
crook/ook 2
croon/oon
crooner/ooner
crop/op
croquet/ay
cross/oss 2
crossed/ost 2
crossfire/ire
crossroad/ode
crosstown/own 2
crosswalk/ock
crosswalks/ox
crossword/erd
crouch/ouch
crow/o
crowd/oud
crowed/ode
crowing/owing
crown/own 2
crowned/ound
crows/ose 2
crucify/y
crud/ud
cruddy/uddy
crude/ude
cruel/uel
crueler/ooler
cruelly/uly
cruise/use 2
cruiser/user
crumb/um
crumble/umble

crummy/ummy
crunch/unch
crusade/ade 1
crusader/ader
crush/ush 1
crust/ust
crusty/usty
crutch/utch
crux/ucks
cry/y
crypt/ipped
cub/ub
cubbyhole/ole
cube/ube
cuckoo/ew
cuckoos/use 2
cucumber/umber 1
cuddle/uddle
cue/ew
cued/ude
cuff/uff
cuisine/een
cul-de-sac/ack
culinary/ary
cull/ull 1
cult/ult
cultivate/ate
culture/ulture
cummerbund/und
cup/up
cupcake/ake
cupid/upid
cupidity/idity
cupped/upt
curable/urable
curb/urb
curdle/urdle
cure/ure
curfew/ew 2
curfews/use
curiosity/ocity
curious/urious
curl/url
curlicue/ew
curly/urly
curry/urry
curse/erse
cursed/irst
curt/ert

curtail/ale 1
curvacious/acious
curvature/ure
curve/erve
cushy/ushy
cuss/us
cussed/ust
customary/ary
cut/ut 1
cute/ute
cuter/uter
cutie/oody
cutoff/off
cutter/utter
cutthroat/ote
cutup/up
cyclone/one 1
cymbal/imble
cynicism/ism
cyst/ist
czar/ar
Czech/eck

D

dab/ab 1
dabble/abble
dad/ad 1
daddy/atty
daffodil/ill
daily/aily
dairy/ary
daisy/azy
dally/alley
Dalmatian/ation
dam/am
damp/amp
damper/amper
dance/ance
dandelion/ion
dang/ang
Daniel Boone/oon
dank/ank
Danny/anny
Danube/ube
dare/air
daredevil/evel
dark/ark
Darlene/een

darn/arn
dart/art 1
dash/ash 1
dashboard/ord 1
date/ate
daub/ob
daughter/otter
daunt/aunt
Davy Crockett/ocket
dawdle/oddle
dawn/awn
dawned/ond
dawns/ons
day/ay
daybreak/ake
daydream/eem
daylight/ight
days/aze
daytime/ime
daze/aze
dead/ed
deadbeat/eet
deadbolt/olt
deader/etter
deadline/ine 1
deadlock/ock
deadlocks/ox
deadpan/an
deadwood/ood 3
deaf/ef
deal/eel
dealt/elt
dean/een
dear/eer
Dear Abby/abby
dearer/earer
dearie/eery
death/eath 1
deathbed/ed
Death Valley/alley
debacle/ackle
debate/ate
debater/ader
debonair/air
debrief/ief
debt/et
debtor/etter
debut/ew
debutante/aunt

decade/ade 1
decaf/aff
decal/al
decathlon/awn
decay/ay
decayed/ade 1
decays/aze
decease/ease 2
deceased/east
deceit/eet
deceive/eave
December/ember
deception/eption
decide/ide
decision/ision
deck/eck
decked/ect
decks/ex
declaration/ation
declare/air
decline/ine 1
declined/ind 1
decode/ode
decompose/ose 2
decomposition/ition
decongest/est
decongestion/estion
decor/ore
decorate/ate
decoration/ation
decorator/ader
decoys/oys
decrease/ease 2
decreased/east
dedicate/
    ate, edicate
dedication/ation
deduce/use 1
deduced/uced
deduct/uct
deduction/uction
deed/eed
deem/eem
deep/eep
deeper/eeper
deep-fried/ide
deer/eer
deface/ace
defaced/aste

defame/aim
default/alt
defaults/alts
defeat/eet
defect/ect
defective/ective
defector/ector
defects/ex
defend/end
defender/ender
defense/ense
defensive/ensive
defer/er
deferential/ential
deferred/erd
defiance/iance
defiant/iant
deficient/icient
defied/ide
defies/ize
define/ine 1
defined/ind 1
definition/ition
deflate/ate
deform/orm 1
defrost/ost 2
defroster/oster
deft/eft
defuse/use 2
defy/y
degree/ee
degrees/eeze
dehydration/ation
dejection/ection
Delaware/air
delay/ay 1
delayed/ade
delays/aze
delegate/ate
delete/eet
deli/elly
deliberate/ate, it
delicious/icious
delight/ight
delirious/erious
deliver/iver 2
Della/ella
delude/ude
deluge/uge

delusion/usion
deluxe/ucks
delve/elve
demand/and
demerit/arrot
democracy/ocracy
democrat/at 1
democratic/atic
demography/ography
demolish/olish
demolition/ition
demonic/onic
demonstrate/ate
demonstration/ation
demonstrator/ader
demoralize/ize
demur/er
demure/ure
demystifies/ize
demystify/y
den/en
denied/ide
denies/ize
Denmark/ark
Denny/enny
denomination/omination
dense/ense
density/ensity
dent/ent
dental/ental
dents/ense
denture/enture
deny/y
deodorize/ize
deodorizer/izer
depart/art 1
departmental/ental
depend/end
dependability/ility
deport/ort
depravity/avity
depress/ess
depressed/est
depression/ession
deprive/ive 1
derail/ale 1
derelict/ict

dermatologist/ologist
dermatology/ology
derogatory/ory
descend/end
descent/ent
describe/ibe
description/iption
desert/ert
deserter/erter
deserve/erve
design/ine 1
designed/ind 1
designer/iner
desire/ire
desk/esque
Des Moines/oin
despair/air
desperation/ation
despise/ize
dessert/ert
destination/ation
destitute/ute
destitution/ution
destroy/oy
destroyed/oid
destroys/oys
destruct/uct
destruction/uction
destructive/uctive
detach/atch 1
detail/ale 1
detect/ect
detective/ective
detector/ector
detects/ex
detention/ention
deter/er
detergent/ergent
determination/ation
deterred/erd
detest/est
dethrone/one 1
detonate/ate
detonator/ader
detour/ure
detox/ox
detrimental/ental
deuce/use 1

devastate/ate
devastation/ation
deviate/ate
device/ice
devil/evel
devise/ize 1
devoid/oid
Devon/even
devote/ote
devotion/otion
devotional/otional
devour/our 1
devoured/owered
devout/out
dew/ew
dewy/ewy
dexterity/arity
diabetic/etic
diabolic/olic
diagnose/ose 1
diagnosed/ost 1
diagram/am
dial/ile 1
dialects/ex
dialed/ild
dialogue/og
Diana/ana 1
diaper/iper
diatribe/ibe
dice/ice 1
diced/iced
dictation/ation
dictator/ader
dictatorial/orial
dictatorship/ip
diction/iction
dictionary/ary
did/id
diddle/iddle
die/y
died/ide
diehard/ard 1
dies/ize
diet/iet
dietary/ary
Diet Coke/oke
Diet Cokes/okes
dietetic/etic
dietician/ition

difficult/ult
dig/ig
digestion/estion
digger/igger
dignified/ide
dignify/y
dignitary/ary
digress/ess
digressed/est
dilettante/aunt
dill/ill
dilute/ute
dim/im
dime/ime
dimension/ention
dimmer/immer
dimple/imple
din/in
Din, Gunga/in
Dinah/ina 2
dine/ine 1
dined/ind 1
diner/iner
dinero/arrow
ding/ing
ding-a-ling/ing
dingbat/at 1
dinghy/ingy 1
dingo/ingo
dingy/ingy 2
dinky/inky
dinner/inner
dinnertime/ime
dinosaur/ore
dip/ip
diphtheria/eria
diploma/oma
diplomat/at 1
diplomatic/atic
dipped/ipped
dipper/ipper
dippy/ippy
dire/ire
direct/ect
direction/ection
director/ector
directs/ex
dirt/ert
dirty/irty

disability/ility
disable/able
disagree/ee
disagreed/eed
disagrees/eeze
disappear/eer
disappoint/oint
disapprove/ove 3
disarm/arm 1
disaster/aster
disband/and
disbar/ar
disbelief/ief
disc/isk
discard/ard 1
discharge/arge
disciplinary/ary
discipline/in
disciplined/inned
disco/isco
disconnect/ect
disconnects/ex
discontent/ent
discord/ord 1
discotheque/eck
discount/ount
discounts/ounce
discreet/eet
discrete/eet
discretion/ession
discriminate/ate
discrimination/ation
discuss/us
discussed/ust
discussion/ussion
disdain/ain
disease/eeze
disembark/ark
disenchants/ance
disfavor/aver
disgrace/ace
disgraced/aste
disguise/ize
disgust/ust
disgusted/usted
dish/ish
dishevel/evel
dishonor/onor
dishpan/an

dishrag/ag
dishwater/otter
disillusion/usion
disinfect/ect
disinherit/arrot
disk/isk
dislike/ike
dislocate/ate
dislodge/odge
disloyal/oil
dismiss/iss
dismissal/istle
dismissed/ist
Disneyland/and
disobey/ay
disobeyed/ade 1
disobeys/aze
disown/one 1
disparity/arity
dispatch/atch 1
dispense/ense
disperse/erse
dispersed/irst
displaced/aste
display/ay
displayed/ade 1
displays/aze
displease/eeze
displeasure/easure
disposal/osal
dispose/ose 2
disposition/ition
disprove/ove 3
dispute/ute
disqualified/ide
disqualifies/ize
disqualify/y
disregard/ard 1
disrespect/ect
disrobe/obe
disrupt/upt
disruption/uption
dissatisfaction/action
dissatisfied/ide
dissatisfies/ize
dissatisfy/y
dissect/ect
dissension/ention
dissent/ent

dissenter/enter
dissolution/ution
dissolve/olve
distance/istance
distaste/aste
distinct/inct
distort/ort
distortion/ortion
distract/act
distraction/action
distracts/ax
distraught/ot
distress/ess
distressed/est
distressful/essful
distribution/ution
distrust/ust
disturb/urb
ditch/itch
ditchdigger/igger
dither/ither
ditty/itty
ditzy/itzy
dive/ive 1
diver/iver 1
diverge/erge
divergent/ergent
diverse/erse
diversion/ersion
diversity/ersity
divert/ert
divide/ide
dividend/end
divider/ider
divine/ine 1
divinity/inity
division/ision
divorce/orse
divulge/ulge
Dixieland/and
dizzy/izzy
do/ew
doc/ock
dock/ock
docket/ocket
docks/ox
Dr. Seuss/use 1
dodge/odge
doe/o

Doe, John/o
does/uzz
dog/og
dog-doo/ew
doggie/oggy
doggone/awn
doggoned/ond
doghouse/ouse
dogtrot/ot
dole/ole
doled/old
doll/all
dollar/aller
dolly/olly
dolt/olt
domain/ain
dome/ome 1
domesticity/icity
domicile/ile 1
dominate/ate
domination/
    omination
dominoes/ose 2
don/awn
Donald Duck/uck
donate/ate
donation/ation
done/un
dong/ong
Don Juan/awn
Donna/onna
donned/ond
donnybrook/ook 2
dons/ons
doodad/ad 1
doodle/oodle
doodlebug/ug
Doody, Howdy/oody
doom/oom
door/ore
doorbell/ell
doorknob/ob
doormat/at 1
doorstep/ep
doorstop/op
dope/ope
dopey/opey
Dora/ora
dork/ork 1

dorm/orm 1
dose/ose 1
dot/ot
dote/ote
Dotty/ody
double/ouble
double-check/eck
double-checked/ect
doubleheader/etter
doubt/out
doubter/owder
dough/o
doughy/owy
douse/ouse
doused/oust
dove/ove 1, ove 2
dovetail/ale 1
down/own 2
downcast/ast
downed/ound
downfall/all
downhill/ill
downpour/ore
downrange/ange
downriver/iver 2
downstream/eem
downtown/own 2
downturn/urn
downwind/inned
doze/ose 1
drab/ab 1
drabber/abber
drabby/abby
draft/aft
drafter/after
drafty/afty
drag/ag
draggy/aggy
dragnet/et
dragonflies/ize
dragonfly/y
drain/ain
drama/ama 1
dramatic/atic
dramatize/ize
drank/ank
drape/ape
drastic/astic
draw/aw

drawback/ack
drawbacks/ax
drawbridge/idge
drawer/ore
drawl/all
drawled/alled
drawn/awn
drawstring/ing
dread/ed
dream/eem
dreamboat/ote
dreamland/and
dreamt/empt
dreamy/eamy
dreary/eery
dredge/edge
drench/ench
dress/ess
dressed/est
dresser/essor
dressy/essy
drew/ew
dribble/ibble
dried/ide
dries/ize
drift/ift
driftwood/ood 3
drill/ill
drilled/illed
drink/ink
drip/ip
dripped/ipped
dripper/ipper
drippy/ippy
drive/ive 1
drivel/ivel
driven/iven
driver/iver 1
drizzle/izzle
dromedary/ary
drone/one 1
drool/ool
drooler/ooler
drooly/uly
droop/oop
drooper/ooper
droopy/oopy
drop/op
dropout/out

dropper/opper
drought/out
drove/ove 1
drown/own 2
drowned/ound
drudge/udge
drug/ug
drugstore/ore
drum/um
drummer/ummer
drumstick/ick
drumsticks/icks
drunk/unk
drunken/unken
drunker/unker
dry/y
dryness/inus
dual/uel
dub/ub
duck/uck
Duck, Donald/uck
ducked/uct
ducks/ucks
ducky/ucky
duct/uct
dud/ud
dude/ude
dudette/et
due/ew
duel/uel
dues/use 2
duet/et
duffel/uffle
dug/ug
dugout/out
duke/uke
dull/ull 1
dullsville/ill
dumb/um
dumbbell/ell
dumber/ummer
dumbfound/ound
dumbstruck/uck
dummy/ummy
dump/ump
dumpy/umpy
Duncan/unken
dunce/unts
dune/oon

dungarees/eeze
dunk/unk
dupe/oop
duplex/ex
duplicate/ate
duplication/ation
duplicator/ader
duplicity/icity
durability/ility
durable/urable
duration/ation
duress/ess
dusk/usk
dust/ust
dusted/usted
duster/uster
dustpan/an
duststorm/orm
dusty/usty
Dutch/utch
duty/oody
dwarf/arf 2
dwell/ell
dweller/eller
Dwight/ight
dwindle/indle
dye/y
dyed/ide
dyes/ize
dynamite/ight
dynamo/o
dynamos/ose 2
dysfunction/unction

E

each/each
eager/eager
eagle/egal
ear/eer
earache/ake
eardrum/um
earful/earful
earl/url
earlobe/obe
early/urly
earmark/ark
earn/urn
Earp, Wyatt/urp

171

earplug/**ug**
earring/**ing**
earth/**irth**
earthbound/**ound**
earthquake/**ake**
earthworm/**erm**
earwax/**ax**
ease/**eeze**
east/**east**
easy/**easy**
easygoing/**owing**
eat/**eet**
eaten/**eaten**
eater/**eeder**
eavesdrop/**op**
eavesdropper/**opper**
eccentricity/**icity**
ecclesiastic/**astic**
ecologist/**ologist**
ecology/**ology**
economic/**omic**
economize/**ize**
economy/**onomy**
ecstatic/**atic**
Ecuador/**ore**
Ed/**ed**
Eddie/**etty**
edge/**edge**
edition/**ition**
editorial/**orial**
educate/**ate**
educator/**ader**
eel/**eel**
eerie/**eery**
effect/**ect**
effective/**ective**
effects/**ex**
effervescent/**escent**
efficient/**icient**
effuse/**use 2**
egad/**ad 1**
egg/**eg**
egghead/**ed**
eggplant/**ant 1**
eggshell/**ell**
egotism/**ism**
Egyptian/**iption**
Eiffel Tower/**our 1**
eight/**ate**

eighteen/**een**
eighty/**ady**
Einstein/**ine 1**
eject/**ect**
ejection/**ection**
ejects/**ex**
elaborate/**ate**
Elaine/**ain**
elastic/**astic**
elasticity/**icity**
elate/**ate**
elation/**ation**
elect/**ect**
election/**ection**
elective/**ective**
electrician/**ition**
electricity/**icity**
electrify/**y**
electrocute/**ute**
electrocution/**ution**
electrode/**ode**
electronic/**onic**
elects/**ex**
elemental/**ental**
elephant/**unt**
elevate/**ate**
elevation/**ation**
elevator/**ader**
eleven/**even**
elf/**elf**
elicit/**icit**
eliminate/**ate**
elimination/**ation**
elite/**eet**
Elizabeth/**eath 1**
Ella/**ella**
elope/**ope**
elsewhere/**air**
elude/**ude**
elusive/**usive**
emancipate/**ate**
embalm/**alm, om**
ember/**ember**
emblazon/**azon**
embody/**ody**
embrace/**ace**
embraced/**aste**
emcee/**ee**
emerge/**erge**

emergency/**urgency**
emergent/**ergent**
emigrate/**ate**
emotion/**otion**
emotional/**otional**
emperor/**er**
emphasize/**ize**
employ/**oy**
employed/**oid**
employee/**ee**
emporium/**orium**
empower/**our 1**
empowered/**owered**
enable/**able**
enact/**act**
enchant/**ant 1**
enchants/**ance**
enchilada/**ada**
enclose/**ose 2**
enclosure/**osure**
encore/**ore**
end/**end**
endeavor/**ever**
endorse/**orse**
endurable/**urable**
endurance/**urance**
endure/**ure**
energetic/**etic**
energize/**ize**
energizer/**izer**
enfold/**old**
enforce/**orse**
engage/**age 1**
engineer/**eer**
engorge/**orge**
engrave/**ave**
engross/**ose 1**
engrossed/**ost 1**
enhance/**ance**
enjoy/**oy**
enjoyed/**oid**
enjoys/**oys**
enlarge/**arge**
enlighten/**ighten**
enlist/**ist**
enmesh/**esh**
enough/**uff**
enrage/**age 1**
enrich/**itch**

enroll/**ole**
enrolled/**old**
ensure/**ure**
enter/**enter**
enterprise/**ize**
entertain/**ain**
enthrall/**all**
enthralled/**alled**
enthuse/**use 2**
enthusiasm/**asm**
enthusiast/**ast, ist**
enthusiastic/**astic**
entice/**ice 1**
enticed/**iced**
entire/**ire**
entitle/**idle**
entomb/**oom**
entourage/**age 2**
entrance/**ance**
entreaty/**eedy**
entrust/**ust**
entwine/**ine 1**
entwined/**ind 1**
envelope/**ope**
environmental/**ental**
envision/**ision**
enzyme/**ime**
episode/**ode**
equality/**ality 2**
equate/**ate**
equation/**asion**
equator/**ader**
equip/**ip**
equipped/**ipped**
erase/**ace**
erased/**aste**
erect/**ect**
erects/**ex**
erode/**ode**
erosion/**osion**
erosive/**osive**
err/**er**
erratic/**atic**
erred/**erd**
error/**arer**
erupt/**upt**
eruption/**uption**
escalate/**ate**
escalator/**ader**

escapade/ade 1
escape/ape
escort/ort
Eskimo Pie/y
Eskimos/ose 2
espionage/age 2
essay/ay
essays/aze
essential/ential
state/ate, it
esteem/eem
sther/ester
stimate/ate, it
tch/etch
ternal/ernal
thiopia/opia
thnicity/icity
ugene/een
uphoric/oric
urasian/asion
vacuate/ate
valuate/ate
valuation/ation
vaporate/ate
vasion/asion
ve/eave
vent/ent
ver/ever
vergreen/een
vermore/ore
verybody/ody
veryday/ay
veryone/un
veryplace/ace
verything/ing
verywhere/air
vict/ict
viction/iction
victs/icks
vidence/ense
vident/ent
vidently/ently
volution/ution
volve/olve
we/ew
x/ex
xact/act
xaggerate/ate
xaggerator/ader

exalt/alt
exam/am
exasperate/ate
exasperation/ation
excavate/ate
exceed/eed
excel/ell
excelled/eld
except/ept
exception/eption
excess/ess
excessive/essive
exchange/ange
excite/ight
exclaim/aim
exclude/ude
exclusion/usion
exclusive/usive
ex-con/awn
ex-cons/ons
excrete/eet
excursion/ersion
excusable/usable
excuse/use 1, use 2
execute/ute
execution/ution
exemplified/ide
exemplifies/ize
exemplify/y
exempt/empt
exercise/ize
exerciser/izer
exert/ert
exhale/ale 1
exhaust/ost 2
exhibit/ibit
exhibition/ition
exhilarate/ate
exhume/oom
exile/ile 1
exiled/ild
exist/ist
existence/istance
exotic/otic
expand/and
expanse/ance
expect/ect
expectation/ation
expects/ex

expedition/ition
expel/ell
expelled/eld
expense/ense
expensive/ensive
experiment/ent
experimental/ental
expire/ire
explain/ain
explanation/ation
explanatory/ory
explicit/icit
explode/ode
exploration/ation
explore/ore
explored/ord 1
explosion/osion
explosive/osive
export/ort
exporter/order
expose/ose 2
exposure/osure
express/ess
expressed/est
expression/ession
expressive/essive
extend/end
extension/ention
extensive/ensive
extent/ent
exterminate/ate
extermination/ation
exterminator/ader
external/ernal
extinct/inct
extol/ole
extolled/old
extract/act
extraction/action
extraordinary/ary
extreme/eem
extrovert/ert
exude/ude
exult/ult
eye/y
eyeball/all
eyebrow/ow 1
eyed/ide
eyedropper/opper

eyelash/ash 1
eyelid/id
eyeliner/iner
eyes/ize
eyesight/ight
eyesore/ore

F

fab/ab 1
fable/able
fabrication/ation
facade/awed
face/ace
faced/aste
facial/acial
facilitator/ader
facility/ility
fact/act
faction/action
facts/ax
fad/ad 1
faddy/addy
fade/ade 1
fahrenheit/ight
fail/ale 1
fair/air
fairer/arer
fairy/ary
fairyland/and
fajita/ita
fake/ake
falafel/awful
fall/all
fallout/out
falsehood/ood 3
falsetto/etto
falsify/y
falter/alter
fame/aim
familiarity/arity
familiarize/ize
fan/an
fanatic/atic
fanfare/air
fang/ang
fanned/and
fantasize/ize
fantastic/astic

fantasyland/and
far/ar
faraway/ay
fare/air
farewell/ell
farm/arm 1
fascinate/ate
fascination/ation
fascism/ism
fast/ast
faster/aster
fastidious/idious
fat/at 1
fatalistic/istic
fatality/ality 1
fate/ate
father/ather 2
fatherhood/ood 3
fatigue/eague
fatten/atin
fatter/atter
fatty/atty
fault/alt
faults/alts
favor/aver
favoritism/ism
fawn/awn
fawned/ond
fawns/ons
fax/ax
faze/aze
FBI/y
fear/eer
fearful/earful
feast/east
feat/eet
feather/eather
featherbrain/ain
feature/eacher
February/ary
fed/ed
fedora/ora
fee/ee
feed/eed
feedback/ack
feeder/eeder
feel/eel
fees/eeze
feet/eet

feline/ine 1
fell/ell
fella/ella
feller/eller
fellow/ellow
fellowship/ip
felt/elt
female/ale 1
femininity/inity
fence/ense
fender/ender
fern/urn
ferocious/ocious
ferocity/ocity
Ferrari/arry 2
ferret/arrot
ferry/ary
fertile/urdle
fertilize/ize
fertilizer/izer
fester/ester
festivity/ivity
fetch/etch
fettucine/ini
feud/ude
feudal/oodle
fever/eaver
few/ew
fiasco/asco
fib/ib
fickle/ickle
fiction/iction
fictitious/icious
fiddle/iddle
fiddlesticks/icks
field/ield
fifteen/een
fifty/ifty
fig/ig
fight/ight
fighter/ider
figurehead/ed
file/ile 1
filed/ild
filibuster/uster
Filipino/ino 2
fill/ill
filled/illed
filler/iller

filly/illy
fin/in
finale/olly
finality/ality 1
finance/ance
finch/inch
find/ind 1
fine/ine 1
fined/ind 1
finesse/ess
finessed/est
finger/inger 1
fingernail/ale 1
fingerprint/int
fingertip/ip
finite/ight
fink/ink
fir/er
fire/ire
firearm/arm 1
firefighter/ider
firefly/y
firehouse/ouse
firelight/ight
fireplace/ace
fireplug/ug
fireproof/oof 1
fireside/ide
firetrap/ap
firm/erm
first/irst
firsthand/and
fish/ish
fishbowl/ole
fishhook/ook 2
fishmonger/unger
fishpond/ond
fist/ist
fistfight/ight
fit/it
fits/its
five/ive 1
fix/icks
fixation/ation
fizz/iz
fizzle/izzle
fizzy/izzy
fjord/ord 1
flab/ab 1

flabbergast/ast
flabby/abby
flack/ack
flag/ag
flagpole/ole
flair/air
flake/ake
flame/aim
flamingo/ingo
flap/ap
flapjack/ack
flare/air
flash/ash 1
flashback/ack
flashlight/ight
flashy/ashy
flask/ask
flat/at 1
flatten/atin
flatter/atter
flattery/attery
flattop/op
flaunt/aunt
flavor/aver
flaw/aw
flawed/awed
flaws/ause
flea/ee
fleas/eeze
fleck/eck
flecked/ect
flecks/ex
fled/ed
flee/ee
fleece/ease 2
flees/eeze
fleet/eet
flesh/esh
flew/ew
flex/ex
flexed/ext
flexibility/ility
flibbertigibbet/ibbit
flick/ick
flicked/ict
flicker/icker
flicks/icks
flies/ize
flight/ight

ighty/idy	fluster/uster	foresees/eeze	franchise/ize
inch/inch	flute/ute	foresight/ight	frank/ank
ing/ing	flutter/utter	forever/ever	Frankenstein/ine 1
int/int	flux/ucks	forevermore/ore	Frankfurt/ert
ip/ip	fly/y	forewarn/orn	frankfurter/erter
ipped/ipped	FM/em	forgave/ave	Frankie/anky
ipper/ipper	foal/ole	forge/orge	frantic/antic
irt/ert	foam/ome 1	forget/et, it	fraternal/ernal
irtation/ation	focal/ocal	forgetter/etter	fraud/awed
irtatious/acious	fodder/otter	forgive/ive 2	fray/ay
irty/irty	foe/o	forgiven/iven	frayed/ade 1
lit/it	foes/ose 2	forgot/ot	freak/eek
lits/its	fog/og	forgotten/otten	freaky/eaky
litty/itty	foggy/oggy	fork/ork 1	freckle/eckle
loat/ote	foghorn/orn	forlorn/orn	Freddie/etty
lock/ock	foil/oil	form/orm 1	free/ee
locks/ox	fold/old	formal/ormal	freed/eed
log/og	folk/oke	formality/ality 1	free-lance/ance
lood/ud	folklore/ore	format/at 1	freeload/ode
loodwater/otter	folks/okes	formation/ation	freely/eally
loor/ore	follow/allow 2	former/ormer	frees/eeze
loored/ord 1	folly/olly	formulate/ate	freestyle/ile 1
lop/op	fond/ond	fort/ort	freewill/ill
loppy/oppy	fonder/onder	forte/ort	freeze/eeze
loral/oral	food/ude	forthright/ight	freezer/eezer
loss/oss 2	foodaholic/olic	fortify/ortify, y	freight/ate
lossed/ost 2	fool/ool	fortune-teller/eller	freighter/ader
lounce/ounce	foolhardy/ardy	forty/orty	French/ench
lour/our 1	foolproof/oof 1	forty-niner/iner	frenetic/etic
low/o	foot/oot 2	forward/erd	frequent/ent
lowed/ode	football/all	foster/oster	fresh/esh
lower/our 1	foothold/old	fought/ot	freshen/ession
lowered/owered	footlocker/ocker	foul/owl	fret/et
lowerpot/ot	footloose/use 1	found/ound	Freud/oid
lowing/owing	footmark/ark	foundation/ation	friction/iction
lown/one 1	footnote/ote	four/ore	Friday/idy
lows/ose 2	footprint/int	fourteen/een	fridge/idge
loyd/oid	footprints/ince	fourth/orth	fried/ide
lu/ew	footwork/erk	four-wheeled/ield	friend/end
lub/ub	for/ore	fox/ox	friendship/ip
luctuate/ate	forbid/id	foxhole/ole	fries/ize
luff/uff	forbidden/idden	foxy/oxy	fright/ight
luffy/uffy	force/orse	fraction/action	frighten/ighten
luke/uke	Ford/ord 1	fragmentary/ary	frill/ill
lung/ung	forecast/ast	frail/ale 1	frilled/illed
lunk/unk	forecaster/aster	frame/aim	frilly/illy
luorescent/escent	forefront/unt	framework/erk	fringe/inge
lurry/urry	foreground/ound	Fran/an	fringy/ingy 2
lush/ush 1	forehead/ed	France/ance	Frisco/isco

frisk/isk
frisky/isky
Frito/edo
fritter/itter
frivolity/ality 2
frizz/iz
frizzy/izzy
frock/ock
frog/og
froggy/oggy
frolic/olic
from/um
front/unt
frontier/eer
fronts/once
frost/ost 2
frostbite/ight
frostbitten/itten
froth/oth 2
frown/own 2
frowned/ound
froze/ose 2
frozen/ozen
fruit/ute
fruitcake/ake
fruity/oody
frumpy/umpy
frustrate/ate
frustration/ation
fry/y
fuddy-duddy/uddy
fudge/udge
fuel/uel
fulfill/ill
fulfilled/illed
full/ull 2
fullback/ack
fully/ully
fumble/umble
fumbling/umbling
fume/oom
fumigate/ate
fun/un
function/unction
fund/und
fundamental/ental
funk/unk
funky/unky
funnel/unnel

funny/unny
fur/er
furious/urious
furry/urry
furthermore/ore
fury/ury
fuse/use 2
fusion/usion
fuss/us
fussed/ust
futile/oodle
futility/ility
future/uture
futuristic/istic
fuzz/uzz

G

gab/ab 1
gabber/abber
gabby/abby
gag/ag
ga-ga/aw
gaily/aily
gain/ain
gait/ate
gal/al
Galahad/ad 1
gale/ale 1
gall/all
gallbladder/atter
galley/alley
gallivant/ant 1
galore/ore
game/aim
gang/ang
gangplank/ank
gangway/ay
gap/ap
gape/ape
garage/age 2
gargoyle/oil
garish/erish
garter/arter 1
Gary/ary
gas/ass
gash/ash
gasket/asket
gasoline/een

gasp/asp
gassed/ast
gastritis/itis
gate/ate
gather/ather 1
gator/ader
Gatorade/ade 1
gaudy/ody
gauge/age 1
gaunt/aunt
gauze/ause
gave/ave
gavel/avel
gawk/ock
gawks/ox
gawky/awky
gay/ay
Gaza Strip/ip
gaze/aze
gazelle/ell
gear/eer
gee/ee
geek/eek
geeky/eaky
geese/ease 2
geezer/eezer
gel/ell
gem/em
gender/ender
gene/een
generate/ate
generation/ation
generator/ader
generosity/ocity
genetic/etic
Genghis Khan/awn
genie/ini
gent/ent
genteel/eel
gentle/ental
gently/ently
gents/ense
geographic/aphic
geography/ography
geological/ogical
geologist/ologist
geology/ology
George/orge
Gepetto/etto

germ/erm
Geronimo/o
Gertie/irty
gesundheit/ight
get/et, it
gets/its
Gettysburg Address/
  ess
geyser/izer
Ghana/onna
ghetto/etto
ghost/ost 1
ghostwriter/ider
ghoul/ool
giant/iant
giants/iance
gibe/ibe
Gibraltar/alter
giddy/itty
gift/ift
giftwrap/ap
gig/ig
gigantic/antic
giggle/iggle
giggly/iggly
gill/ill
Gina/ena
ginger/inger 2
gingerbread/ed
gingersnap/ap
Ginny/inny
giraffe/aff
girdle/urdle
girl/url
girlfriend/end
girth/irth
gist/ist
give/ive 2
given/iven
giver/iver 2
gizzard/izard
glacial/acial
gladder/atter
gladiola/ola
glance/ance
gland/and
glare/air
glass/ass
glassy/assy

aze/aze
eam/eem
ean/een
ee/ee
ib/ib
ide/ide
ider/ider
immer/immer
int/int
itch/itch
itter/itter
ittery/ittery
itzy/itzy
oat/ote
ob/ob
obal/oble
obe/obe
obetrotter/otter
ockenspiel/eel
oom/oom
oomy/oomy
orified/ide
orifies/ize
orify/orify, y
orious/orious
ory/ory
oss/oss 2
ossed/ost 2
ossy/ossy
ove/ove 2
ow/o
owed/ode
owing/owing
ows/ose 2
owworm/erm
ue/ew
ued/ude
ues/use 2
ug/ug
um/um
lut/ut 1
nash/ash 1
nat/at 1
naw/aw
nawed/awed
nome/ome 1
nu/ew
o/o
oad/ode

goal/ole
goalie/oly
goalpost/ost 1
goaltender/ender
goat/ote
gob/ob
gobble/obble
gobbledygook/
    ook 2, uke
gobbler/obbler
God/awed
godchild/ild
godfather/ather 2
Godiva/iva
godmother/other
goes/ose 2
go-getter/etter
goggle/oggle
going/owing
gold/old
Golden retriever/
    eaver
goldenrod/awed
goldfish/ish
Goldilocks/ox
golly/olly
gone/awn
goner/onor
gong/ong
gonna/onna
goo/ew
good/ood 3
goodwill/ill
gooey/ewy
goof/oof 1
goofball/all
goofy/oofy
goon/oon
goop/oop
goopy/oopy
goose/use 1
gooseflesh/esh
gore/ore
gorge/orge
gorilla/illa
gory/ory
gosh/osh
got/ot
gotten/otten

gourd/ord 1
governmental/ental
gown/own 2
grab/ab 1
grabber/abber
grabby/abby
grace/ace
graced/aste
Gracie/acy
gracious/acious
grad/ad 1
grade/ade 1
graduate/ate, it
graduation/ation
graffiti/eedy
graft/aft
grain/ain
gram/am
Grammy/ammy
Granada/ada
grand/and
granddad/ad 1
granddaddy/atty
grandfather/ather 2
grandiose/ose 1
grandma/aw
grandmother/other
grandpa/aw
grandpappy/appy
grandparent/arent
grandson/un
grandstand/and
granny/anny
grant/ant 1
grants/ance
grape/ape
grapefruit/ute
grapevine/ine 1
graph/aff
graphic/aphic
grapple/apple
grasp/asp
grass/ass
grasshopper/opper
grassy/assy
grate/ate
Grateful Dead/ed
gratifies/ize
gratify/y

gratitude/ude
grave/ave
gravel/avel
graveyard/ard 1
gravitate/ate
gravity/avity
gravy/avy
gray/ay
grayed/ade 1
grayer/ayer
graze/aze
grease/ease 2
greased/east
great/ate
Great Britain/itten
Great Dane/ain
greater/ader
Greece/ease 2
greed/eed
greedy/eedy
Greek/eek
green/een
greenhorn/orn
greet/eet
Greg/eg
gregarious/arious
grenade/ade 1
Gretel/eddle
grew/ew
greyhound/ound
grid/id
griddle/iddle
gridlock/ock
grief/ief
grieve/eave
grill/ill
grilled/illed
grim/im
grime/ime
grimmer/immer
grin/in
grind/ind 1
grindstone/one 1
gringo/ingo
grinned/inned
grinner/inner
grip/ip
gripe/ipe
griper/iper

gristle/istle
grit/it
grits/its
gritty/itty
groan/one 1
grog/og
groggy/oggy
groin/oin
groom/oom
groomer/umor
groove/ove 3
grope/ope
gross/ose 1
grossed/ost 1
grotesque/esque
grotto/otto
grouch/ouch
ground/ound
groundhog/og
groundwork/erk
group/oop
grove/ove 1
grow/o
growing/owing
growl/owl
grown/one 1
grows/ose 2
growth/oth 1
gr-r-r/er
grub/ub
grubby/ubby
grudge/udge
gruel/uel
gruff/uff
gruffer/uffer
grumble/umble
grumbling/umbling
grump/ump
grunt/unt
grunts/unts
guacamole/oly
Guam/om
guarantee/ee
guaranteed/eed
guarantees/eeze
guard/ard 1
guardianship/ip
guerilla/illa
guess/ess

guessed/est
guesser/essor
guesswork/erk
guest/est
guide/ide
guideline/ine 1
guidepost/ost 1
guild/illed
guillotine/een
guilt/ilt
guise/ize
guitar/ar
gull/ull 1
gullibility/ility
gulp/ulp
gum/um
gumdrop/op
gummy/ummy
gumption/
    umption
gumshoes/use 2
gun/un
gung ho/o
Gunga Din/in
gunned/und
gunner/unner
gunnysack/ack
gunshot/ot
gunslinger/inger 1
gunsmith/ith
guppy/uppy
gush/ush 1
gushy/ushy
gust/ust
gusty/usty
gut/ut 1
gutter/utter
guttersnipe/ipe
guy/y
guys/ize
guzzle/uzzle
gymnast/ast, ist
gymnastic/astic
gyp/ip
gypped/ipped
gypsy/ipsy
gyrate/ate

H

habitat/at 1
hack/ack
had/ad 1
hah/aw
ha ha/aw
hail/ale 1
hair/air
hairbrush/ush 1
haircut/ut 1
hairdo/ew
hairdresser/essor
hairline/ine 1
hairpiece/ease 2
hairpin/in
hairy/ary
Haiti/ady
Hal/al
half/aff
halfmast/ast
halfway/ay
halibut/ut 1
hall/all
hallow/allow 1
Halloween/een
hallucinate/ate
hallucination/ation
hallway/ay
hallways/aze
halt/alt
halter/alter
halts/alts
ham/am
hamper/amper
hand/and
handball/all
handbook/ook 2
handcuff/uff
handicap/ap
handiwork/erk
handkerchief/ief
handlebar/ar
handout/out
handpick/ick
handpicked/ict
handshake/ake
handstand/and
handwrite/ight

handwritten/itten
handyman/an
hang/ang
hangman/an
hangnail/ale 1
hangout/out
hangover/over
hankie/anky
hanky-panky/anky
Hans/ons
Hanukkah/onica
happy/appy
hara-kiri/eery
harangue/ang
harass/ass
harassed/ast
hard/ard 1
hard-boil/oil
harder/arter 1
hardhat/at 1
hardhead/ed
hardship/ip
hardy/ardy
hare/air
hark/ark
harm/arm 1
harmonic/onic
harmonica/onica
harmonize/ize
harpoon/oon
harpsichord/ord 1
Harry/ary
has/azz
hash/ash
haste/aste
hasten/ason
hasty/asty
hat/at 1
hatch/atch 1
hate/ate
hater/ader
haughty/ody
haul/all
hauled/alled
haunch/aunch
haunt/aunt
Havana/ana 1
Hawaiian/ion
hawk/ock

awks/ox	heavyweight/ate	hiccup/up	hive/ive 1
ay/ay	heck/eck	hiccupped/upt	hoard/ord 1
aystack/ack	heckle/eckle	hicupper/upper	hoarder/order
aystacks/ax	Hector/ector	hid/id	hoarse/orse
aywire/ire	hedge/edge	hidden/idden	hoax/okes
aze/aze	heed/eed	hide/ide	hobble/obble
azy/azy	heel/eel	hideous/idious	hobbler/obbler
e/ee	Heidi/idy	hi-fi/y	hobby/obby
ead/ed	height/ight	hi-fis/ize	hobnob/ob
eadache/ake	heighten/ighten	high/y	Hoboken/oken
eadband/and	heir/air	high-heeled/ield	hockey/awky
eadfirst/irst	heirloom/oom	highlight/ight	hodgepodge/odge
eadhunter/unter	heist/iced	highlighter/ider	hoedown/own 2
eadlight/ight	held/eld	highs/ize	hog/og
eadline/ine 1	heliport/ort	highway/ay	hogwash/osh
eadlined/ind 1	hell/ell	hijack/ack	hogwild/ild
eadliner/iner	hello/ellow, o	hijacked/act	hold/old
eadlock/ock	help/elp	hike/ike	holdout/out
eadlong/ong	helpmate/ate	hiker/iker	hole/ole
eadmaster/aster	Helsinki/inky	hilarious/arious	holey/oly
eadphone/one 1	helter-skelter/elter	hilarity/arity	holiday/ay
eadstone/one 1	hem/em	hill/ill	holidays/aze
eadstrong/ong	hemisphere/eer	hilltop/op	holistic/istic
eadway/ay	hemline/ine 1	hilly/illy	holler/aller
eady/etty	hen/en	hilt/ilt	hollow/allow 2
eal/eel	her/er	him/im	holly/olly
ealed/ield	herb/urb	himself/elf	Hollywood/ood 3
eap/eep	Hercules/eeze	hindsight/ight	holocaust/ost 2
ear/eer	herd/erd	hinge/inge	holster/olster
eard/erd	herder/erter	hint/int	holy/oly
earse/erse	here/eer	hints/ince	Holy Grail/ale 1
eart/art 1	hereafter/after	hip/ip	home/ome 1
eartache/ake	hereditary/ary	hippie/ippy	homebody/ody
eartbeat/eet	heretic/ick	hire/ire	homefront/unt
eartbreak/ake	herewith/ith	his/iz	homegrown/one 1
eartbroken/oken	hero/ero 1	hiss/iss	homeland/and
eartburn/urn	heroic/oic	hissed/ist	homemade/ade 1
eartfelt/elt	heroism/ism	hissy/issy	homeroom/oom
eartsick/ick	heron/aron	historic/oric	homesick/ick
eartstopper/opper	herself/elf	history/istory	homespun/un
eartthrob/ob	hesitant/esident	hit/it	homestead/ed
earty/ardy	hesitate/ate	hitch/itch	homestretch/etch
eat/eet	hesitation/ation	Hitchcock/ock	hometown/own 2
eater/eeder	hex/ex	hitchhike/ike	homework/erk
eather/eather	hexagon/awn	hitchhiker/iker	homicidal/idle
eatstroke/oke	hexed/ext	hi-tech/eck	homonym/im
eave/eave	hey/ay	hither/ither	hon/un
eave-ho/o	hi/y	hits/its	honcho/oncho
eaven/even	hibernate/ate	hitter/itter	hone/one 1

honey/unny
honeybun/un
honeybunch/unch
honeycomb/ome 1
honeymoon/oon
honeymooner/ooner
honeysuckle/uckle
Hong Kong/ong
honk/onk
honor/onor
honorary/ary
honorbound/ound
hood/ood 3
Hood, Robin/ood 3
hoodwink/ink
hoodwinked/inct
hoof/oof 2
hook/ook 2
hooky/ookie
hoop/oop
hoopla/aw
hoot/ute
hop/op
hope/ope
Hopi/opey
hopscotch/otch
Horatius/acious
hormone/one 1
horn/orn
horoscope/ope
horrific/ific
horrified/ide
horrifies/ize
horrify/orify, y
hors d'oeuvre/erve
horse/orse
horsefly/y
horsepower/our 1
horseshoe/ew
horticulture/ulture
hose/ose 2
hospital/iddle
hospitality/ality 1
host/ost 1
hostility/ility
hot/ot
hotel/ell
hotfoot/oot 2
hotrod/awed

hot rodder/otter
hotter/otter
hotwire/ire
Houdini/ini
hound/ound
hounddog/og
hour/our 1
hourglass/ass
house/ouse
housebreak/ake
housebroken/oken
household/old
housekeeper/eeper
housewife/ife
housework/erk
how/ow 1
Howard/owered
Howdy Doody/oody
however/ever
howl/owl
hub/ub
hubbub/ub
hubby/ubby
hubcap/ap
huddle/uddle
hue/ew
hued/ude
hues/use 2
huff/uff
huffy/uffy
hug/ug
huge/uge
hulk/ulk
hull/ull 1
hullabaloo/ew
hum/um
humane/ain
humankind/ind 1
humble/umble
humbling/umbling
humbug/ug
humdinger/inger 1
humdrum/um
humidity/idity
humiliate/ate
humiliation/ation
humility/ility
hummer/ummer
hummingbird/erd

humor/umor
humorous/umorous
hump/ump
Hun/un
hunch/unch
hung/ung
hunger/unger
hunk/unk
hunker/unker
hunky-dory/ory
hunt/unt
hunter/unter
hunts/unts
hurdle/urdle
hurl/url
hurrah/aw
hurricane/ain
hurry/urry
hurt/ert
hurtle/urdle
hush/ush 1
hushaby/y
husk/usk
hustle/ustle
hut/ut 1
hutch/utch
hybrid/id
hydraulic/olic
hyena/ena
hygiene/een
hymn/im
hype/ipe
hyper/iper
hyperactive/active
hypertension/ention
hyphenate/ate
hypnotic/otic
hypnotism/ism
hypnotize/ize
hypocrisy/ocracy
hypocrite/it
hypocrites/its
hypocritical/itical
hysteria/area

I

I/y
ice/ice 1

iced/iced
icepack/ack
icicle/ickle
icky/icky
iconoclast/ast
icons/ons
icy/icy
ID/ee, idy
id/id
Idaho/o
ideal/eel
idealism/ism
idealistic/istic
idealize/ize
ideally/eally
identified/ide
identifies/ize
identify/y
idiosyncratic/atic
idiotic/otic
idle/idle
idol/idle
idolize/ize
if/iff
iffy/iffy
ignite/ight
ignition/ition
ignore/ore
ignored/ord 1
iguana/onna
ilk/ilk
I'll/ile 1
ill/ill
illegal/egal
illegality/ality 1
illicit/icit
Illinois/oy
illogical/ogical
illuminate/ate
illusion/usion
illusive/usive
illustrate/ate
illustration/ation
illustrator/ader
I'm/ime
imaginary/ary
imagination/ation
imbibe/ibe
imitate/ate

imitation/ation	impressive/essive	indirect/ect	initiate/ate
imitator/ader	imprint/int	indiscreet/eet	initiation/ation
immature/ure	imprints/ince	indiscretion/ession	inject/ect
immaturity/urity	impromptu/ew	individualism/ism	injection/ection
immense/ense	improper/opper	individuality/ality 1	injects/ex
immensity/ensity	improve/ove 3	indoor/ore	injure/inger 2
immerse/erse	improvise/ize	induce/use 1	injurious/urious
immersed/irst	improviser/izer	indulge/ulge	ink/ink
immersion/ersion	impulsive/ulsive	industrialism/ism	inkblot/ot
immigrate/ate	impunity/unity	ineffective/ective	inked/inct
immigration/ation	impure/ure	inefficient/icient	inkwell/ell
immobile/oble	impurity/urity	inept/ept	inmate/ate
immoral/oral	in/in	inequality/ality 2	inn/in
immorality/ality 1	inability/ility	inexcusable/usable	innate/ate
immortality/ality 1	inaction/action	inexpensive/ensive	inner/inner
immune/oon	inactive/active	infantile/ile 1	innermost/ost 1
immunity/unity	inattention/ention	infect/ect	innovation/ation
imp/imp	inborn/orn	infection/ection	innovator/ader
impact/act	inbound/ound	infects/ex	inoculate/ate
impair/air	inbred/ed	infer/er	input/oot 2
impale/ale 1	incense/ense	inferiority/ority	inquire/ire
impart/art 1	incentive/entive	inferred/erd	inquisition/ition
impasse/ass	incessant/escent	infiltrate/ate	insane/ain
impeach/each	inch/inch	infinity/inity	inscribe/ibe
impede/eed	incidental/ental	inflame/aim	inscription/iption
impeder/eeder	incidentally/ently	inflammation/ation	insect/ect
imperfection/ection	incision/ision	inflate/ate	insecticide/ide
impersonate/ate	incisor/izer	inflation/ation	insects/ex
impersonation/ation	incite/ight	inflection/ection	insecure/ure
impersonator/ader	incline/ine 1	inflict/ict	insecurity/urity
implant/ant 1	include/ude	influential/ential	insensitivity/ivity
implement/ent	inclusion/usion	info/o	insert/ert
implicit/icit	incognito/edo	inform/orm 1	inside/ide
implied/ide	incomplete/eet	informal/ormal	insider/ider
implies/ize	inconclusive/usive	informality/ality 1	insidious/idious
implode/ode	incorrect/ect	information/ation	insight/ight
implosion/osion	increase/ease 2	informer/ormer	insincere/eer
imply/y	increased/east	infraction/action	insincerity/arity
impolite/ight	incurable/urable	infrared/ed	insinuate/ate
import/ort	indecision/ision	infringe/inge	insist/ist
importer/order	indeed/eed	infuse/use 2	insistence/istance
impose/ose 2	indent/ent	ingrate/ate	insomniac/ack
imposition/ition	index/ex	inhale/ale 1	inspect/ect
impossibility/ility	indexed/ext	inherent/arent	inspection/ection
impostor/oster	Indiana/ana 1	inherit/arrot	inspector/ector
impractical/actical	indicate/ate	inhibit/ibit	inspects/ex
impress/ess	indicator/ader	inhibition/ition	inspiration/ation
impressed/est	indict/ight	inhumane/ain	inspire/ire
impression/ession	indigestion/estion	initial/icial	install/all

installed/alled
installer/aller
Instamatic/atic
instead/ed
instigate/ate
instigator/ader
instill/ill
instinct/inct
institute/ute
institution/ution
instruct/uct
instruction/uction
instructive/uctive
instructor/uctor
instrumental/ental
insufficient/icient
insult/ult
insurance/urance
insure/ure
insurgency/urgency
insurgent/ergent
intake/ake
integrate/ate
integration/ation
intellect/ect
intend/end
intense/ense
intensifies/ize
intensify/y
intensity/ensity
intensive/ensive
intent/ent
intention/ention
intently/ently
interact/act
interaction/action
interacts/ax
intercept/ept
interception/eption
interchange/ange
intercom/om
interfere/eer
interferer/earer
interjection/ection
interlaced/aste
interlude/ude
intermission/ition
intern/urn
internal/ernal

internship/ip
interpretation/ation
interracial/acial
interrogate/ate
interrogation/ation
interrupt/upt
interruption/uption
interscholastic/astic
intersect/ect
intersection/ection
intersects/ex
interspaced/aste
intersperse/erse
interstellar/eller
intertwine/ine 1
intertwined/ind 1
intervene/een
intervention/ention
interview/ew
interviewed/ude
interviews/use 2
intimidate/ate
intimidation/ation
into/ew
intoxicate/ate
intoxication/ation
intramural/ural
intrigue/eague
introduce/use 1
introduced/uced
introduction/uction
introvert/ert
intrude/ude
intrusion/usion
intrusive/usive
intuition/ition
invade/ade 1
invader/ader
invasion/asion
invent/ent
invention/ention
inventive/entive
inventor/enter
inverse/erse
invert/ert
invest/est
investigate/ate
investigation/ation
investigator/ader

investor/ester
invigorate/ate
invite/ight
involve/olve
iodine/ine 1
iota/ota
IQ/ew
Iran/awn
Iraq/ack
Irene/een
iridescent/escent
irk/erk
ironclad/ad 1
ironic/onic
ironical/onical
irregularity/arity
irrigate/ate
irritate/ate
irritation/ation
is/iz
Isabel/ell
Isabella/ella
isle/ile 1
isolate/ate
isolation/ation
Israeli/aily
issue/issue
Istanbul/ull 2
it/it
itch/itch
itinerary/ary
its/its
itself/elf
itsy-bitsy/itzy
Ivanhoe/o
I've/ive 1

J

jab/ab 1
jabber/abber
Jabberwocky/awky
jack/ack
jackal/ackle
jackknife/ife
jackpot/ot
jacks/ax
Jacques/ock
Jacques Cousteau/o

jade/ade 1
jag/ag
jaguar/ar
jail/ale 1
jailbird/erd
jailbreak/ake
Jake/ake
jalopy/oppy
jam/am
jamboree/ee
jamborees/eeze
James Bond/ond
Jan/an
Jane/ain
January/ary
Japan/an
Japanese/eeze
jar/ar
jarred/ard 1
Jason/ason
jaunt/aunt
jaw/aw
jawbone/one 1
jaws/ause
jaywalk/ock
jaywalker/ocker
jaywalks/ox
jazz/azz
jazzy/azzy
jealous/ealous
Jean/een
Jeanette/et
Jeanie/ini
jeep/eep
jeer/eer
Jeff/ef
Jekyll/eckle
jell/ell
jelled/eld
Jell-O/ellow
jelly/elly
jellyfish/ish
Jenny/enny
jeopardize/ize
jerk/erk
jerky/erky
Jessie/essy
jest/est
jester/ester

et/et	Joyce/oice	Karen/aron	eeder, ometer
etliner/iner	joyride/ide	Kate/ate	kilt/ilt
etsetter/etter	joys/oys	Kathleen/een	Kim/im
ewel/uel	Juanita/ita	Katie/ady	kimono/ona
eweler/ooler	Judah/uda	kayak/ack	kin/in
ffy/iffy	judge/udge	kayaks/ax	kind/ind 1
g/ig	judgmental/ental	kazoo/ew	kindle/indle
ggle/iggle	judicial/icial	kazoos/use 2	kinfolk/oke
ggly/iggly	judicious/icious	keel/eel	king/ing
gsaw/aw	Judy/oody	keen/een	King Kong/ong
gsaws/ause	jug/ug	keep/eep	King Tut/ut 1
ll/ill	juggle/uggle	keeper/eeper	kink/ink
lt/ilt	juggler/uggler	keepsake/ake	kinked/inct
m/im	juice/use 1	keg/eg	kinship/ip
ngle/ingle	juiced/uced	Keith/eath 2	Kirk/erk
tterbug/ug	jujitsu/ew	Kelly/elly	kiss/iss
ttery/ittery	Jules Verne/urn	kelp/elp	kissed/ist
ve/ive 1	Juliet/et	Kenny/enny	kissy/issy
an/one 1	July/y	Kentucky/ucky	kit/it
an of Arc/ark	July Fourth/orth	kept/ept	kite/ight
ob/ob	jumble/umble	kernel/ernal	kits/its
ob/obe	jumbling/umbling	kerosene/een	kitten/itten
ock/ock	jump/ump	kerplop/op	kitty/itty
ockey/awky	jumpy/umpy	kerplunk/unk	Kleenex/ex
ocks/ox	junction/unction	kettle/eddle	knack/ack
oe/o	June/oon	Kevin/even	knapsack/ack
oel/ole	jungle/ungle	key/ee	knave/ave
oey/owy	junk/unk	keyboard/ord 1	knead/eed
og/og	junkheap/eep	keyhole/ole	knee/ee
oggle/oggle	junky/unky	keynote/ote	kneecap/ap
ohn/awn	junkyard/ard 1	keys/eeze	kneed/eed
ohn Doe/o	Jupiter/upiter	Khan, Genghis/aun	kneel/eel
ohnny/awny	jurisdiction/iction	kibble/ibble	knees/eeze
oin/oin	jury/ury	kick/ick	knelt/elt
oint/oint	just/ust	kicked/ict	knew/ew
oke/oke	justifiable/iable	kicker/icker	knife/ife
oker/oker	justification/ation	kickoff/off	knight/ight
okes/okes	justified/ide	kicks/icks	knit/it
olly/olly	justifies/ize	kickstand/and	knits/its
olt/olt	justify/y	kid/id	knitter/itter
onah/ona	jut/ut 1	kidder/itter	knob/ob
osephine/een	juvenile/ile 1	kiddie/itty	knobby/obby
osh/osh		kidnap/ap	knock/ock
ot/ot	**K**	kill/ill	knockabout/out
urnal/ernal		killed/illed	knockdown/own 2
urnalism/ism	kangaroo/ew	killer/iller	knocker/ocker
ust/oust	kangaroos/use 2	killjoy/oy	knockout/out
viality/ality 1	kaput/oot 2	killjoys/oys	knocks/ox
y/oy	karate/ody	kilometer/	knockwurst/urst

183

knoll/ole
knot/ot
knotty/ody
know/o
knowing/owing
knowledge/owledge
known/one 1
knows/ose 2
knuckle/uckle
knucklehead/ed
konk/onk
kook/uke
Kool-Aid/ade 1
kowtow/ow 1
kowtowed/oud
Kriss Kringle/ingle
Kringle, Kriss/ingle
kung fu/ew

L

lab/ab 1
label/able
laboratory/ory
laborious/orious
lace/ace
laced/aste
lack/ack
lacked/act
lackluster/uster
lacks/ax
lacy/acy
lad/ad 1
ladder/atter
lady/ady
ladybird/erd
ladybug/ug
ladylike/ike
lag/ag
lagoon/oon
laid/ade 1
lair/air
lake/ake
lamb/am
lame/aim
lament/ent
lamp/amp
lampoon/oon
lampshade/ade 1

lance/ance
Lancelot/ot
land/and
landlord/ord 1
landlubber/ubber
landmark/ark
Land Rover/over
landscape/ape
landslide/ide
lane/ain
lanky/anky
Laos/ose 1
lap/ap
lapel/ell
Lapland/and
lard/ard 1
large/arge
lark/ark
Larry/ary
laryngitis/itis
lash/ash 1
lass/ass
last/ast
latch/atch 1
late/ate
latecomer/ummer
later/ader
lather/ather 1
Latin/atin
Latino/ino 2
latitude/ude
latter/atter
laugh/aff
laughed/aft
laughingstock/ock
laughter/after
launch/aunch
launder/onder
laundromat/at 1
laurel/oral
Laurie/ory
lavatory/ory
law/aw
lawful/awful
lawman/an
lawn/awn
lawns/ons
laws/ause
lawsuit/ute

lax/ax
lay/ay
layer/ayer
layover/over
layperson/erson
laze/aze
lazy/azy
lead/ed, eed
leader/eeder
leadership/ip
leaf/ief
league/eague
leak/eek
leaky/eaky
lean/een
leap/eep
leapfrog/og
learn/urn
lease/ease 2
least/east
leather/eather
leatherneck/eck
leave/eave
led/ed
ledge/edge
leech/each
leer/eer
leery/eery
left/eft
leftover/over
leg/eg
legal/egal
legality/ality 1
legalize/ize
legendary/ary
legion/egion
legislate/ate
legislation/ation
legislator/ader
legit/it
legwork/erk
lemonade/ade 1
lend/end
lender/ender
length/ength
Lent/ent
lentil/ental
leotard/ard 1
leprechaun/awn

leprechauns/ons
less/ess
lesser/essor
Lester/ester
letdown/own 2
letter/etter
letterhead/ed
level/evel
lever/ever
Levi's/ize
liability/ility
liable/iable
liaison/awn
liberate/ate
liberation/ation
liberator/ader
library/ary
libretto/etto
lice/ice 1
lick/ick
licked/ict
licks/icks
lid/id
lie/y
lied/ide
lies/ize
life/ife
lifeboat/ote
lifeguard/ard 1
lifelike/ike
lifeline/ine 1
lifelong/ong
lifesaver/aver
life-style/ile 1
lifetime/ime
lift/ift
liftoff/off
light/ight
lighten/ighten
lighter/ider
lighthouse/ouse
like/ike
likelihood/ood 3
likewise/ize
lilacs/ax
Lilliput/ut 1
lilt/ilt
lily/illy
limb/im

imbo/imbo
ime/ime
imelight/ight
imitation/ation
imousine/een
imp/imp
ine/ine 1
ined/ind 1
ineup/up
inger/inger 1
ingo/ingo
inguine/ini
inguistic/istic
ink/ink
inked/inct
int/int
.inus/inus
ion/ion
ip/ip
ippy/ippy
ip-read/eed
ipstick/ick
ipsticks/icks
iqueur/ure
iquidate/ate
iquor/icker
isp/isp
isper/isper
ist/ist
it/it
iter/eeder
iterary/ary
itter/itter
itterbag/ag
itterbug/ug
ittle/iddle
ive/ive 1, ive 2
ivelihood/ood 3
iver/iver 2
.iverpool/ool
ivestock/ock
.iz/iz
izard/izard
lama/ama
.loyd/oid
oad/ode
oaf/oaf
oan/one 1
ob/ob

lobby/obby
lobe/obe
local/ocal
locale/al
locality/ality 1
locate/ate
location/ation
Loch Ness/ess
lock/ock
locker/ocker
locket/ocket
locks/ox
locksmith/ith
loco/oco
locomotion/otion
lodge/odge
log/og
logical/ogical
loin/oin
Lola/ola
loll/all
lolled/alled
lollipop/op
lollygag/ag
lone/one 1
lonely/only
long/ong
Longfellow/ellow
longhand/and
longitude/ude
look/ook 2
lookout/out
loom/oom
loon/oon
loop/oop
loophole/ole
loose/use 1
loot/ute
looter/uter
lop/op
lope/ope
loquacious/acious
lord/ord 1
lore/ore
Lorraine/ain
lose/use 2
loser/user
loss/oss 2
lost/ost 2

lot/ot
lotion/otion
lottery/ottery
lotto/otto
loud/oud
louder/owder
loudmouth/outh 1
loudspeaker/eaker
Louise/eeze
Louisiana/ana 1
louse/ouse
love/ove 2
lovebird/erd
lovelorn/orn
lovesick/ick
lovestruck/uck
low/o
low-cal/al
lowdown/own 2
Lowell/ole
lows/ose 2
loyal/oil
Loyola/ola
luau/ow 1
lube/ube
lubricate/ate
luck/uck
lucky/ucky
lug/ug
Luke/uke
lukewarm/orm 1
lull/ull 1
lullabies/ize
lullaby/y
lumber/umber 1
lumberjack/ack
lump/ump
lumpy/umpy
lunar/ooner
lunatic/ick
lunch/unch
lunchbox/ox
lung/ung
lunge/unge
lurch/urch
lure/ure
lurk/erk
lush/ush 1
luster/uster

lute/ute
luxurious/urious
lynch/inch

M

ma/aw
ma'am/am
macabre/obber
macaroni/ony
macaroon/oon
Macbeth/eath 1
machete/etty
machine/een
mad/ad 1
madame/am
madcap/ap
madder/atter
made/ade 1
mademoiselle/ell
Mad Hatter/atter
madhouse/ouse
madman/an
Madrid/id
magazine/een
Maggie/aggy
magician/ition
magnetic/etic
magnetism/ism
magnified/ide
magnifies/ize
magnify/y
magpie/y
maid/ade 1
mail/ale 1
mailbag/ag
mailbox/ox
maim/aim
main/ain
Maine/ain
mainstream/eem
maintain/ain
majorette/et
majority/ority
make/ake
makeshift/ift
makeup/up
malaria/area
malcontent/ent

male/ale 1
malfunction/unction
Malibu/ew
malicious/icious
mall/all
malnutrition/ition
malt/alt
malts/alts
mama/ama 1
man/an
mañana/onna
mandate/ate
mandatory/ory
mandolin/in
mane/ain
Manhattan/atin
manhole/ole
manhunt/unt
manhunter/unter
maniac/ack
maniacs/ax
manicure/ure
manifest/est
Manila/illa
manipulate/ate
manipulation/ation
manipulator/ader
manner/anner
mannerism/ism
manor/anner
manslaughter/otter
manuscript/ipped
many/enny, inny
map/ap
mar/ar
marathon/awn
marathons/ons
March/arch
march/arch
Mardi Gras/aw
mare/air
Marge/arge
Marie/ee
marina/ina
marine/een
maritime/ime
mark/ark
Mark Twain/ain
Marlene/een

marmalade/ade 1
maroon/oon
marred/ard 1
marrow/arrow
marry/ary
marshmallow/
    allow 1, ellow
mart/art 1
martini/ini
Marty/ardy
martyr/arter 1
Marv/arve
Mary/ary
Mary Jo/o
Masai/y
mascara/ara
mascot/ot
masculinity/inity
mash/ash 1
mask/ask
mason/ason
masquerade/ade 1
masquerader/ader
mass/ass
massacred/erd
massage/age 2
masseur/ure
masseuse/use 1
mast/ast
master/aster
mastermind/ind 1
masterpiece/ease 2
mat/at 1
matador/ore
match/atch 1
mate/ate
materialism/ism
maternal/ernal
matey/ady
math/ath
mathematic/atic
mathematician/ition
matinee/ay
Matisse/ease 2
matrimonial/onial
matrimony/ony
matter/atter
Matterhorn/orn
mature/ure

maturity/urity
maul/all
mauled/alled
Maurice/ease 2
mauve/ove 1
Maxine/een
Maxwell/ell
may/ay
maybe/aby
Maybelline/een
Mayflower/our 1
mayonnaise/aze
mayor/ayer
Mazatlán/awn
maze/aze
me/ee
meadow/etto
meager/eager
meal/eel
mean/een
meant/ent
meantime/ime
meanwhile/ile 1
meany/ini
measure/easure
meat/eet
meatball/all
meaty/eedy
medal/eddle
meddle/eddle
mediator/ader
medicate/
    ate, edicate
medication/ation
mediocre/oker
meditate/ate
meditation/ation
meek/eek
meet/eet
Meg/eg
melancholy/olly
meld/eld
mellow/ellow
melodic/otic
melodious/odious
melodrama/ama
melodramatic/atic
melt/elt
meltdown/own 2

member/ember
membership/ip
memoir/ar
memorial/orial
memorize/ize
men/en, in
mend/end
menorah/ora
mental/ental
mentality/ality 1
mention/ention
mentor/enter, ore
meow/ow 1
meowed/oud
mercenary/ary
merchandise/ice 1
mere/eer
merge/erge
meringue/ang
merit/arrot
mermaid/ade 1
merry/ary
mesh/esh
mesmerize/ize
mess/ess
messed/est
messy/essy
met/et
metal/eddle
metaphor/ore
meteorite/ight
meteorology/ology
meter/eeder
metronome/ome 1
mew/ew
mewed/ude
mews/use 2
Mexico/o
mezzanine/een
Miami/ammy
mic/ike
mice/ice 1
Mickey/icky
microphone/one 1
microscope/ope
microscopic/opic
microwave/ave
midair/air
middle/iddle

midnight/ight
midriff/iff
midsummer/ummer
midterm/erm
midweek/eek
midwinter/inter
miff/iff
miffed/ift
might/ight
mighty/idy
migraine/ain
migrate/ate
migration/ation
mild/ild
mildewy/ewy
mile/ile 1
milestone/one 1
military/ary
milk/ilk
Milk Dud/ud
mill/ill
milled/illed
Millie/illy
milligram/am
million/illion
millionaire/air
Milwaukee/awky
mime/ime
Mimi/eamy
mince/ince
mind/ind 1
mine/ine 1
mined/ind 1
miner/iner
minestrone/ony
mingle/ingle
mini/inny
minimart/art 1
miniscule/ool
miniskirt/ert
minister/inister
mink/ink
Minnesota/ota
Minnie/inny
minor/iner
minority/ority
mint/int
mints/ince
minuet/et

minus/inus
minuscule/ool
minute/ute
mirage/age 2
mirror/earer
mirth/irth
misapprehension/ention
misbehave/ave
miscast/ast
misconception/eption
misconstrue/ew
misconstrued/ude
miscue/ew
miscued/ude
miscues/use 2
misdeal/eel
misdialed/ild
misdo/ew
miser/izer
misfiled/ild
misfit/it
misfits/its
misguide/ide
mishap/ap
mishmash/ash 1
misinform/orm 1
misjudge/udge
mislabel/able
mislead/eed
mismatch/atch 1
misplace/ace
misplaced/aste
misprint/int
misprints/ince
mispronounce/ounce
misquote/ote
misread/ed
misrepresent/ent
miss/iss
missed/ist
missile/istle
mission/ition
missionary/ary
Mississippi/ippy
missive/issive
Missouri/ury, urry
misspeak/eek

misspell/ell
misspelled/eld
misspent/ent
misspoken/oken
missy/issy
mist/ist
mistake/ake
Mister/ister
mistletoe/o
mistook/ook 2
mistreat/eet
mistrust/ust
mistrusted/usted
misunderstand/and
misunderstood/ood 3
misuse/use 1, use 2
mitt/it
mitten/itten
mitts/its
Mitzi/itzy
mix/icks
moan/one 1
moat/ote
mob/ob
Mobil/oble
mobile/oble, eel
mobility/ility
mobilize/ize
Moby Dick/ick
mock/ock
mockingbird/erd
mocks/ox
mod/awed
mode/ode
model/oddle
moderation/ation
moderator/ader
modernize/ize
modified/ide
modifies/ize
modify/y
module/ool
Mohawk/ock
Mohawks/ox
molar/olar
mold/old
mole/ole
molecule/ool
Molly/olly

mom/om
momentary/ary
mommy/ommy
Mona/ona
monarch/ark
monastery/ary
money/unny
mongoose/use 1
monk/unk
monkey/ee, unky
monkeys/eeze
monocle/onical
monologue/og
monopolize/ize
monorail/ale 1
monotone/one 1
monsoon/oon
monstrosity/ocity
Montana/ana 1
months/once
Montreal/all
monumental/ental
moo/ew
mooch/ooch
moocher/uture
mood/ude
moody/oody
mooed/ude
moon/oon
moonbeam/eem
moonchild/ild
moonlight/ight
moonlighter/ider
moonlit/it
moonstruck/uck
moos/use 2
moose/use 1
moot/ute
mop/op
mope/ope
moped/ed
mopey/opey
moral/oral
morale/al
morality/ality 1
moratorium/orium
morbidity/idity
more/ore
morn/orn

morning/orning
moronic/onic
morons/ons
morose/ose 1
Morse Code/ode
mortality/ality 1
mortar/order
mortifies/ize
mortify/ortify, y
mortuary/ary
Moscow/ow 1
mosey/osy
moss/oss 2
mossy/ossy
most/ost 1
motel/ell
moth/oth 2
mother/other
Mother Goose/use 1
motherhood/ood 3
motif/ief
motion/otion
motivate/ate
motivation/ation
motorbike/ike
motto/otto
mound/ound
mount/ount
mountaintop/op
mounts/ounce
mourn/orn
mourning/orning
mouse/ouse
mouseketeer/eer
mousetrap/ap
mousse/use 1
mouth/outh 1
mouthwash/osh
move/ove 3
mow/o
mowed/ode
mowing/owing
mows/ose 2
Mozart/art 1
mozzarella/ella
Ms./iz
much/utch
muck/uck
mucky/ucky

mud/ud
muddle/uddle
muddy/uddy
mudhole/ole
muff/uff
muffle/uffle
mug/ug
mukluk/uck
mule/ool
multiplication/ation
multiplied/ide
multiplies/ize
multiply/y
multitude/ude
mum/um
mumble/umble
mumbling/umbling
mummify/y
mummy/ummy
munch/unch
mundane/ain
municipality/ality 1
mural/ural
murder/erter
murky/erky
muscle/ustle
musclebound/ound
muse/use 2
muser/user
mush/ush 1
mushroom/oom
musicale/al
musician/ition
musk/usk
musketeer/eer
muskrat/at 1
muss/us
mussed/ust
mussel/ustle
must/ust
mustache/ash 1
mustang/ang
muster/uster
musty/usty
mute/ute
mutilate/ate
mutilation/ation
mutineer/eer
mutt/ut 1

mutter/utter
muumuu/ew
muumuus/use 2
muzzle/uzzle
my/y
myself/elf
mysterious/erious
mystery/istory
mystic/istic
mysticism/ism
mystifies/ize
mystify/y
mystique/eek
myth/ith
mythological/ogical
mythology/ology

N

nab/ab 1
Nabisco/isco
nadir/ader
nag/ag
nail/ale 1
naive/eave
name/aim
namesake/ake
name-tag/ag
Nan/an
nanny/anny
nap/ap
napalm/alm
narcotic/otic
narrate/ate
narrator/ader
narrow/arrow
nation/ation
nationality/ality 1
nationalize/ize
nativity/ivity
naughty/ody
nauseate/ate
Navajo/o
navigate/ate
navigator/ader
navy/avy
nay/ay
nays/aze
Neanderthal/all

near/eer
nearby/y
Near East/east
nearer/earer
neat/eet
neaten/eaten
neater/eeder
neat-o/edo
necessary/ary
neck/eck
neckline/ine 1
necks/ex
necktie/y
neckties/ize
nectar/ector
nectarine/een
need/eed
needle/eedle
needlepoint/oint
needy/eedy
neglect/ect
neglects/ex
negotiator/ader
neigh/ay
neighborhood/ood 3
neighed/ade 1
Nell/ell
Nellie/elly
neophyte/ight
Neptune/oon
nerdy/urdy
Nero/ero 1
nerve/erve
nest/est
net/et
network/erk
neurotic/otic
neuter/uter
neutrality/ality 1
neutralize/ize
neutrons/ons
never/ever
nevermore/ore
nevertheless/ess
new/ew
newborn/orn
newcomer/ummer
New Delhi/elly
newfound/ound

New Guinea/inny
newly/uly
newlywed/ed
New Mexico/o
Newport/ort
news/use 2
newsbreak/ake
newscast/ast
newscaster/aster
newsletter/etter
newsprint/int
newsreel/eel
newt/ute
New York/ork 1
next/ext
NFL/ell
nib/ib
nibble/ibble
nice/ice 1
nicey-nicey/icy
niche/itch
nick/ick
nicked/ict
nickel/ickle
nickname/aim
nicks/icks
Nicky/icky
nicotine/een
niece/ease 2
nifty/ifty
Nigeria/eria
night/ight
nightclub/ub
nightfall/all
nightgown/own 2
nightie/idy
nightingale/ale 1
nightlife/ife
nightmare/air
nightshirt/ert
nighttime/ime
nil/ill
Nile/ile 1
nimble/imble
nincompoop/oop
nine/ine 1
ninny/inny
nip/ip
nipped/ipped

nippy/ippy
nitpick/ick
nitpicked/ict
nitpicker/icker
nitpicks/icks
nitwit/it
nitwits/its
nix/icks
no/o
Nobel Prize/ize
nobility/ility
noble/oble
nobody/ody
nocturnal/ernal
nocturne/urn
nod/awed
Noel/ell
noise/oys
Nolan/olen
nomad/ad 1
nominate/ate
nomination/ation, omination
nominee/ee
nominees/eeze
nonbeliever/eaver
nonchalant/aunt
noncommittal/iddle
nondescript/ipped
none/un
nonetheless/ess
nonfat/at 1
nonfiction/iction
nonplus/us
nonplussed/ust
nonsense/ense
nonstop/op
nonuser/user
noodle/oodle
nook/ook 2
noon/oon
noose/oose
nope/ope
nor/ore
Nora/ora
norm/orm 1
normal/ormal
normality/ality 1
north/orth

North Carolina/ina 2
North Dakota/ota
North Pole/ole
Norway/ay
Norwegian/egion
nose/ose 2
nosebleed/eed
nosedive/ive 1
nose-thumber/ummer
nosh/osh
nosy/osy
not/ot
notch/otch
note/ote
notebook/ook 2
notification/ation
notified/ide
notifies/ize
notify/y
notion/otion
notoriety/iety
notorious/orious
Notre Dame/aim
noun/own 2
November/ember
Novocain/ain
now/ow 1
nowadays/aze
nowhere/air
nubby/ubby
nude/ude
nudge/udge
nuke/uke
null/ull 1
nullify/y
numb/um
number/umber 1
numerous/umorous
numskull/ull 1
nun/un
nurse/erse
nursed/irst
nursemaid/ade 1
nut/ut 1
nutrition/ition
nutritious/icious
nutshell/ell
nutty/uddy

nuzzle/uzzle

O

oaf/oaf
Oahu/ew
oak/oke
oaken/oken
oaks/okes
oar/ore
oat/ote
oath/oth 1
oatmeal/eel
obese/ease 2
obey/ay
obeyed/ade 1
obeys/aze
obituary/ary
object/ect
objection/ection
objective/ective
objectivity/ivity
objects/ex
obligation/ation
obligatory/ory
oblique/eek
oblong/ong
O'Brien/ion
obscene/een
obscure/ure
obscurity/urity
observation/ation
observatory/ory
observe/erve
obsessed/est
obsession/ession
obsessive/essive
obstetrician/ition
obstruct/uct
obstruction/uction
obtain/ain
obtrusive/usive
occasion/asion
occult/ult
occupation/ation
occupied/ide
occupies/ize
occupy/y
occur/er

occurred/erd
ocean/otion
oceanography/ography
o'clock/ock
octagon/awn
octopus/uss 1
odd/awed
oddball/all
odder/otter
ode/ode
odious/odious
odometer/ometer
Oedipus/uss 1
of/ove 2
off/off
offend/end
offender/ender
offense/ense
offensive/ensive
offhand/and
official/icial
officiate/ate
offspring/ing
offstage/age 1
offtrack/ack
often/often
ogle/oggle
oh/o
oil/oil
okay/ay
okayed/ade 1
okays/aze
okey-doke/oke
Oklahoma/oma
old/old
older/older
old King Cole/ole
Oldsmobile/eel
oldster/olster
Olympiad/ad 1
Omaha/aw
omit/it
omniscient/icient
on/awn
once/unts
one/un
ongoing/owing
only/only

ooze/use 2
opaque/ake
operate/ate
operation/ation
operator/ader
opossum/ossum
opportune/oon
opportunistic/istic
opportunity/unity
oppose/ose 2
oppress/ess
oppressed/est
oppression/ession
oppressive/essive
oppressor/essor
optician/ition
optimism/ism
optimistic/istic
option/option
or/ore
oral/oral
orangoutang/ang
orangutan/an
ordeal/eel
order/order
ordinary/ary
Oreo/o
Oreos/ose 2
organism/ism
organization/ation
organize/ize
organizer/izer
origami/ommy
originality/ality 1
oriole/orial
Orion/ion
ornamental/ental
ornate/ate
orthodox/ox
orthopedic/edic
ostentatious/acious
ostracize/ize
other/other
otherwise/ize
otter/otter
ouch/ouch
ought/ot
ounce/ounce
our/our 1

oust/oust
out/out
outbid/id
outbound/ound
outbreak/ake
outburst/irst
outcast/ast
outclassed/ast
outcome/um
outcries/ize
outcry/y
outdid/id
outdo/ew
outdone/un
outdoor/ore
outdraw/aw
outfit/it
outfits/its
outfox/ox
outgoing/owing
outgrew/ew
outgrossed/ost 1
outgrow/o
outguess/ess
outguessed/est
outhouse/ouse
outlast/ast
outlaw/aw
outlawed/awed
outlaws/ause
outline/ine 1
outlined/ind 1
outlive/ive 2
outlook/ook 2
outloud/oud
outnumber/umber 1
outpost/ost 1
output/oot 2
outrage/age 1
outrageous/ageous
outran/an
outrank/ank
outreach/each
outright/ight
outrun/un
outscore/ore
outscored/ord 1
outshine/ine 1
outshone/one 1

outshoot/ute
outside/ide
outsider/ider
outsmart/art 1
outspoken/oken
outswam/am
outtalk/ock
outvote/ote
outwear/air
outweighed/ade 1
outweighs/aze
outwit/it
outwits/its
outworn/orn
ovation/ation
over/over
overachiever/eaver
overact/act
overactive/active
overacts/ax
overall/all
overate/ate
overbite/ight
overboard/ord 1
overbuild/illed
overcame/aim
overcast/ast
overcharge/arge
overcoat/ote
overcome/um
overcrowd/oud
overdid/id
overdo/ew
overdone/un
overdrawn/awn
overdress/ess
overdressed/est
overdue/ew
overeager/eager
overeat/eet
overeater/eeder
overexert/ert
overexpose/ose 2
overfed/ed
overfeed/eed
overflow/o
overflowed/ode
overflowing/owing
overflows/ose 2

191

overgrown/one 1
overgrowth/oth 1
overhang/ang
overhaul/all
overhauled/alled
overhead/ed
overhear/eer
overheard/erd
overindulge/ulge
overjoy/oy
overjoyed/oid
overkill/ill
overlap/ap
overload/ode
overlook/ook 2
overmuch/utch
overnight/ight
overpaid/ade 1
overpass/ass
overpower/our 1
overpowered/owered
overpriced/iced
overprotective/ective
overran/an
overrate/ate
overreact/act
overreacts/ax
overridden/idden
overripe/ipe
overrule/ool
overseas/eeze
oversee/ee
oversees/eeze
overshoot/ute
oversight/ight
oversleep/eep
overslept/ept
overspend/end
overstate/ate
overstep/ep
overstepped/ept
overstuff/uff
overt/ert
overtake/ake
overtime/ime
overtire/ire
overture/ure
overturn/urn

overweight/ate
overwork/erk
overzealous/ealous
ow/ow 1
owe/o
owed/ode
owes/ose 2
owl/owl
own/one 1
ownership/ip
ox/ox
ozone/one 1

P

pa/aw
pace/ace
paced/aste
pachyderm/erm
Pacific/ific
pacified/ide
pacifies/ize
pacifism/ism
pacify/y
pack/ack
packed/act
packs/ax
Pac-Man/an
pact/act
pad/ad 1
paddle/attle
padlock/ock
page/age 1
pagoda/ota
paid/ade 1
pail/ale 1
pain/ain
pair/air
pajama/ama 1, ama 2
Pakistan/an
pal/al
pale/ale 1
Palestine/ine 1
palindrome/ome 1
pallbearer/arer
palm/alm, om
palomino/ino 2
Pam/am

pamper/amper
pan/an
Panama/aw
Panasonic/onic
pancake/ake
pane/ain
panic-stricken/icken
panned/and
panorama/ama 2
pant/ant 1
pantomime/ime
pants/ance
paperback/ack
paperweight/ate
papoose/use 1
pappy/appy
par/ar
parachute/ute
parade/ade 1
paradise/ice 1
paradox/ox
paragon/awn
paragons/ons
paragraph/aff
Paraguay/y
parakeet/eet
parallel/ell
paralyze/ize
paramount/ount
paranoid/oid
paraphrase/aze
parasite/ight
parasitic/itic
parasol/all
paratrooper/ooper
parch/arch
Parcheesi/easy
parent/arent
parental/ental
Parisian/ision
park/ark
parmesan/awn
parole/ole
paroled/old
parolee/oly
parrot/arrot
part/art 1
participate/ate
participation/ation

party/ardy
partygoing/owing
Pasadena/ena
pass/ass
passed/ast
passerby/y
passport/ort
password/erd
past/ast
paste/aste
pastel/ell
pasteurize/ize
pastime/ime
pastor/aster
pastoral/oral
pastrami/ommy
pat/at 1
patch/atch 1
patchwork/erk
patchy/atchy
paternal/ernal
path/ath
pathetic/etic
pathology/ology
patriotic/otic
patriotism/ism
patrol/ole
patrolled/old
patroller/olar
patronize/ize
patty/atty
Paul/all
Paulette/et
Paul Revere/eer
paunch/aunch
pauper/opper
pause/ause
pave/ave
pavilion/illion
paw/aw
pawed/awed
pawn/awn
pawnbroker/oker
pawned/ond
pawns/ons
pawnshop/op
paws/ause
pay/ay
paycheck/eck

payoff/off
payola/ola
payroll/ole
pays/aze
pea/ee
peace/ease 2
Peace Corps/ore
peacetime/ime
peach/each
peacock/ock
peacocks/ox
peak/eek
peanutty/uddy
pear/air
pearl/url
pearly/urly
peas/eeze
peashooter/uter
pebble/ebble
pecan/awn
pecans/ons
peck/eck
pecks/ex
peculiarity/arity
pedal/eddle
peddle/eddle
pediatrician/ition
pedicure/ure
pedigree/ee
pedigrees/eeze
peek/eek
peek-a-boo/ew
peeker/eaker
peel/eel
peeled/ield
peep/eep
peephole/ole
peer/eer
peewee/ee
peg/eg
pelt/elt
pen/en
penalize/ize
pencil/encil
penetrate/ate
penmanship/ip
penned/end
penny/enny
pension/ention

pensive/ensive
pentagon/awn
penthouse/ouse
pep/ep
pepped/ept
peppermint/int
pepperoni/ony
Pepsi-Cola/ola
per/er
perceive/eave
percent/ent
percents/ense
perception/eption
perch/urch
percolate/ate
percussion/ussion
perfect/ect
perfection/ection
perfects/ex
perform/orm 1
performer/ormer
perfume/oom
perfumy/oomy
periscope/ope
perish/erish
periwinkle/inkle
perk/erk
perky/erky
perm/erm
permission/ition
permissive/issive
permit/it
permits/its
perpetrator/ader
perplex/ex
perplexed/ext
persecute/ute
persecution/ution
persecutor/uter
persevere/eer
Persian/ersion
persist/ist
persistence/istance
person/erson
personality/ality 1
personified/ide
personifies/ize
personify/y
personnel/ell

perspective/ective
perspiration/ation
perspire/ire
persuade/ade 1
persuader/ader
persuasion/asion
pert/ert
perturb/urb
Peru/ew
peruse/use 2
pessimism/ism
pest/est
pester/ester
pet/et
petal/eddle
Pete/eet
Peter/eeder
Peter Pan/an
petite/eet
petition/ition
petrified/ide
petrify/y
petticoat/ote
petty/etty
pew/ew
pewter/uter
pharaoh/arrow
phase/aze
Ph.D./ee
phenomenon/awn
Phil/ill
phone/one 1
phonetic/etic
phonic/onic
phonograph/aff
phony/ony
phony-baloney/ony
phooey/ewy
photograph/aff
photographed/aft
photographic/aphic
photography/
   ography
phrase/aze
physician/ition
physique/eek
piccolo/o
pick/ick
picked/ict

picker/icker
picker-upper/upper
picket/icket
pickle/ickle
pickpocket/ocket
picks/icks
pickup/up
picky/icky
picnic/ick
picnicked/ict
picnicker/icker
picnics/icks
pictorial/orial
picturesque/esque
piddle/iddle
pie/y
piece/ease 2
pieced/east
piecemeal/eel
pier/eer
Pierre/air
pies/ize
piety/iety
pig/ig
pigeonhole/ole
pigeonholed/old
pigeon-toed/ode
piggyback/ack
pigpen/en
pigskin/in
pigsties/ize
pigsty/y
pigtail/ale 1
pike/ike
pile/ile 1
piled/ild
pill/ill
pillar/iller
pillow/illow
pimple/imple
pin/in
piñata/ada
pinball/all
pinch/inch
pine/ine 1
pinecone/one 1
pined/ind
ping/ing
Ping-Pong/ong

pink/ink
pinkie/inky
pinned/inned
Pinocchio/o
pinochle/uckle
pinpoint/oint
pinpricks/icks
pinstripe/ipe
pioneer/eer
pip/ip
pipe/ipe
pipeline/ine
piper/iper
pip-squeak/eek
pique/eek
piranha/onna
pirouette/et
pistachio/o
pit/it
pita/ita
pitch/itch
pitchfork/ork 1
pitfall/all
pits/its
pitter-patter/atter 1
pity/itty
pizzazz/azz
place/ace
placed/aste
plagiarism/ism
plagiarize/ize
plaid/ad 1
plain/ain
plainspoken/oken
plan/an
plane/ain
planetary/ary
plank/ank
planned/and
planner/anner
plant/ant 1
plantation/ation
plants/ance
plaque/ack
plaques/ax
plaster/aster
plastic/astic
plate/ate
platform/orm 1

Platonic/onic
platoon/oon
platter/atter
platypus/uss 1
play/ay
played/ade 1
player/ayer
playground/ound
playmate/ate
play-off/off
playpen/en
plays/aze
plaything/ing
playwright/ight
plea/ee
plead/eed
pleas/eeze
please/eeze
pleasure/easure
pleat/eet
pledge/edge
pliable/iable
pliant/iant
plight/ight
plod/awed
plop/op
plot/ot
plotter/otter
plow/ow 1
plowed/oud
ploy/oy
ploys/oys
pluck/uck
plucked/uct
plucks/ucks
plucky/ucky
plug/ug
plum/um
plumber/ummer
plume/oom
plump/ump
plunder/under
plunge/unge
plunk/unk
plural/ural
plus/us
plush/ush 1
P.M. /em
pneumonia/onia

poach/oach
pocket/ocket
pod/awed
poem/ome 1
poetic/etic
point/oint
poise/oys
poke/oke
poker/oker
pokes/okes
polar/olar
Polaroid/oid
pole/ole
police/ease 2
policed/east
polish/olish
polite/ight
political/itical
politician/ition
politics/icks
poll/ole
polled/old
pollster/olster
pollute/ute
polluter/uter
pollution/ution
Polly/olly
Pollyanna/ana 1
polo/olo
poltergeist/iced
polyester/ester
pompom/om
poncho/oncho
pond/ond
ponder/onder
ponds/ons
pontoon/oon
pony/ony
pooch/ooch
poodle/oodle
poof/oof 1
poofy/oofy
pooh/ew
poohed/ude
pool/ool
poop/oop
pooper/ooper
poor/ore, ure
pop/op

popcorn/orn
pope/ope
Popeye/y
popper/opper
poppy/oppy
poppycock/ock
Popsicle/ickle
Pop Tart/art 1
popularity/arity
popularize/ize
populate/ate
population/ation
porch/orch
porcupine/ine 1
pore/ore
por favor/or
pork/ork 1
port/ort
porter/order
portfolio/o
porthole/ole
portion/ortion
portrayed/ade 1
portrays/aze
pose/ose 2
posh/osh
position/ition
posse/ossy
possess/ess
possessed/est
possession/ession
possessive/essive
possessor/essor
possibility/ility
possum/ossum
post/ost 1
postcard/ard 1
posterity/arity
postmark/ark
postmaster/aster
postpone/one 1
postscript/ipped
postwar/ore
pot/ot
potbelly/elly
potential/ential
pothole/ole
potion/otion
potluck/uck

potter/otter
pottery/ottery
potty/ody
pouch/ouch
pounce/ounce
pound/ound
pour/ore
poured/ord 1
pout/out
pouter/owder
pow/ow 1
powder/owder
power/our 1
power-driven/iven
powered/owered
powerhouse/ouse
powwow/ow
pox/ox
practical/actical
practicality/ality 1
prairie/ary
praise/aze
prance/ance
prank/ank
prattle/attle
pray/ay
prayed/ade 1
prayer/air
prays/aze
preach/each
preacher/eacher
prearrange/ange
precarious/arious
precautionary/ary
precede/eed
precinct/inct
precise/ice 1
precision/ision
precocious/ocious
precut/ut 1
predecessor/essor
predict/ict
prediction/iction
predictor/ictor
predicts/icks
preemie/eamy
prefer/er
preferential/ential
preferred/erd

prehistoric/oric
prejudge/udge
prejudicial/icial
preliminary/ary
premature/ure
premier/eer
premonition/ition
preoccupied/ide
preoccupies/ize
preoccupy/y
prep/ep
preparation/ation
prepare/air
preposition/ition
preschool/ool
preschooler/ooler
prescribe/ibe
prescription/iption
present/ent
presentation/ation
presenter/enter
presents/ense
preservation/ation
preserve/erve
preshrunk/unk
president/esident
presidential/ential
press/ess
pressed/est
presume/oom
presumption/
    umption
preteen/een
pretend/end
pretender/ender
pretense/ense
pretension/ention
pretty/iddy
prevail/ale 1
prevent/ent
prevention/ention
preventive/entive
prey/ay
price/ice 1
priced/iced
pricey/icy
prick/ick
pricked/ict
prickly/ickly

pricks/icks
pride/ide
pried/ide
priest/east
prim/im
prima donna/onna
primary/ary
primate/ate
prime/ime
primp/imp
prince/ince
principality/ality 1
print/int
printer/inter
prints/ince
priority/ority
Priscilla/illa
prism/ism
prissy/issy
prize/ize
prizefight/ight
prizewinner/inner
pro/o
probability/ility
probation/ation
probe/obe
problematic/atic
proceed/eed
procession/ession
processor/essor
procrastinate/ate
procrastination/ation
procrastinator/ader
prod/awed
prodder/otter
produce/use 1
produced/uced
production/uction
productive/uctive
productivity/ivity
profane/ain
profess/ess
professed/est
profession/ession
professionalism/ism
professor/essor
profile/ile 1
profound/ound
program/am

progress/ess
progressed/est
progression/ession
progressive/essive
prohibit/ibit
prohibition/ition
project/ect
projector/ector
projects/ex
prolific/ific
prologue/og
prolong/ong
prom/om
promenade/
    ade 1, awed
promote/ote
promotion/otion
promotional/otional
prone/one 1
pronoun/own 2
pronounce/ounce
pronto/onto
pronunciation/ation
proof/oof 1
proofread/ed, eed
proofreader/eeder
prop/op
propel/ell
propelled/eld
propeller/eller
proper/opper
proportion/ortion
proposal/osal
propose/ose 2
proposition/ition
propriety/iety
pros/ose 2
prose/ose 2
prosecute/ute
prosecution/ution
prosecutor/uter
prospect/ect
prospects/ex
prosperity/arity
protect/ect
protection/ection
protector/ector
protects/ex
protégé/ay

protein/een
protest/est
protestor/ester
protocol/all
prototype/ipe
protrude/ude
protrusion/usion
proud/oud
prouder/owder
prove/ove 3
proverb/urb
provide/ide
provider/ider
provision/ision
provoke/oke
provoker/oker
provokes/okes
prowl/owl
proxy/oxy
prude/ude
prudent/udent
prune/oon
pry/y
psalm/alm, om
pseudonym/im
psych/ike
psychological/ogical
psychologist/ologist
psychology/ology
psychopath/ath
psychosomatic/atic
psychotic/otic
PTA/ay
P.U./ew
pub/ub
publicity/icity
publicize/ize
puck/uck
pucker/ucker
pucks/ucks
puddle/uddle
pueblo/o
puff/uff
puffy/uffy
pug/ug
puke/uke
pull/ull 2
pulley/ully
pulp/ulp

pulsate/ate
pump/ump
pumpernickel/ickle
pumpkin/umpkin
pun/un
punch/unch
punctuality/ality 1
punctuate/ate
punctuation/ation
punk/unk
punker/unker
punky/unky
punned/und
punner/unner
punt/unt
punter/unter
punts/unts
pup/up
pupil/uple
puppy/uppy
pure/ure
purebred/ed
purgatory/ory
purge/erge
purify/y
purity/urity
purloin/oin
Purple Heart/art 1
purr/er
purred/erd
purse/erse
pursue/ew
pursued/ude
pursues/use 2
pursuit/ute
pus/us
push/ush 2
pushover/over
pushy/ushy
puss/uss 1
pussycat/at 1
pussyfoot/oot 2
put/oot 2
put-down/own 2
putt/ut 1
putter/utter
putty/uddy
puzzle/uzzle
pyramid/id

python/awn
pythons/ons

Q

Q-Tip/ip
quack/ack
quacked/act
quacks/ax
quad/awed
quadruple/uple
quail/ale 1
quake/ake
qualification/ation
qualified/ide
qualifies/ize
qualify/y
quality/ality 2
qualm/alm, om
quarantine/een
quarrel/oral
quarry/ory
quart/ort
quarter/order
quarterback/ack
quartet/et
quash/osh
queasy/easy
Quebec/eck
queen/een
quelled/eld
quench/ench
quencher/enture
query/eery
quest/est
question/estion
questionnaire/air
quibble/ibble
quick/ick
quicken/icken
quicker/icker
quickie/icky
quickly/ickly
quicksand/and
quiet/iet
quilt/ilt
quip/ip
quipped/ipped
quirk/erk

quirky/erky
quit/it
quite/ight
quits/its
quitter/itter
quiver/iver 2
quiz/iz
quota/ota
quotation/ation
quote/ote

R

rabbi/y
rabble/abble
raccoon/oon
race/ace
raced/aste
racehorse/orse
racetrack/ack
racial/acial
racism/ism
rack/ack
racketeer/eer
racks/ax
radiate/ate
radiation/ation
radiator/ader
radio/o
radioactive/active
radioactivity/ivity
radios/ose 2
raft/aft
rafter/after
rag/ag
rage/age 1
ragtag/ag
raid/ade 1
raider/ader
rail/ale 1
railroad/ode
railway/ay
railways/aze
rain/ain
rainbow/o
rainbows/ose 2
raincheck/eck

raincoat/ote
raindrop/op
rainfall/all
rainswept/ept
raise/aze
raisin/azon
rake/ake
rally/alley
ram/am
Rama/ama 1
Ramon/one 1
ramp/amp
rampage/age 1
rampageous/ageous
ramshackle/ackle
ran/an
rang/ang
range/ange
Rangoon/oon
rank/ank
ransack/ack
ransacked/act
rant/ant 1
rap/ap
Raphael/ell
rapport/ore
Raquel/ell
rare/air
rarer/arer
rarity/arity
rash/ash 1
rasp/asp
raspberry/ary
rat/at 1
rate/ate
rather/ather 1
ratifies/ize
ratify/y
ratio/o
rationale/al
rationality/ality 1
rattle/attle
rattlesnake/ake
ratty/atty
ravage/avage
rave/ave
ravine/een
ravioli/oly
raw/aw

ray/ay
rays/aze
razz/azz
razzmatazz/azz
reach/each
react/act
reaction/action
reactive/active
reacts/ax
read/ed, eed
reader/eeder
ready/etty
real/eel
realism/ism
realistic/istic
reality/ality 1
realization/ation
realize/ize
really/eally
ream/eem
reap/eep
reaper/eeper
reappear/eer
rear/eer
rearrange/ange
reason/eason
reassurance/urance
reassure/ure
reattach/atch 1
rebate/ate
rebel/ebble, ell
rebelled/eld
rebirth/irth
reborn/orn
rebound/ound
rebuff/uff
rebuild/illed
rebuke/uke
rebut/ut 1
recall/all
recalled/alled
recap/ap
recede/eed
receipt/eet
receive/eave
receiver/eaver
reception/eption
recess/ess
recessed/est

recession/ession
recharge/arge
reciprocity/ocity
recital/idle
recite/ight
reclaim/aim
recline/ine 1
recliner/iner
recluse/use 1
reclusive/usive
recognition/ition
recognize/ize
recoil/oil
recollect/ect
recollection/ection
recommend/end
recommendation/
  ation
reconcile/ile 1
reconsider/itter
reconstruct/uct
reconstruction/
  uction
record/ecord, ord 1
recorder/order
recreation/ation
recruit/ute
recruiter/uter
rectify/y
recuperate/ate
red/ed
redder/etter
redeem/eem
red-faced/aste
redhead/ed
redid/id
redo/ew
redone/un
redshirt/ert
reduce/use 1
reduced/uced
reduction/uction
redwood/ood 3
Reeboks/ox
reed/eed
reef/ief
reek/eek
reel/eel
reelect/ect

reelects/ex
reeled/ield
reenter/enter
ref/ef
refer/er
referee/ee
refereed/eed
referees/eeze
referred/erd
refill/ill
refine/ine 1
refined/ind 1
reflect/ect
reflection/ection
reflective/ective
reflector/ector
reflects/ex
reflex/ex
reform/orm 1
reformatory/ory
reformer/ormer
refrain/ain
refresh/esh
refreshen/ession
refrigerator/ader
refuge/uge
refugee/ee
refund/und
refuse/use 1, use 2
refute/ute
regain/ain
regal/egal
regard/ard 1
regatta/ada
regime/eem
region/egion
registrar/ar
registration/ation
regress/ess
regret/et
regroup/oop
regrowth/oth 1
regularity/arity
regulate/ate
regulation/ation
regulator/ader
rehab/ab 1
rehearse/erse
rehearsed/irst

eign/ain
eimburse/erse
eimbursed/irst
ein/ain
eindeer/eer
einforce/orse
eiterate/ate
eject/ect
ejection/ection
ejects/ex
ejoice/oice
ejoin/oin
elate/ate
elation/ation
elativity/ivity
elax/ax
elaxation/ation
elay/ay
elease/ease 2
eleased/east
eliable/iable
eliance/iance
eliant/iant
elied/ide
elief/ief
elies/ize
elieve/eave
elive/ive 2
ely/y
emain/ain
emake/ake
emark/ark
emarry/ary
embrandt/ant 1
emember/ember
emind/ind 1
eminisced/ist
emorse/orse
emote/ote
emove/ove 3
ender/ender
endezvous/ew
endezvoused/ude
endition/ition
enegade/ade 1
enege/eg
enew/ew
enewal/uel
enewed/ude

Reno/ino 2
Renoir/ar
renounce/ounce
renown/own 2
renowned/ound
rent/ent
rental/ental
reoccurred/erd
reorganize/ize
repaid/ade 1
repair/air
repay/ay
repays/aze
repeat/eet
repeater/eeder
repel/ell
repelled/eld
repent/ent
repercussion/ussion
repetition/ition
repetitious/icious
rephrase/aze
replace/ace
replaced/aste
replied/ide
replies/ize
reply/y
report/ort
reporter/order
repossess/ess
represent/ent
represents/ense
repress/ess
repressed/est
repression/ession
reprimand/and
reproach/oach
reproduce/use 1
reproduced/uced
reproduction/uction
reproductive/uctive
reptile/ile 1
reptilian/illion
repulsive/ulsive
reputation/ation
repute/ute
request/est
require/ire
rerun/un

research/urch
resemble/emble
resent/ent
resents/ense
reservation/ation
reserve/erve
reservoir/ar, ore
reset/et
reshape/ape
reside/ide
resident/esident
residential/ential
residue/ew
resign/ine 1
resignation/ation
resigned/ind 1
resist/ist
resistance/istance
resolute/ute
resolution/ution
resolve/olve
resort/ort
resource/orse
respect/ect
respects/ex
respond/ond
responds/ons
responsibility/ility
rest/est
restart/art 1
restaurant/aunt, unt
restore/ore
restored/ord 1
restrain/ain
restrict/ict
restriction/iction
restricts/icks
result/ult
resurrection/ection
retail/ale 1
retain/ain
retaliate/ate
retaliation/ation
retch/etch
retell/ell
rethink/ink
retire/ire
retold/old
retouch/utch

retrace/ace
retraced/aste
retreat/eet
retribution/ution
retrieve/eave
retroactive/active
retrospective/ective
return/urn
reunion/union
reunite/ight
reusable/usable
reveal/eel
revealed/ield
revel/evel
revelation/ation
revenue/ew
revenues/use 2
reverberate/ate
Revere, Paul/eer
reverse/erse
reversed/irst
review/ew
reviewed/ude
reviews/use 2
revise/ize
revision/ision
revitalize/ize
revival/ival
revive/ive 1
revolt/olt
revolution/ution
revolutionary/ary
revolve/olve
revue/ew
reward/ord 1
rewrote/ote
rhinestone/one 1
rhino/ino 1
rhyme/ime
rib/ib
rice/ice 1
rich/itch
ricocheted/ade 1
ricotta/ota
rid/id
riddle/iddle
ride/ide
rider/ider
ridge/idge

ridicule/ool
riffraff/aff
rift/ift
rig/ig
rigatoni/ony
right/ight
rigor/igger
rile/ile 1
riled/ild
rim/im
rind/ind 1
ring/ing
ringer/inger 1
ringleader/eeder
Ringo/ingo
rink/ink
rinky-dink/ink
rinky-dinky/inky
rinse/ince
Rin Tin Tin/in
Rio de Janeiro/arrow
Rio Grande/and
riot/iet
rip/ip
ripe/ipe
rip-off/off
ripped/ipped
ripple/ipple
riptide/ide
Rip Van Winkle/inkle
rise/ize
riser/izer
risk/isk
risky/isky
Rita/ita
rite/ight
ritualistic/istic
ritzy/itzy
rival/ival
river/iver 2
roach/oach
road/ode
roadblock/ock
roadblocks/ox
roadrunner/unner
roadside/ide
roam/ome 1
roar/ore
roared/ord 1

roast/ost 1
rob/ob
robber/obber
robe/obe
Robin Hood/ood 3
robot/ot
robust/ust
rock/ock
rockaby/y
Rockefeller/eller
rocker/ocker
rocket/ocket
rocks/ox
rocky/awky
rod/awed
rode/ode
rodeo/o
rodeos/ose 2
rogue/ogue 1
role/ole
roll/ole
rolled/old
roller/olar
Rolls-Royce/oice
roly-poly/oly
romance/ance
romantic/antic
romanticism/ism
romanticize/ize
Rome/ome 1
Romeo/o
romp/omp
Ron/awn
roof/oof 1, oof 2
rooftop/op
rook/ook 2
rookie/ookie
room/oom
roomy/oomy
roost/uced
rooster/ooster
root/oot 2, ute
rooter/uter
rope/ope
rose/ose 2
Rose Bowl/ole
rosebud/ud
rosebush/ush 2
Rosemarie/ee

Rosemary/ary
Rose Parade/ade 1
Rosie/osy
Ross/oss 2
roster/oster
rosy/osy
rot/ot
rotate/ate
rotation/ation
rotten/otten
rouge/uge
rough/uff
rougher/uffer
roughhouse/ouse
roughneck/eck
round/ound
roundabout/out
roundup/up
roust/oust
rout/out
route/out, ute
routine/een
rover/over
row/o, ow 1
rowboat/ote
rowed/ode
rowing/owing
rows/ose 2
Roy/oy
royal/oil
rub/ub
rubber/ubber
rubberneck/eck
rubbernecks/ex
rubble/ouble
rudder/utter
rude/ude
rue/ew
rued/ude
ruffle/uffle
rug/ug
rule/ool
ruler/ooler
rum/um
rumble/umble
rumbling/umbling
rummy/ummy
rumor/umor
rumormonger/unger

rump/ump
Rumpelstiltskin/in
run/un
runabout/out
runaround/ound
runaway/ay
runaways/aze
rung/ung
runner/unner
runny/unny
runt/unt
runts/unts
runway/ay
rural/ural
ruse/use 2
rush/ush 1
Russell/ustle
Russian/ussion
rust/ust
rusted/usted
rustle/ustle
rusty/usty
rut/ut 1
Ruth/ooth
Ruth, Babe/ooth
RV/ee
Ryan/ion
rye/y

S

sable/able
sabotage/age 2
saboteur/ure
sack/ack
sacked/act
sacks/ax
sacrifice/ice 1
sacrificed/iced
sad/ad 1
sadder/atter
saddle/attle
saddlebag/ag
safari/arry 2
safeguard/ard 1
sag/ag
sagacity/acity
sage/age 1
saggy/aggy

Sagittarius/arious
Sahara/ara
said/ed
Saigon/awn
sail/ale 1
St. Bernard/ard 1
St. Jude/ude
St. Nick/ick
St. Patrick's Day/ay
St. Peter/eeder
sainthood/ood 3
sake/ake
sale/ale 1
salesmanship/ip
saliva/iva
Sally/alley
salon/awn
saloon/oon
salt/alt
Salt Lake City/itty
salts/alts
salute/ute
Sam/am
same/aim
samurai/y
sanctimony/ony
sanctuary/ary
sand/and
sandbag/ag
sandblast/ast
sandblaster/aster
sandbox/ox
San Jose/ay
sandman/an
sandpiper/iper
sane/ain
San Francisco/isco
sang/ang
sanitary/ary
sank/ank
Santa Anita/ita
Santa Claus/ause
Santa Fe/ay
Santa Monica/onica
sap/ap
sapphire/ire
sappy/appy
Sarah/ara
sarcasm/asm

sarcastic/astic
sardine/een
sarge/arge
sari/arry 2
sarong/ong
sash/ash 1
sashimi/eamy
Saskatchewan/awn
sass/ass
sassafras/ass
sassed/ast
sassy/assy
sat/at 1
satellite/ight
satin/atin
satire/ire
satirize/ize
satisfaction/action
satisfied/ide
satisfies/ize
satisfy/y
sauce/oss 2
saucy/ossy
Saudi/ody
sauerkraut/out
Saul/all
sauna/onna
savage/avage
Savannah/ana 1
save/ave
savor/aver
savory/avery
saw/aw
sawdust/ust
sawed/awed
sax/ax
saxophone/one 1
say/ay
scab/ab 1
scald/alled
scale/ale 1
scaly/aily
scam/am
scamp/amp
scamper/amper
scan/an
scanner/anner
scant/ant 1
scapegoat/ote

scar/ar
scare/air
scarecrow/o
scarecrows/ose 2
scarf/arf 1
scarred/ard 1
scary/ary
scatter/atter
scatterbrain/ain
scene/een
scent/ent
scents/ense
scheme/eem
schism/ism
schlep/ep
scholar/aller
scholarship/ip
scholastic/astic
school/ool
schoolbell/ell
schoolmaster/aster
schoolwork/erk
schooner/ooner
schuss/uss 1
science/iance
scientific/ific
sci-fi/y
scoff/off
scold/old
scoop/oop
scooper/ooper
scoot/ute
scooter/uter
scope/ope
scorch/orch
score/ore
scoreboard/ord 1
scorecard/ard 1
scored/ord 1
scorn/orn
Scot/ot
Scotch/otch
Scottie/ody
scour/our 1
scoured/owered
scout/out
scoutmaster/aster
scowl/owl
Scrabble/abble

scram/am
scrap/ap
scrapbook/ook 2
scrape/ape
scrappy/appy
scratch/atch 1
scratchy/atchy
scrawl/all
scrawled/alled
scrawny/awny
scream/eem
screech/each
screecher/eacher
screen/een
screw/ew
screwdriver/iver 1
screws/use 2
screwy/ewy
scribble/ibble
scribe/ibe
script/ipped
scroll/ole
Scrooge/uge
scrub/ub
scrubber/ubber
scruff/uff
scrunch/unch
scruple/uple
scrutinize/ize
scud/ud
scuff/uff
scuffle/uffle
scum/um
scummy/ummy
scurry/urry
scuttle/uddle
scuttlebutt/ut 1
sea/ee
seafarer/arer
seafood/ude
seal/eel
sealed/ield
seam/eem
seaport/ort
search/urch
searchlight/ight
seas/eeze
seashore/ore
seasick/ick

season/eason	senility/ility	shade/ade 1	shillelagh/aily
seat/eet	seniority/ority	shadowbox/ox	shimmer/immer
Seattle/attle	señor/ore	shady/ady	shin/in
seaweed/eed	señora/ora	shaft/aft	shindig/ig
seclude/ude	señorita/ita	shag/ag	shine/ine 1
seclusion/usion	sensationalism/ism	shaggy/aggy	shiner/iner
seclusive/usive	sense/ense	shake/ake	shingle/ingle
secondary/ary	sensibility/ility	Shake 'n Bake/ake	shiny/iny
secondhand/and	sensitivity/ivity	Shakespeare/eer	ship/ip
secretary/ary	sensitize/ize	shall/al	shipped/ipped
secrete/eet	sent/ent	shallow/allow 1	shipper/ipper
sect/ect	sentimental/ental	sham/am	shipshape/ape
section/ection	sentimentality/	shame/aim	shipwreck/eck
securable/urable	ality 1	shampoo/ew	shipwrecked/ect
secure/ure	separate/ate, it	shampooed/ude	shipyard/ard 1
security/urity	separation/ation	shampoos/use 2	shirk/erk
sedan/an	September/ember	shamrock/ock	Shirley/urly
sedate/ate	serape/oppy	shamrocks/ox	shirt/ert
sedentary/ary	serenade/ade 1	Shanghai/y	shirtsleeve/eave
see/ee	serenader/ader	shape/ape	shirttail/ale 1
seed/eed	serene/een	share/air	shish kebab/ob
seedy/eedy	serf/urf	sharecropper/opper	shiver/iver 2
seek/eek	serious/erious	shareholder/older	shock/ock
seem/eem	serpentine/een	shark/ark	shocker/ocker
seen/een	serve/erve	Sharon/aron	shocks/ox
seep/eep	servitude/ude	sharpshooter/uter	shockwave/ave
sees/eeze	Sesame Street/eet	shatter/atter	shoddy/ody
seesaw/aw	session/ession	shave/ave	shoe/ew
seesawed/awed	set/et	shaver/aver	shoehorn/orn
seesaws/ause	setback/ack	shawl/all	shoelace/ace
seethe/eethe	settle/eddle	she/ee	shoes/use 2
segregate/ate	setup/up	shed/ed	shoeshine/ine 1
segregation/ation	seven/even	sheen/een	shoeshiner/iner
seize/eeze	seventeen/een	sheep/eep	shoestring/ing
select/ect	7-Up/up	sheepskin/in	shone/one 1
selection/ection	sever/ever	sheer/eer	shook/ook 2
selective/ective	severe/eer	sheet/eet	shoot/ute
selects/ex	severer/earer	shelf/elf	shooter/uter
self/elf	severity/arity	shell/ell	shop/op
sell/ell	sew/o	shelled/eld	shoplift/ift
seller/eller	sewed/ode	Shelley/elly	shopper/opper
semester/ester	sewing/owing	shelter/elter	shore/ore
semiautomatic/atic	sewn/one 1	shelve/elve	short/ort
semicolon/olen	sews/ose 2	Sherlock/ock	shortcake/ake
semiformal/ormal	sex/ex	shied/ide	shortchange/ange
seminar/ar	shabby/abby	shield/ield	shortcut/ut 1
send/end	shack/ack	shies/ize	shorter/order
sender/ender	shackle/ackle	shift/ift	shorthand/and
senile/ile 1	shacks/ax	shifty/ifty	shortstop/op

horty/orty
hoshone/ony
hot/ot
hotgun/un
hotput/oot 2
hould/ood 3
houlder/older
hout/out
houter/owder
hove/ove 2
how/o
howbiz/iz
howed/ode
hower/our 1
howered/owered
howing/owing
hown/one 1
how-off/off
hows/ose 2
howtime/ime
howy/owy
hrank/ank
hred/ed
hredder/etter
hrewd/ude
hriek/eek
hrill/ill
hrilly/illy
hrimp/imp
hrimpy/impy
hrine/ine 1
hrink/ink
hrivel/ivel
hroud/oud
hrub/ub
hrug/ug
hrunk/unk
hrunken/unken
hucks/ucks
hudder/utter
huffle/uffle
hun/un
hunned/und
hush/ush 1
hut/ut 1
hutter/utter
huttle/uddle
hy/y
hyness/inus

Siamese/eeze
Siberia/eria
Sibyl/ibble
Sicilian/illion
sick/ick
sickbed/ed
sicken/icken
sicker/icker
sickle/ickle
sickly/ickly
Sid/id
side/ide
sidekick/ick
sideline/ine 1
sidesaddle/attle
sideshow/o
sideshows/ose 2
sidestep/ep
sidestepped/ept
sideswipe/ipe
sidetrack/ack
sidetracked/act
sidewalk/ock
sideways/aze
sieve/ive 2
sift/ift
sigh/y
sighed/ide
sighs/ize
sight/ight
sightsee/ee
sign/ine 1
signed/ind 1
signifies/ize
signify/y
signpost/ost 1
silhouette/et
silicon/awn
silk/ilk
silkworm/erm
sill/ill
silly/illy
Silly Putty/uddy
silverware/air
similarity/arity
simmer/immer
simple/imple
simplicity/icity
simplifies/ize

simplify/y
simplistic/istic
sin/in
Sinbad/ad 1
since/ince
sincere/eer
sincerer/earer
sincerity/arity
sing/ing
Singapore/ore
singe/inge
singer/inger 1
single/ingle
Sing Sing/ing
sinister/inister
sink/ink
sinned/inned
sinner/inner
sinus/inus
sip/ip
sipped/ipped
sipper/ipper
sir/er
sire/ire
sirloin/oin
sis/iss
sissy/issy
sister/ister
sisterhood/ood 3
sit/it
sitcom/om
site/ight
sits/its
sitter/itter
Sitting Bull/ull 2
situate/ate
situation/ation
six/icks
sixteen/een
size/ize
sizzle/izzle
skate/ate
skateboard/ord 1
skater/ader
skedaddle/attle
skepticism/ism
sketch/etch
ski/ee
skid/id

skied/eed
skies/ize
skill/ill
skilled/illed
skim/im
skimp/imp
skimpy/impy
skin/in
skinned/inned
skinny/inny
skintight/ight
skip/ip
skipped/ipped
skipper/ipper
Skippy/ippy
skirt/ert
skis/eeze
skit/it
skits/its
skittery/ittery
skulk/ulk
skull/ull 1
skunk/unk
sky/y
skydive/ive 1
skydiver/iver1
skylark/ark
skyline/ine 1
skyrocket/ocket
slack/ack
slacks/ax
slain/ain
slam/am
slang/ang
slant/ant 1
slap/ap
slaphappy/appy
slapstick/ick
slash/ash 1
slate/ate
slaughter/otter
slave/ave
slavery/avery
slay/ay
slays/aze
sled/ed
sleek/eek
sleep/eep
sleepaholic/olic

sleeper/eeper
Sleepy Beauty/oody
sleepwalk/ock
sleepwalker/ocker
sleepwalks/ox
sleepy/eepy
sleepyhead/ed
sleet/eet
sleeve/eave
sleigh/ay
sleighbell/ell
slender/ender
slept/ept
sleuth/ooth
slew/ew
slice/ice 1
sliced/iced
slick/ick
slicked/ict
slicker/icker
slid/id
slide/ide
slight/ight
slighter/ider
slim/im
slime/ime
slimmer/immer
sling/ing
slingshot/ot
slink/ink
slinky/inky
slip/ip
slipped/ipped
slipper/ipper
slipshod/awed
slit/it
slither/ither
slits/its
sliver/iver 2
slob/ob
slobber/obber
sloop/oop
slop/op
slope/ope
sloppy/oppy
Sloppy Joe/o
slosh/osh
slot/ot
sloth/oth 2

slouch/ouch
slow/o
slowdown/own 2
slowed/ode
slowly/oly
slowpoke/oke
slows/ose 2
sludge/udge
slug/ug
slum/um
slumber/umber 1
slumlord/ord 1
slump/ump
slunk/unk
slur/er
slurp/urp
slurred/erd
slush/ush 1
sly/y
slyness/inus
smack/ack
smacked/act
smacks/ax
small/all
smaller/aller
smallish/olish
smart/art 1
smarter/arter
smarty/ardy
smash/ash 1
smear/eer
smell/ell
smelly/elly
smelter/elter
smile/ile 1
smiled/ild
smirk/erk
smith/ith
smitten/itten
smock/ock
smocks/ox
smoggy/oggy
smoke/oke
smoker/oker
smokes/okes
smokescreen/een
Smokey the Bear/air
smolder/older
smooch/ooch

smorgasbord/ord 1
smother/other
smudge/udge
smug/ug
smuggle/uggle
smuggler/uggler
Smurf/urf
smut/ut 1
snack/ack
snacked/act
snacks/ax
snafu/ew
snag/ag
snaggletooth/ooth
snail/ale 1
snake/ake
snakebite/ight
snakeskin/in
snap/ap
snappy/appy
snapshot/ot
snare/air
snatch/atch 1
snazzy/azzy
sneak/eek
sneaker/eaker
sneaky/eaky
sneer/eer
sneeze/eeze
sneezy/easy
snide/ide
sniff/iff
sniffed/ift
snigger/igger
snip/ip
sniper/iper
snipped/ipped
snippy/ippy
snitch/itch
snivel/ivel
snob/ob
snobby/obby
snoop/oop
snooper/ooper
snoopy/oopy
snoot/ute
snooty/oody
snooze/use 2
snoozer/user

snore/ore
snored/ord 1
snort/ort
snot/ot
snotty/ody
snout/out
snow/o
snowball/all
snowballed/alled
snowbound/ound
snowdrift/ift
snowed/ode
snowfall/all
snowflake/ake
snowing/owing
snowplow/ow 1
snows/ose 2
snowstorm/orm 1
Snow White/ight
snowy/owy
snub/ub
snuff/uff
snuffle/uffle
snug/ug
snuggle/uggle
snuggler/uggler
so/o
soak/oke
soap/ope
soapy/opey
soar/ore
soared/ord 1
sob/ob
sobber/obber
soccer/ocker
socialism/ism
socialite/ight
socialize/ize
society/iety
sociologist/ologist
sociology/ology
sock/ock
socket/ocket
socks/ox
Socrates/eeze
soda/ota
soften/often
soggy/oggy
soil/oil

sojourn/urn	soul/ole	spearmint/int	spitfire/ire
solar/olar	sound/ound	specialize/ize	spits/its
Solarcaine/ain	soundproof/oof 1	specific/ific	spitter/itter
sold/old	soundtrack/ack	specifies/ize	spittoon/oon
sole/ole	soup/oop	specify/y	splash/ash 1
solely/oly	soupy/oopy	speck/eck	splashdown/own 2
solicit/icit	sour/our 1	spectator/ader	splashy/ashy
solidarity/arity	source/orse	specter/ector	splat/at 1
solidifies/ize	sourdough/o	speculate/ate	splatter/atter
solidify/y	soured/owered	speculation/ation	splendor/ender
solitaire/air	sourpuss/uss 1	speculator/ader	splice/ice 1
solitary/ary	south/outh 1	sped/ed	splint/int
solitude/ude	South Carolina/ina 2	speech/each	splinter/inter
solo/olo	South Dakota/ota	speed/eed	split/it
solution/ution	southpaw/aw	speeder/eeder	splits/its
solve/olve	souvenir/eer	speedometer/ometer	splurge/erge
sombrero/arrow	Soviet/et	speed-read/eed	spoil/oil
some/um	sow/ow 1	speedy/eedy	spoilsport/ort
somebody/ody	sox/ox	spell/ell	Spokane/an
somehow/ow 1	soy/oy	spellbound/ound	spoke/oke
someone/un	spa/aw	spelled/eld	spoken/oken
somersault/alt	space/ace	speller/eller	spokes/okes
somersaults/alts	spacecraft/aft	spend/end	spokesperson/erson
something/ing	spaced/aste	spendthrift/ift	sponge/unge
sometime/ime	spaceship/ip	spent/ent	spoof/oof 1
someway/ay	spacey/acy	spewed/ude	spoofy/oofy
somewhat/ot, ut 1	spacious/acious	sphere/eer	spook/uke
somewhere/air	spackle/ackle	spice/ice 1	spool/ool
son/un	spade/ade 1	spiced/iced	spoon/oon
song/ong	spaghetti/etty	spicy/icy	spoonfed/ed
songbird/erd	Spain/ain	spider/ider	sport/ort
songwriter/ider	span/an	spied/ide	sportsmanship/ip
Sonia/onia	spank/ank	spies/ize	sporty/orty
sonic/onic	spanned/and	spiffy/iffy	spot/ot
sonny/unny	spar/ar	spike/ike	spot-check/eck
sony/ony	spare/air	spill/ill	spotlight/ight
soon/oon	sparerib/ib	spilled/illed	spotty/ody
sooner/ooner	spark/ark	spillover/over	spouse/ouse
soot/oot 2	sparred/ard 1	spilt/ilt	spout/out
soothsayer/ayer	sparrow/ero 2	spin/in	sprain/ain
sophistication/ation	spasm/asm	spindle/indle	sprang/ang
sophomore/ore	spastic/astic	spine/ine 1	sprawl/all
sophomoric/oric	spat/at 1	spinner/inner	sprawled/alled
sore/ore	spatial/acial	spiny/iny	spray/ay
sorority/ority	spawn/awn	spire/ire	sprayed/ade 1
sorry/arry 2	speak/eek	spiritualism/ism	sprays/aze
sort/ort	speaker/eaker	spit/it	spread/ed
s.o.s./ess	spear/eer	spitball/all	spree/ee
ought/ot	spearhead/ed	spite/ight	sprees/eeze

spring/ing	squirt/ert	starvation/ation	stewed/ude
springtime/ime	squirter/erter	starve/arve	stews/use 2
springy/ingy 1	squirty/irty	stash/ash 1	stick/ick
sprinkle/inkle	squish/ish	state/ate	sticker/icker
sprint/int	stab/ab 1	static/atic	sticks/icks
sprinter/inter	stabilize/ize	station/ation	stickup/up
sprints/ince	stability/ility	stationary/ary	sticky/icky
sprite/ight	stable/able	stationery/ary	stiff/iff
spritz/its	stack/ack	statistic/istic	stiletto/etto
sprout/out	stacked/act	status quo/o	still/ill
spruce/use 1	stacks/ax	staunch/aunch	stilled/illed
spruced/uced	staff/aff	stay/ay	stilt/ilt
sprung/ung	staffed/aft	stayed/ade 1	stimulate/ate
spry/y	stag/ag	stays/aze	stimulation/ation
spryness/inus	stage/age 1	steadfast/ast	sting/ing
spud/ud	stagecoach/oach	steady/etty	stinger/inger 1
spun/un	stagestruck/uck	steak/ake	stingray/ay
spunk/unk	stagnate/ate	steal/eel	stingy/ingy 2
spunky/unky	stain/ain	steam/eem	stink/ink
spur/er	stair/air	steamboat/ote	stinkaroo/ew
spurred/erd	staircase/ace	steamroll/ole	stinky/inky
spurt/ert	stairway/ay	steamrolled/old	stint/int
sputter/utter	stake/ake	steamroller/olar	stir/er
spy/y	stakeout/out	steamy/eamy	stirred/erd
spyglass/ass	stale/ale 1	steed/eed	stitch/itch
squabble/obble	stalemate/ate	steel/eel	stock/ock
squabbler/obbler	stall/all	steep/eep	stockbroker/oker
squad/awed	stalled/alled	steeper/eeper	Stockholm/ome 1
squall/all	stamp/amp	steer/eer	stockpile/ile 1
squalled/alled	stampede/eed	Stella/ella	stockpiled/ild
squalor/aller	Stan/an	stellar/eller	stocks/ox
squander/onder	stance/ance	stem/em	stocky/awky
square/air	stand/and	stench/ench	stoic/oic
squash/osh	standby/y	stencil/encil	stoke/oke
squat/ot	standout/out	step/ep	stokes/okes
squawk/ock	standstill/ill	stepchild/ild	stole/ole
squawks/ox	star/ar	stepdaughter/otter	stolen/olen
squeak/eek	starch/arch	stepmother/other	stomachache/ake
squeaky/eaky	stardust/ust	stepped/ept	stomp/omp
squeal/eel	stare/air	stepsister/ister	stone/one 1
squeezer/eezer	stargaze/aze	stereo/o	stonewall/all
squelch/elch	stark/ark	stereophonic/onic	stony/ony
squid/id	starlight/ight	stereos/ose 2	stood/ood 3
squiggle/iggle	starred/ard 1	stereotype/ipe	stooge/uge
squiggly/iggly	starry/arry 2	sterilize/ize	stool/ool
squint/int	starstruck/uck	stern/urn	stoolie/uly
squire/ire	start/art 1	stethoscope/ope	stoop/oop
squirm/erm	starter/arter 1	Steve/eave	stop/op
squirrel/url	Star Trek/eck	stew/ew	stoplight/ight

,topper/opper
,topwatch/otch
,tore/ore
,tored/ord 1
tork/ork 1
torm/orm 1
tory/ory
toryline/ine 1
tout/out
touter/owder
tove/ove 1
tow/o
towaway/ay
towed/ode
traddle/attle
traight/ate
traighter/ader
train/ain
trait/ate
traitlaced/aste
trand/and
trange/ange
tranglehold/old
trangulate/ate
trap/ap
tratosphere/eer
traw/aw
trawberry/ary
traws/ause
tray/ay
trays/aze
treak/eek
tream/eem
treamline/ine 1
treamlined/ind 1
treet/eet
treetcar/ar
trength/ength
trep/ep
tress/ess
tressed/est
tressful/essful
tretch/etch
trewn/oon
tricken/icken
trict/ict
tricter/ictor
tride/ide
trife/ife

strike/ike
striker/iker
string/ing
strip/ip
stripe/ipe
stripped/ipped
strive/ive 1
striven/iven
strode/ode
stroganoff/off
stroke/oke
strokes/okes
stroll/ole
strolled/old
stroller/olar
strong/ong
stronghold/old
struck/uck
strudel/oodle
struggle/uggle
struggler/uggler
strum/um
strummer/ummer
strut/ut 1
stub/ub
stubble/ouble
stubby/ubby
stuck/uck
student/udent
studio/o
study/uddy
stuff/uff
stuffy/uffy
stumble/umble
stumbling/umbling
stump/ump
stumpy/umpy
stun/un
stung/ung
stunk/unk
stunned/und
stunner/unner
stunt/unt
stunts/unts
stupefies/ize
stupefy/y
stupid/upid
stupider/upiter
stupidity/idity

stupor/ooper
sturdy/urdy
stutter/utter
sty/y
style/ile 1
styled/ild
sub/ub
subdue/ew
subdued/ude
subdues/use 2
subject/ect
subjective/ective
subjects/ex
sublime/ime
submarine/een
submerge/erge
submerse/erse
submersion/ersion
submission/ition
submissive/issive
submit/it
subpoena/ena
subscribe/ibe
subscription/iption
subside/ide
substitute/ute
substitution/ution
subterfuge/uge
subtitle/idle
subtle/uddle
subtopic/opic
subtract/act
subtraction/action
subtracts/ax
suburb/urb
subvert/ert
subway/ay
subways/aze
succeed/eed
success/ess
successful/essful
succession/ession
successor/essor
succinct/inct
succotash/ash 1
succumb/um
such/utch
suck/uck
sucked/uct

sucker/ucker
sucks/ucks
suction/uction
Sudafed/ed
sue/ew
sued/ude
suede/ade 1
sues/use 2
Suess, Dr./use 1
suffer/uffer
suffice/ice 1
sufficed/iced
sufficient/icient
suffocate/ate
suffragette/et
sugarcoat/ote
suggest/est
suggestion/estion
suit/ute
suitcase/ace
suite/eet
suitor/uter
sulk/ulk
sum/um
summarize/ize
summation/ation
summer/ummer
summertime/ime
sun/un
sunbeam/eem
sunblock/ock
sunburn/urn
sunburst/irst
sundown/own 2
sung/ung
sunk/unk
sunken/unken
sunlight/ight
sunlit/it
sunned/und
sunny/unny
sunrise/ize
sunscreen/een
sunset/et
Sunset Strip/ip
sunshine/ine 1
sunstroke/oke
suntan/an
suntanned/and

super/ooper
superb/urb
supercool/ool
Superdome/ome 1
super-duper/ooper
superficial/icial
superiority/ority
superman/an
supermom/om
superpower/our 1
supersede/eed
supersonic/onic
superstar/ar
superstition/ition
superstitious/icious
supervise/ize
supervision/ision
supervisor/izer
supper/upper
supplant/ant 1
supplied/ide
supplies/ize
supply/y
support/ort
supporter/order
suppose/ose 2
suppress/ess
suppressed/est
suppression/ession
supreme/eem
Supreme Court/ort
sure/ure
surefire/ire
surety/urity
surf/urf
surfboard/ord 1
surge/erge
surly/urly
surname/aim
surpass/ass
surpassed/ast
surprise/ize
surrender/ender
surround/ound
survey/ay
surveyed/ade 1
surveyor/ayer
surveys/aze
survival/ival

survive/ive 1
survivor/iver 1
Susanna/ana 1
suspect/ect
suspects/ex
suspend/end
suspender/ender
suspense/ense
suspension/ention
suspicion/ition
suspicious/icious
sustain/ain
suture/uture
svelte/elt
Svengali/olly
swab/ob
Swahili/eally
swallow/allow 2
swam/am
swami/ommy
swamp/omp
swan/awn
swanky/anky
swans/ons
swap/op
swarm/orm 1
swashbuckle/uckle
swat/ot
swatch/otch
sway/ay
swayed/ade 1
sways/aze
swear/air
swearword/erd
sweat/et
sweater/etter
sweaty/etty
sweep/eep
sweeper/eeper
sweet/eet
sweeten/eaten
sweeter/eeder
sweetheart/art 1
sweetie/eedy
swell/ell
swelter/elter
swept/ept
swerve/erve
swift/ift

swig/ig
swim/im
swimmer/immer
swindle/indle
swine/ine 1
swing/ing
swipe/ipe
swirl/url
swirly/urly
swish/ish
Swiss/iss
switch/itch
switcheroo/ew
swivel/ivel
swollen/olen
swoon/oon
swoop/oop
sword/ord 1
swore/ore
sworn/orn
swung/ung
symbol/imble
symbolic/olic
symbolism/ism
sympathetic/etic
sympathize/ize
symphonic/onic
symptomatic/atic
synagogue/og
syndrome/ome 1
synonym/im
synthetic/etic
Syria/eria
syringe/inge
syrup/urp
systematic/atic
Szechwan/awn

T

tab/ab 1
Tabasco/asco
tabby/abby
tabernacle/ackle
table/able
tabloid/oid
taboo/ew
taboos/use 2
tack/ack

tacked/act
tackle/ackle
tact/act
tactical/actical
tad/ad 1
tadpole/ole
tag/ag
tagalong/ong
Tahiti/eedy
tail/ale 1
tailgate/ate
tailgater/ader
tailpipe/ipe
tailspin/in
tailwind/inned
Taipei/ay
Taiwan/awn
Taj Mahal/all
take/ake
tale/ale 1
talk/ock
talkathon/awn
talker/ocker
talks/ox
tall/all
Tallahassee/assy
taller/aller
tallish/olish
tally/alley
tamale/olly
tambourine/een
tame/aim
Tammy/ammy
tamper/amper
tan/an
Tang/ang
tangerine/een
tank/ank
tanned/and
tanner/anner
tantalize/ize
tantamount/ount
tap/ap
tape/ape
tar/ar
tardy/ardy
tarred/ard 1
tarry/ary
tart/art 1

Tartar/arter 1	teenybopper/opper	terrify/y	thing/ing
arter/arter 1	teeny weeny/ini	territorial/orial	thingamabob/ob
ask/ask	teepee/ee	territory/ory	thingamajig/ig
aste/aste	teepees/eeze	terror/arer	think/ink
asty/asty	teeter/eeder	terrorism/ism	thinned/inned
atter/atter	teeth/eath 2	terrorize/ize	thinner/inner
attle/attle	teethe/eethe	Terry/ary	third/erd
attletale/ale 1	Tel Aviv/eave	terse/erse	thirst/irst
attoo/ew	telecast/ast	Tess/ess	thirteen/een
attooed/ude	telegram/am	test/est	thirty/irty
attoos/use 2	telegraph/aff	tester/ester	this/iss
aught/ot	telephone/one 1	testify/y	thistle/istle
aunt/aunt	telephonic/onic	testimonial/onial	thong/ong
aupe/ope	telescope/ope	testimony/ony	thorn/orn
aut/ot	telescopic/opic	tether/eather	thoroughbred/ed
auter/otter	televise/ize	text/ext	those/ose 2
awny/awny	television/ision	textbook/ook 2	though/o
ax/ax	tell/ell	Thailand/and	thought/ot
axation/ation	teller/eller	than/an, en	thrash/ash 1
axi/axi	telltale/ale 1	thank/ank	thread/ed
axicab/ab 1	Tell, William/ell	that/at 1	threadbare/air
axpayer/ayer	temperamental/ental	thatch/atch 1	threat/et
ea/ee	temporary/ary	thaw/aw	three/ee
each/each	tempt/empt	theft/eft	threshold/old
eacher/eacher	ten/en	their/air	threw/ew
eacup/up	tenacious/acious	them/em	thrift/ift
eakettle/eddle	tenacity/acity	theme/eem	thrifty/ifty
eal/eel	tend/end	then/en	thrill/ill
eam/eem	tender/ender	Theodore/ore	thrilled/illed
eamwork/erk	tenderfoot/oot 2	theorize/ize	thriller/iller
eapot/ot	tenderize/ize	theory/eery	thrive/ive 1
ear/air, eer	tenderloin/oin	there/air	throat/ote
eardrop/op	Tennessee/ee	thereafter/after	throb/ob
earful/earful	tense/ense	therefore/ore	throne/one 1
earstain/ain	tension/ention	thermometer/	throng/ong
eary/eery	tent/ent	ometer	throttle/oddle
eas/eeze	tents/ense	thermostat/at 1	through/ew
ease/eeze	tepee/eepy	these/eeze	throughout/out
echnicality/ality 1	tepees/eeze	they/ay	throw/o
echnician/ition	teriyaki/awky	thick/ick	throwaway/ay
echnique/eek	term/erm	thicken/icken	throwing/owing
echnology/ology	terminate/ate	thicker/icker	thrown/one 1
ed/ed	terminator/ader	thicket/icket	throws/ose 2
eddy/etty	terminology/ology	thickly/ickly	thrust/ust
ee/ee	termite/ight	thief/ief	thud/ud
eem/eem	terrain/ain	thigh/y	thug/ug
een/een	terrific/ific	thighs/ize	thumb/um
eenage/age 1	terrified/ide	thimble/imble	thumbnail/ale 1
eeny/ini	terrifies/ize	thin/in	thumbtack/ack

207

thumbtacks/ax	timeworn/orn	tom/om	touch/utch
thump/ump	timidity/idity	tomahawk/ock	touchdown/own
thunder/under	tin/in	tomahawks/ox	tough/uff
thundercloud/oud	Tina/ena	tomb/oom	tougher/uffer
thunderstorm/orm 1	tinfoil/oil	tombstone/one 1	toughie/uffy
thunderstruck/uck	tinge/inge	tomcat/at 1	tour/ure
thus/us	tingle/ingle	Tommy/ommy	tow/o
thwart/ort	Tinkertoys/oys	ton/un	toward/ord 1
thyme/ime	tinny/inny	tone/one 1	towed/ode
Tibet/et	tint/int	tongue/ung	towel/owl
tick/ick	tints/ince	tonic/onic	tower/our 1
ticked/ict	tiny/iny	tonight/ight	towered/owered
ticker/icker	tip/ip	tonsillitis/itis	towing/owing
ticket/icket	tipped/ipped	Tonto/onto	town/own 2
tickle/ickle	tipper/ipper	Tony/ony	towrope/ope
tickly/ickly	tippytoe/o	too/ew	tows/ose 2
ticks/icks	tipsy/ipsy	toodle-oo/ew	toxicity/icity
Tic Tac/ack	tiptoe/o	took/ook 2	toy/oy
ticktock/ock	tiptoed/ode	tool/ool	toyed/oid
ticktocks/ox	tiptoeing/owing	toot/ute	Toyota/ota
tidal/idle	tiptoes/ose 2	tooth/ooth	toys/oys
tidbits/its	tiptop/op	toothache/ake	trace/ace
tide/ide	tirade/ade 1	toothbrush/ush 1	traced/aste
tidepool/ool	tire/ire	toothpaste/aste	track/ack
tidy/idy	'tis/iz	toothpick/ick	tracked/act
tie/y	tissue/issue	toothpicks/icks	tracks/ax
tied/ide	titanosaur/ore	top/op	tract/act
tier/eer	title/idle	topaz/azz	traction/action
ties/ize	titter/itter	topic/opic	Tracy/acy
tiff/iff	tizzy/izzy	topmost/ost 1	trade/ade 1
tight/ight	to/ew	topnotch/otch	trademark/ark
tighten/ighten	toad/ode	topper/opper	trader/ader
tighter/ider	toadstool/ool	torch/orch	tradition/ition
tight-lipped/ipped	toast/ost 1	torchbearer/arer	traffic/aphic
tightrope/ope	today/ay	tore/ore	trail/ale 1
tightwad/awed	Todd/awed	torment/ent	trailblaze/aze
Tijuana/onna	toddle/oddle	tormentor/enter	train/ain
tile/ile 1	toe/o	torn/orn	trait/ate
tiled/ild	toehold/old	Toronto/onto	traitor/ader
till/ill	toenail/ale 1	torpedo/edo	tram/am
tilled/illed	toes/ose 2	torrential/ential	tramp/amp
tilt/ilt	together/eather	tortellini/ini	trampoline/een
Tim/im	toil/oil	toss/oss 2	trance/ance
Timbuktu/ew	token/oken	tossed/ost 2	tranquilize/ize
time/ime	Tokyo/o	tostada/ada	tranquillity/ility
timekeeper/eeper	told/old	tot/ot	transact/act
timepiece/ease 2	Toledo/edo	totality/ality 1	transaction/action
time-saver/aver	tolerate/ate	tote/ote	transatlantic/antic
timetable/able	toll/ole	totter/otter	transcend/end

ranscendental/ental	trekked/ect	trounce/ounce	turnstile/ile 1
ranscribe/ibe	treks/ex	troupe/oop	turquoise/oice, oys
ranscript/ipped	tremble/emble	trouper/ooper	turtle/urdle
ransferred/erd	trench/ench	trout/out	turtledove/ove 2
ransfix/icks	trend/end	Troy/oy	turtleneck/eck
ransform/orm 1	trendsetter/etter	truce/use 1	tusk/usk
ransformer/ormer	trespass/ass	truck/uck	tussle/ustle
ransfusion/usion	Trevor/ever	trucked/uct	Tut, King/ut 1
ransistor/ister	trial/ile 1	trucker/ucker	tutor/uter
ransition/ition	tribe/ibe	truckload/ode	tutorial/orial
ranslate/ate	tribute/ute	trucks/ucks	tutti-frutti/oody
ranslator/ader	trick/ick	trudge/udge	tutu/ew
ransmission/ition	tricked/ict	Trudy/oody	tux/ucks
ransmit/it	trickle/ickle	true/ew	tuxedo/edo
ransmits/its	tricks/icks	truffle/uffle	TVs/eeze
ransmittal/iddle	tricky/icky	truism/ism	TWA/ay
ransparent/arent	tricycle/ycle	truly/uly	twang/ang
ranspire/ire	tried/ide	trump/ump	tweak/eek
ransplant/ant 1	tries/ize	trunk/unk	tweed/eed
ransplants/ance	trigger/igger	trust/ust	tweet/eet
ransport/ort	trill/ill	trusted/usted	tweezer/eezer
ransportation/ation	trilled/illed	trustee/usty	twelve/elve
ransporter/order	trillion/illion	truth/ooth	twice/ice 1
ransverse/erse	trim/im	try/y	twiddle/iddle
rap/ap	trimmer/immer	tryout/out	twig/ig
rapdoor/ore	Trinidad/ad 1	tsk tsk/isk	twilight/ight
rapeze/eeze	trinity/inity	tsunami/ommy	twin/in
rash/ash 1	trip/ip	tub/ub	twine/ine 1
rashcan/an	triple/ipple	tube/ube	twined/ind 1
rashy/ashy	tripod/awed	tucked/uct	twinge/inge
rauma/ama 1	tripped/ipped	Tucson/awn	Twinkie/inky
raumatic/atic	tripper/ipper	tug/ug	twinkle/inkle
raumatize/ize	trite/ight	tuition/ition	twirl/url
ravel/avel	triviality/ality 1	tumble/umble	twirly/urly
ravelogue/og	trod/awed	tumbleweed/eed	twist/ist
ray/ay	troll/ole	tumbling/umbling	twister/ister
rays/aze	trolley/olly	tummy/ummy	twitch/itch
read/ed	trombone/one 1	tumor/umor	twitter/itter
readmill/ill	tromp/omp	tumult/ult	two/ew
reason/eason	troop/oop	tune/oon	two-seater/eeder
reasure/easure	trooper/ooper	tuner/ooner	tycoon/oon
reat/eet	tropic/opic	tunnel/unnel	tyke/ike
reaty/eedy	trot/ot	turf/urf	Tylenol/all
reble/ebble	trotter/otter	Turk/erk	type/ipe
ree/ee	troubadour/ore	turkey/erky	typecast/ast
reed/eed	trouble/ouble	turmoil/oil	typewriter/ider
rees/eeze	troubleshoot/ute	turn/urn	typewritten/itten
reetop/op	troubleshooter/uter	turncoat/ote	typhoon/oon
rek/eck	trough/off	turnover/over	

U

udder/utter
ugh/ug
Ukraine/ain
ukulele/aily
umbrella/ella
ump/ump
umpire/ire
unable/able
unafraid/ade 1
unapparent/arent
unaware/air
unbend/end
unborn/orn
unbroken/oken
uncanny/anny
unchain/ain
uncivil/ivel
unclear/eer
unclench/ench
uncontrolled/old
uncouth/ooth
uncut/ut 1
undeniable/iable
under/under
underachiever/eaver
underarm/arm 1
undercut/ut 1
underdog/og
underdone/un
underfed/ed
underfoot/oot 2
undergrad/ad 1
underground/ound
underlie/y
underline/ine 1
underlined/ind 1
undermine/ine 1
undermined/ind 1
underneath/eath 2
underpaid/ade 1
underpants/ance
underrate/ate
underscore/ore
undershirt/ert
understand/and
understood/ood 3
understudy/uddy

undertow/o
underwater/otter
underway/ay
underwear/air
underweight/ate
underwent/ent
undo/ew
undone/un
undress/ess
undressed/est
unearth/irth
uneasy/easy
unemotional/otional
unemployed/oid
unexplored/ord 1
unfair/air
unfit/it
unfold/old
unfulfilled/illed
unfurl/url
unglued/ude
unhappy/appy
unheard/erd
unhitch/itch
unholy/oly
unhook/ook 2
unhurt/ert
unicorn/orn
unifies/ize
uniform/orm 1
unify/y
unimpressed/est
union/union
unique/eek
unite/ight
unity/unity
universe/erse
university/ersity
unjust/ust
unkind/ind 1
unknown/one 1
unlace/ace
unlaced/aste
unlatch/atch 1
unlawful/awful
unless/ess
unlike/ike
unload/ode
unlock/ock

unlocks/ox
unlucky/ucky
unmade/ade 1
unnecessary/ary
unnerve/erve
unobtrusive/usive
unofficial/icial
unorthodox/ox
unpack/ack
unpacked/act
unpacks/ax
unpaid/ade 1
unparalleled/eld
unpin/in
unplug/ug
unproductive/uctive
unravel/avel
unreal/eel
unrealistic/istic
unrefined/ind 1
unrehearsed/irst
unreliable/iable
unripe/ipe
unroll/ole
unromantic/antic
unruly/uly
unsaid/ed
unsatisfied/ide
unsavory/avery
unscrew/ew
unseen/een
unsettle/eddle
unskilled/illed
unspoken/oken
unstable/able
unsteady/etty
unsung/ung
unsure/ure
unsurpassed/ast
untidy/idy
untie/y
untied/ide
unties/ize
until/ill
unto/ew
untold/old
untrue/ew
untruth/ooth
unusable/usable

unveil/ale 1
unwed/ed
unwell/ell
unwind/ind 1
unwise/ize
unwrap/ap
unwritten/itten
unzip/ip
up/up
upbeat/eet
update/ate
upend/end
upgrade/ade 1
upheld/eld
uphill/ill
uplift/ift
upon/awn
upped/upt
uppercut/ut 1
upright/ight
uproar/ore
uproarious/orious
uproot/ute
upscale/ale 1
upset/et
upstage/age 1
upstart/art 1
uptight/ite
up-to-date/ate
upturn/urn
urge/erge
urgency/urgency
urgent/ergent
urn/urn
Uruguay/y
us/us
USA/ay
usable/usable
use/use 1, use 2
user/user
usurp/urp
Utah/aw
utensil/encil
utility/ility
utilize/ize
utmost/ost 1
utopia/opia
utter/utter

V

vacate/ate
vacation/ation
vaccinate/ate
vaccine/een
vagabond/ond
vagabonds/ons
vain/ain
valentine/ine 1
validate/ate
validity/idity
valley/alley
vamoose/use 1
vamoosed/uced
vamp/amp
vampire/ire
van/an
vandalism/ism
vane/ain
vanguard/ard 1
vanilla/illa
Van Winkle, Rip/inkle
vaporizer/izer
variation/ation
variety/iety
various/arious
vary/ary
vase/ace
vaseline/een
vast/ast
vaster/aster
vat/at 1
vaudeville/ill
vault/alt
vaulter/alter
vaults/altz
VCR/ar
veal/eel
veer/eer
veg/edge
vegetarianism/ism
vehicle/ickle
veil/ale 1
vein/ain
velocity/ocity
velour/ure
vendor/ender

vent/ent
ventilator/ader
vents/ense
venture/enture
veracity/acity
verb/urb
verbalize/ize
verbose/ose 1
verge/erge
verification/ation
verified/ide
verifies/ize
verify/y
Vermont/aunt
Verne, Jules/urn
Veronica/onica
versatility/ility
verse/erse
version/ersion
verve/erve
very/ary
vest/est
vet/et
veto/edo
vex/ex
vexed/ext
viable/iable
vibrate/ate
vibration/ation
vicarious/arious
vice/ice 1
vicinity/inity
vicious/icious
Vicki/icky
victimize/ize
victor/ictor
victorious/orious
video/o
videos/ose 2
vied/ide
Vietnam/om
view/ew
viewed/ude
viewpoint/oint
views/use 2
vigor/igger
vile/ile 1
villa/illa
vindicate/ate

vine/ine 1
viola/ola
violate/ate
violation/ation
violin/in
VIP/ee
viper/iper
vise/ize
vision/ision
visionary/ary
visor/izer
visualize/ize
vital/idle
vitality/ality 1
vitalize/ize
vivacious/acious
vocabulary/ary
vocal/ocal
vocalize/ize
vogue/ogue 1
voice/oice
void/oid
volley/olly
volleyball/all
voluntary/ary
volunteer/eer
volunteerism/ism
voodoo/ew o
vote/ote
vouch/ouch
vow/ow 1
vowed/oud
vowel/owl
vulgarity/arity
vulture/ulture

W

wad/awed
waddle/oddle
wade/ade 1
waffle/awful
wag/ag
wage/age 1
wail/ale 1
waist/aste
wait/ate
waiter/ader
waive/ave

waiver/aver
wake/ake
walk/ock
walker/ocker
walkie-talkie/awky
walks/ox
wall/all
walled/alled
wallflower/our 1
wallow/allow 2
Wally/olly
Walter/alter
waltz/alts
wand/ond
wander/onder
wanderlust/ust
wands/ons
wane/ain
wanna/onna
want/aunt
war/ore
ward/ord 1
wardrobe/obe
ware/air
warehouse/ouse
warfare/air
warlike/ike
warm/orm 1
warmer/ormer
warmonger/unger
warn/orn
warning/orning
warpath/ath
warred/ord 1
wart/ort
wartime/ime
warty/orty
wary/ary
was/uzz
wash/osh
washboard/ord 1
Washington, D.C./ee
washrag/ag
waste/aste
wasteland/and
watch/otch
watchdog/og
watchword/erd
water/otter

waterbed/ed
waterfall/all
Waterloo/ew
watery/ottery
wave/ave
waver/aver
wavy/avy
wax/ax
waxy/axi
way/ay
wayfarer/arer
ways/aze
we/ee
weak/eek
weaker/eaker
wear/air
weary/eery
weather/eather
weatherbeaten/
    eaten
weathervane/ain
weatherworn/orn
weave/eave
weaver/eaver
wed/ed
wedge/edge
weed/eed
weeder/eeder
weedy/eedy
week/eek
weekday/ay
weep/eep
weeper/eeper
weepy/eepy
weigh/ay
weighed/ade 1
weighs/aze
weight/ate
weighty/ady
welch/elch
weld/eld
welfare/air
well/ell
well-versed/irst
welt/elt
went/ent
wept/ept
were/er
west/est

wet/et
wetter/etter
we've/eave
whack/ack
whacked/act
whale/ale 1
wham/am
whammy/ammy
wharf/arf 2
what/ot, ut 1
whatever/ever
whatnot/ot
wheat/eet
wheedle/eedle
wheel/eel
wheelbarrow/arrow
wheelchair/air
wheelie/eally
wheeze/eeze
when/en
whenever/ever
where/air
wherever/ever
whet/et
whether/eather
which/itch
whichever/ever
whiff/iff
whiffed/ift
while/ile 1
whim/im
whine/ine 1
whined/ind 1
whiner/iner
whinny/inny
whiny/iny
whip/ip
whiplash/ash 1
whipped/ipped
whippoorwill/ill
whirl/url
whirlpool/ool
whirlwind/inned
whisk/isk
whiskey/isky
whisper/isper
whistle/istle
white/ight
whiten/ighten

whiter/ider
whitewash/osh
whittle/iddle
whiz/iz
who/ew
whoa/o
whoever/ever
whole/ole
wholesale/ale 1
wholly/oly
whom/oom
whomp/omp
whoop/oop
whoopee/oopy
whoosh/ush 2
whopper/opper
whose/use 2
why/y
Wichita/aw
wicker/icker
wicket/icket
wicks/icks
wide/ide
wider/ider
widespread/ed
wienie/ini
wife/ife
wig/ig
wiggle/iggle
wiggly/iggly
wigwam/om
wild/ild
wildcat/at 1
wildebeest/east
wildflower/our 1
wildlife/ife
will/ill
willed/illed
William Tell/ell
willow/illow
willpower/our 1
willy-nilly/illy
wilt/ilt
wimp/imp
wimpy/impy
win/in
wince/ince
wind/ind 1, inned
windbag/ag

windblown/one 1
windmill/ill
windowpane/ain
windowsill/ill
windpipe/ipe
windshield/ield
windswept/ept
wine/ine 1
wing/ing
wingding/ing
wingdinger/inger 1
wink/ink
winked/inct
winner/inner
Winnie the Pooh/ew
Winnipeg/eg
winter/inter
wipe/ipe
wiper/iper
wire/ire
wiretap/ap
wise/ize
wisecrack/ack
wisecracked/act
wisecracks/ax
wiser/izer
wish/ish
wishbone/one 1
wisp/isp
wit/it
witch/itch
witchcraft/aft
with/ith
withdraw/aw
withdrawn/awn
withdrew/ew
wither/ither
withheld/eld
withhold/old
within/in
without/out
wits/its
witticism/ism
witty/itty
wizard/izard
Wizard of Oz/ause
wobble/obble
wobbler/obbler
woe/o

woebegone/awn
woes/ose 2
wok/ock
woke/oke
woks/ox
womb/oom
wombat/at 1
won/un
wonder/under
won ton/awn
woo/ew
wood/ood 3
woodblock/ock
woodchopper/opper
woodchuck/uck
woodcutter/utter
woodpile/ile 1
woodwind/inned
woodwork/erk
wooed/ude
woof/oof 2
wool/ull 2
woolly/ully
word/erd
wordy/urdy
wore/ore
work/erk
workaholic/olic
workload/ode
workout/out
workplace/ace
workshop/op
worldwide/ide
worm/erm
worn/orn
worry/urry
worrywart/ort
worse/erse
worsen/erson
worst/irst
worth/irth
worthwhile/ile 1
would/ood 3
wound/ound
wove/ove 1
wow/ow 1
wowed/oud
wrap/ap
wrath/ath

wreath/eath 2
wreck/eck
wrecked/ect
wrecks/ex
wrench/ench
wretch/etch
wring/ing
wrinkle/inkle
wrist/ist
wristwatch/otch
write/ight
writer/ider
written/itten
wrong/ong
wrote/ote
wrung/ung
wry/y
Wyatt Earp/urp

X

Xerox/ox
x-ray/ay
x-rayed/ade 1
x-rays/aze
xylophone/one 1

Y

yacht/ot
yak/ack
yakked/act
yaks/ax
Yale/ale 1
yam/am
yank/ank
Yankee/anky
Yankee Doodle/
    oodle
yap/ap
yard/ard 1
yardstick/ick
yarn/arn
yawn/awn
yawned/ond
yawner/onor
yawns/ons
year/eer
yearn/urn

yeast/east
yell/ell
yelled/eld
yeller/eller
yellow/ellow
Yellowstone/one 1
yelp/elp
yen/en
yep/ep
yes/ess
yesterday/ay
yet/et
yield/ield
yippee/ippy
yokel/ocal
Yokohama/ama 1
yolk/oke
yolks/okes
yonder/onder
yoo-hoo/ew
you/ew
young/ung
younger/unger
your/ore, ure
you're/ure
yourself/elf
youth/ooth
you've/ove 3
yo-yo/o
yo-yos/ose 2
yuck/uck
yucky/ucky
Yukon/awn
yule/ool
yum/um
yummy/ummy
yuppie/uppy
Yvonne/awn

Z

zag/ag
Zambezi/easy
Zanzibar/ar
zap/ap
zeal/eel
zealous/ealous
zero/ero 1
zest/est

Zeus/use 1
zigzag/ag
zillion/illion
zinc/ink
zing/ing
zinger/inger 1
zingy/ingy 1
zip/ip
zipped/ipped
zipper/ipper
zippy/ippy
zit/it
zither/ither
zits/its
zone/one 1
zonk/onk
zoo/ew
zoologist/ologist
zoology/ology
zoom/oom
zoos/use 2
zucchini/ini